Gentle Annie

With all good wishes.
Anne Ravenook

Darlene.
Enjoy!
love you,
aunt A.

By the author of:

The Storyteller and His Story
Marten River Hideaway
The Returning
Secrets of the Bluebird Inn

Gentle Annie

A Novel

Anne Ravenoak

House of   RavenOak

iUniverse, Inc.
New York   Bloomington   Shanghai

Gentle Annie

iUniverse books may be ordered through booksellers or by contacting:

iUniverse
1663 Liberty Drive
Bloomington, IN 47403
www.iuniverse.com
1-800-Authors (1-800-288-4677)

Because of the dynamic nature of the Internet, any Web addresses
or links contained in this book may have changed
since publication and may no longer be valid.

This is a work of fiction. All of the characters, names, incidents,
organizations, and dialogue in this novel are either the products of the
author's imagination or are used fictitiously.

ISBN: 978-0-595-47176-8 (pbk)
ISBN: 978-0-595-70962-5 (cloth)
ISBN: 978-0-595-91455-5 (ebk)

Printed in the United States of America

for Ruby

ACKNOWLEDGMENTS

Thank you to the wonderful people of Australia, who made our trip there in 1999 such a memorable one. We would also like to thank Rudy and Lady Diana at Coober Pedy and the Ellertons whom we met at East's Beach and the Pearts in Dubbo. Thank you to the gentleman who lent us his cell phone when our camper broke down outside of Sydney. Thank you to the many managers in the superb Australian campgrounds, and thank you to the delightful woman in the Gemini Mountains who said, when asked about the naming of Gentle Annie, a road in North Queensland, *I can tell you this. Gentle Annie ain't so gentle. She bucks and twists and turns.* You are the people who make Australia unique.

Thank you to my supporters and readers for your loyalty. And, as always, a loving thank-you to HG, *the wind beneath my wings.*

This story is fiction, but I am indebted to the following articles for local color:

Breeden, Stanley. "The First Australians." *National_Geographic*, vol. 173, No. 2, Feb. 1988: 267+.

Davidson, Robyn. "Alone." *National Geographic*, vol. 153. No. 5, May 1978: 58+.

Funk and Wagnall's New Encyclopedia, vol. 2, 3. 1979.

Parfit, Michael. "A Harsh Awakening." *National Geographic*, vol. 198, No. 1, July 2000: 2+.

Terrill, Ross. "Australia at 200." *National Geographic*, vol. 173, No. 2, Feb. 1988: 183+.

PROLOGUE

As above, so below. That was the plan. But when the Master Dreamer, whom Annie irreverently called the MD, decided to give his dreams free will, anything was liable to happen. And it did. He looked about him. Annie, for instance, needed toughening up. Even after all this time, she still didn't understand the earthly world. She had incarnated several times already but was still timid. She had to learn to speak out for herself. Yes, he would need to have her dream again to strengthen her backbone a bit. He knew he favored her. She was so beautiful in all her incarnations, but she was too content to romp and play in the Dreamtime without taking that next step to perfect her soul.

Jerosh, or whatever he called himself these days, needed help too. So far, Annie hadn't been able to help him achieve his goal of being of service to people in the physical world, even though she had worked with him periodically through the millennia. Jerosh could do with some humility. He had too much pride, and Annie didn't have enough. Being together again would do them both good. The MD figured three more incarnations should suffice. It would be rough on both Annie and Jerosh, but it was necessary if they wanted to enjoy the perfection of the Dreamtime.

In his omniscient mind he scanned his created world and knew that the red timeless land in the southern hemisphere would be ideal. It was still evolving from prehistoric ages and offered ample opportunity for growth. It looked as though the members of the Sea-turtle clan were still fighting among themselves. And there was Jerosh, being reclusive as usual. He saw Jerosh's problem, and, yes, he would need Annie's help again.

Annie could be sent fully grown this time. It wasn't the MD's usual way of doing things, but often this was just what was needed. It got around a lot of childhood baggage.

> Flowers make a garden,
> Water makes a sea,
> Thoughts make everything —
> Them, and you, and me.
> Come, Wallaby,
> Come dance with me.
> Romp in the grass
> And be carefree

Annie and her friends sang and skipped among the white daisies, yellow buttercups, and red poppies waving their petals in time to the music. Wallaby frolicked with her, tossing a daisy chain into the air and catching it with its tail.

"You're always so happy, Annie, and you never make fun of us the way others do."

She laughed merrily with her face to the warm spring sunshine. She had earned this rest, and she had chosen spring because it was such a free-spirited time. In this place, people milled happily about, doing what they most enjoyed.

"Sometimes I make fun of you all, especially the MD."

"But you aren't serious about it, Annie. We all laugh with you."

In the meadow, Joe played a ragtime tune on his piano while Liz clapped her hands and stamped her feet in rhythm. Two diamondback pythons rose six feet and swayed back and forth to the music. Margo was conducting a financial workshop, though Annie couldn't think why. But if Margo was content, who was she to criticize? About one hundred people showed up for the seminar, and she wouldn't have carried on if the MD was against it.

Mike was pulling weeds from his many-shades-of-blue garden. Even the MD was here. He didn't usually make an appearance at these affairs. Last time, he had downed too much of

Ken's free-flowing wine, and she had found him later with his head buried in Wallaby's pouch.

Today, he reveled in the bubbly atmosphere, flitting about here and there, acknowledging one person and waving to another. He sailed right by Annie as she and Wallaby dipped and skipped to Joe's melodious tunes.

Can't face me, can you? Annie thought.

The next time she landed a pirouette, she looked, but he was gone.

Annie and Wallaby joined the two pythons as Joe switched to a square dance. "Do-si-do your partner, swing her off her feet." They all lifted a few feet off the grass and swung around each other. The pythons glided, and Wallaby hopped.

Suddenly, she began to feel the presence. One minute she was dancing with free abandon, and the next she felt that familiar tingling coursing through her body. She wasn't ready yet, but obviously the MD thought she was. Gradually, the revelry receded to a distant corner of her mind. Part of her wanted to hold on to the scene forever, but an inner voice told her to get on with her task. The quicker she did, the sooner she could return to the Dreamtime.

CHAPTER 1

She became aware of discomfort. Her mind gradually awakened to this new existence, and she looked at herself in amazement. Her two legs were long, slim, and brown. Her two arms were well shaped and the same lovely brown as her legs. She looked at the rest of herself and knew she was beautiful. She had done a good job this time. She was getting the knack of reincarnating after eons of persistence. The MD didn't give out much help in that department. She gulped air into her lungs and forced it out, scattering the attack of flies that were the source of her irritation. She had forgotten about those pesky things. She looked about her and noticed Python.

"Hello, Python. You're here, too? I thought I left you in the Dreamtime."

His mouth turned into a sinister grin, and for the first time, she felt apprehensive in his presence. Moving to stand on her new legs, she discovered they were stiff. She nearly fell onto the red stones in the canyon where she had awakened. Flexing her muscles, she felt more freedom in her movements. She looked around.

"Python, this is a remarkable part of the country. Where is it, exactly?"

"It will have several names but not for many seasons yet. Right now it is the gap where the water comes after the rains, and it is where I and Lizard live." He folded himself around her legs and began to creep up to her waist. She stepped quickly out of his embrace before it tightened.

"You haven't changed. Look elsewhere for your dinner."

"It's not easy, She-woman."

"Well, you're not having me for lunch. I just got here, and I have work to do," she said. "Centuries of work."

She left him and climbed among the dark red rocks on the floor of the canyon. Lizard hid beneath an overhanging rock, and she nodded in his direction but kept climbing. She was in search of something, but she didn't quite know what. There was an indistinct image in the back of her mind. He had planted it there, but it was vague and ephemeral. The old MD was certainly offering limited information.

She gingerly picked her way between the rocks and stopped for a moment to admire the two appendages at the ends of her legs. They were odd-looking things, but they did their job adequately. Flexing her toes, she stood on the balls of her feet. She turned her gaze to her hands and wiggled her fingers. They would do. Already she knew how to grab a branch and discourage those horrendous flies.

She looked at the features of the canyon. The sight was not the gently rolling hills and green meadows of the Dreamtime, but it had its own strong, stark beauty. Gum trees stood grayish white, their long, stringy bark sweeping the dark red canyon floor. She looked to the top of the canyon walls. A sensation in her lower abdomen reminded her that she would have to urinate. Squatting among the stones, she relieved herself, fascinated with the clear, warm liquid streaming from her body. It would take time to remember all these inconveniences of being a human on earth.

The sun's hot rays found her at the bottom of the canyon, and rivulets of sweat trickled down her face, attracting even more flies than before. She picked up another fallen branch to drive the flies in another direction. The way her fingers wrapped around the wood intrigued her, and she nearly forgot about the flies as she stood mesmerized by the mechanics of her hand. A nagging thought forced her onward. She had a purpose to fulfill.

By the time she reached an opening, she was panting. This was going to be harder than she had thought. It seemed to get more difficult each time she did this. It came to her that she was here to help her beloved in his dreaming. Surely there would come a time when it would be unnecessary. The MD had said something about her toughening up and learning, too. She would just have to be patient, she supposed.

She climbed from the canyon floor, grasping at jutting red rocks and finding toeholds in the steep cliff walls. As she neared the top, the hot winds kept the flies away. Thankful for the small blessing, she thought about the bothersome creatures. She couldn't fault them for landing on her eyes and mouth. They were looking for moisture, and any source would do. It was the dry season, she remembered, and she also had to search for cooling water. Dehydration was taking its toll on her new body, and the hot winds were even more gluttonous than the flies in sucking moisture from her skin.

She stood upright, presenting less of her mahogany body to the burning sun. A piece of stringy bark from a kauri tree kept the torrid sun from her head. The pungent smell of eucalyptus assailed her nostrils, and memories of other times flooded back. Nowhere else on earth had such a captivating aroma and beauty as this ancient land. No wonder Jerosh had come back to this place, with its red volcanic soil and empty spaces crying out for hardy souls to inhabit it. His was a stalwart soul. There was no denying it. After all this time, she still felt tenderness for him. At the top of the canyon, she paused to glance around. She remembered the red soil, spinifex, and saltbushes from other times. In disjointed images, the remembrances came back. Lodged deep in her soul, it was knowledge deeper than any other. Thrusting the memories aside, she faced more immediate tasks. She had to find water. She should have asked Python. Python, however, was at the bottom of the canyon, searching for sustenance of his own. A new feeling of wariness overcame her. She would do this by herself. Looking at her feet, she thrust one and then the other before her, heading toward a distantly remembered spring.

Under the burning sun, her halting footsteps caught on a clump of spinifex, and she fell. As she lay face-down in the red dust, the ubiquitous flies landed. If the Master Dreamer was playing a prank on her, she wasn't finding it funny. She tried to focus on him, but he grew hazy in her mind. That had happened the last time she had found herself in this role.

Well, she thought, *I can play the game too. It won't be long before I'm back romping in the cool grass with Wallaby and the rest of my friends.*

This land wasn't half as much fun as the Dreamtime. With new resolve, she pushed herself up from the red soil.

A funny rumbling feeling in her middle body reminded her she needed food as well as water. *One step at a time, Annie, old girl, one step at a time. Show the MD what you're made of. Show him you're tough.*

While she found her way across the red desert, her keen eye discerned a shift in the sand beside a spinifex bush. Digging into the sand, she lifted out a bloated toad. With two hands, she lifted it above her mouth and squeezed firmly. The toad's stored water flowed down her throat.

"Don't squeeze me so hard! You don't know the strength of your hands."

"Sorry," she apologized. "I'm not used to my body yet." Leaving the toad with a little water for its own needs, she thanked it and continued on her way.

The sand emitted waves of heat that distorted all images around her. Eucalyptus trees danced in exotic patterns, and galahs flew into the few desert oaks. The sun neared the western horizon, reminding her that darkness would come. She looked for shelter while she could still see. Finding none, she curled into a ball in the open air. Before long, she was asleep with images of the Dreamtime remaining in the shadows.

After much wrangling, the members of the Sea-turtle clan, who had gone south into the desert on their search, decided to return to their village. Shabar and Wil-Wil, Rach and Tolo, and Una and Hamar, the senior members of the group, had not found what they were looking for, and this was going to cause some dissension when they returned.

Before they left their village, there had been a tribal council with the shaman, kalbin, and elders trying to decide what to do with Jerosh, the village elder's son. They had tried to find him a mate twice, and it had been a disaster each time. Jerosh continued to go about the village with his aloof, superior smile. It was true he did his share of communal tasks in the village and could be relied upon to help those in need. But as for mating and fathering a child, he was a failure. He spent hours with the shaman, studying plants and medicines, and then he disappeared into the forest for days.

The village was concerned for both his welfare and the camp's. If he was to become the next village elder, he needed to prove he could sire an offspring. If he didn't, there was the possibility he would become a kalbin. This caused a great disturbance in the incumbent kalbin. Jerosh was outspoken against the initiation rites at puberty, both for girls and young men. His views caused much debate. The kalbin and older tribal members fought against any change, and for the moment, Jerosh seemed to accept the arguments of the majority.

Then both the kalbin and the shaman had the same dream in which the Master Dreamer told them he was sending a helpmate for Jerosh, and she would be found near the canyon in the desert to the west. Several members volunteered to find her. They traveled almost to the Pitjantjatjara clan but found no mate for Jerosh. As they returned home, Shabar noticed the rounded, brown shape lying on the desert floor.

Singsong voices interrupted Annie's sleep, and she felt a sharp stick in her side. She awoke with a start. The desert air was cooler now, almost cold. Startled, she looked into the dark brown, staring eyes of several people. Three men and three women were looking at her with curiosity.

"Who are you?" The question came from a large man. Memories came back to her. Ah, yes. This would be a patriarchal group. Surprisingly, she understood him. She looked him over before answering. Around his neck he wore an amulet. As she rose and went to him to examine it more clearly, the other tribe members became restless. The women tittered as they looked her over. One came close and pinched Annie's breasts, muttering in an undertone to the others. Annie couldn't hear what the woman said, but the entire tribe broke into howls of laughter. Annie had forgotten those appendages, because she was so intent on her arms and legs. Now she glanced down and saw that her breasts were small but nicely rounded.

"Who are you?" The lead male asked again, controlling his laughter.

"I am An-ee. I come from the Before Time."

Abruptly, the giggling and harassment stilled. Looking at her in awe, the group bowed before her. She frowned. What was this? She formed it into a question. "Why are you paying homage to me? I am not the Master Dreamer. He sent me here to find the man who needs me."

"Yes. We know. We were expecting you, but we didn't expect to find you this far from home."

"Yes I suppose he can be quite arbitrary." An-ee chuckled, but they looked at her in horror. It was obvious they had forgotten the Before World and viewed the old MD with awe. It would take time to forget and think of him as a remarkable figure. If only they had seen him the other day, looking washed-out from his hangover and moaning into the pouch of Wallaby, "Oh, what have I done? My dream has become a nightmare."

CHAPTER 2

Over the three-week journey, An-ee enjoyed the company of the six members of the tribe. Shabar was an ebullient young woman who took to An-ee immediately, becoming her mentor in the new, earthly environment. "You are so clumsy when you try to walk," Shabar said, placing her hand over her mouth and trying not to giggle.

An-ee wasn't offended. She knew she was having difficulty and slowing down the return journey of the others. When she concentrated on putting one foot in front of the other, she often stumbled and had to be pulled up by Wil-Wil, Shabar's mate. "Don't think about walking. Think about something else, and you'll be fine," Wil-Wil advised her.

When she spotted the bright pink of a desert rose, An-ee's steps quickened. She veered from the path to investigate, and Shabar followed. "Be careful. It's beautiful, but often snakes and other poisonous creatures lie under it, seeking shade." An-ee smiled, thinking the pink flower was beautiful against the red desert sand. She decided to pick a flower and put it in her hair. This made Shabar laugh. "You are so beautiful. I better watch Wil-Wil." The trek was full of giggles with Wil-Wil and Shabar. The others were friendly but more reserved.

After several days, they entered the northern rain forest, where a small village came into view. Twenty huts made from the branches of surrounding trees encircled a central fire pit, around which people sat and concentrated on weaving skirts and baskets and preparing food.

"Here we are. This is our home." Shabar's lilting words mixed with the raucous greetings of several youngsters. Shabar, who didn't look old enough to have one child, was the mother of five. An-ee could easily recognize all of Shabar's children. Although not all resembled their mother, all had her joie de vivre, and they inherited a love for teasing from Wil-Wil.

The other four members of An-ee's group were greeted as warmly. Una and Hamar were greeted by their two children, while Rach and Tolo were slapped on the back by a tribal senior. After the trading party was welcomed home, all eyes turned to An-ee. The elder frowned in An-ee's direction. Although it wasn't Shabar's place to introduce her, she couldn't resist. "Elder, this is An-ee. We found her asleep in the desert when we were returning home." Instead of rebuking Shabar as she expected, the elder grinned.

"Aah." It was a sigh of profound relief. An-ee felt trepidation and wondered what was in store. The elder continued to look her over, carefully taking her arm and turning her around.

"Where have you come from, child?" His tone implied that he already knew her answer. "I am from the Before Time, Elder. I came just as you see me. As Shabar said, they found me in the desert, newly arrived."

He turned from her and ordered the women to prepare a feast in her honor. *Do I feel resentment in the tribe?* An-ee wondered. *Fear?* An uneasy wave swept over her. Part of her task was to dispel that resentment and fear. "I understand I am to help a man named Jerosh. Is that correct?" He nodded, still assessing her. "Jerosh is not here at the moment, but I will send one of the young ones to find him. You must be tired. Perhaps you could stay with Shabar until the evening meal." He looked toward the young woman smiling her assent. "Until this evening, then." Nodding to An-ee, he walked away.

An-ee looked at Shabar, mystified. "Why do I feel I'm resented here, Shabar? Surely I've done nothing to these people?"

Shabar looked at the red soil under her feet. "Please do not be hurt. Yes, there is resentment, especially from the women hoping to mate with Jerosh. He is next in line as clan leader but has shown no inclination to mate, to partake in our rites, or anything. Mostly he goes into the bush by himself. He has very sad eyes.

"So the resentment is because I am an outsider?"

"Yes. I would be jealous also, but my Wil-Wil is a handsome man. The two of us make a good team." She giggled and gestured toward her five young children.

The children had drawn a circle in the earth and placed a flat rock in the center. Each was taking a turn tossing a pebble into the circle to see who came closest to the flat stone. An-ee watched solemnly, wondering what the Master Dreamer was getting her into.

"Soon you will have a tribe of your own," An-ee joked with Shabar

Shabar laughed and changed the subject. "What would you like to do until the meal is ready? This is a celebration in your honor, and the elder will formally introduce you to Jerosh."

A sudden thought occurred to An-ee. "What if we do not like each other, Shabar? What then?"

"Let me warn you. You *must* like each other, for there is no other way. Your mating is decreed, and they will not allow otherwise."

An-ee frowned. "What are you trying to tell me?"

Shabar looked frightened. "Do not mention what I tell you to anyone, but if either you or Jerosh turn your back on the other, Jerosh will be driven from the tribe. I cannot say definitely what fate will await you. I doubt the kalbin will defy the Master Dreamer."

"What have I gotten myself into?"

"You didn't have a choice. I rather thought one went wherever the Master Dreamer desired."

An-ee laughed. "That's true to a certain extent. As we progress, though, we do have some choice."

An-ee stopped herself before saying that this time she hadn't had a choice, and she thought she had progressed through her climb to perfection quite well. One minute she had been romping with wallaby in the fields, and the next she was back in this land. Where was her choice?

"Jerosh and I will help each other," An-ee vowed. "I promise."

What is this Jerosh like? An-ee wondered. Lying under a jac-aranda tree, she sighed and closed her eyes. There was time enough to find out. The thing to do now was stay away from the others lest she inadvertently cause their resentment to boil over into anger.

She heard Shabar shushing her youngest child, a boy about eighteen months old. The others had gone off to play with the other tribal children. Opening one eye, An-ee surveyed them from her shaded spot. The boys held miniature throwing sticks and pretended to stalk an animal. An-ee turned and noticed that the girls were learning to grind nuts and fetch water from a nearby spring. The boys' game evoked laughter, while the girls' task was more serious, but An-ee knew both were learn-ing valuable skills for their adulthood.

Shabar came to An-ee. "It is nearly time for Wilsha to be ini-tiated into manhood. I think he will take the rites well. I'm not so sure about Lana undergoing the women's ceremony. She is tender and sensitive. Our rites may be too much for her."

An-ee watched concern pass over the features of her new friend. "Are the rites of passage for women so difficult?" She was astonished to see a tear trickling down the young woman's cheek.

"Some have requested that the circumcision rite for women be discontinued. The men don't know how painful and unnec-essary it is for us." An-ee said nothing and let Shabar continue. "Are we so different from men? They seem to think we should not enjoy bedding with them. That we have no feelings."

An-ee remained quiet. She wasn't sure what Shabar was saying. An-ee had no memory of this initiation rite. Perhaps it was something the Master Dreamer had dreamed recently. She thought back to him. He was too gentle and sensitive to expect pain from his creations. It was the free will he allowed them that caused much of the pain. An-ee often saw him in tears over the happenings he witnessed. Hadn't she seen him shake his head sadly when there was an atrocity in his world? At such times, he looked to Wallaby for comfort. Yes, it was far better for An-ee to withhold comment for the time being. She had more immediate concerns. "I don't understand your rituals yet. When I see them, I will discuss it with you." She touched Shabar's shoulder. "But in the meantime, could you lend me a skirt? All your people are wearing clothing, and I'm beginning to feel uncomfortable."

"Oh, I thought you knew. Because you were sent to us, you are not allowed to wear clothing until Jerosh sees you. If he doesn't like your body, he may disown you immediately. If he chooses to keep you, he will request a piece of clothing for you. It will be given by his mother or a senior woman as a badge of honor. If he renounces you, you will be the third. There is something wrong with Jerosh, but no one knows exactly what."

"It's only a few hours until I meet Jerosh. I guess I can wait until then."

Fishtails! This is the first time I've heard about Jerosh's fear of mating. I have to make him like me. I don't mind returning to the Dreamtime, but now that I'm here, I would like to look around a bit.

"What can I do to make sure this Jerosh will like me?" An-ee asked her friend.

Shabar spent several moments assessing her. "I think you will be to Jerosh's liking just as you are. He hates it when we put red and yellow color in our hair. But I do know he likes his women to wash themselves in water from the river in the forest and to rub their bodies with the bark of that medicine tree that lives close to the river. I am sure you can find it. You must pass the elder's hut and walk 150 paces into those trees there." She pointed to a path through the trees.

"That doesn't sound too difficult." An-ee rose, but Shabar detained her with one hand.

"As you pass the elder's home you must ask his permission. He may prevent you from going."

Why would the elder, who seemed overjoyed to see me, prevent me from pleasing Jerosh? She didn't voice her doubts, unsure if Shabar's information was accurate or the figment of the youthful awe in which she held the elder. An-ee was sure she could handle him. After all, even the old Master Dreamer let her get away with a few things, although he often did so with a scowl.

But she hadn't counted on the elder's harridan of a mate.

"What you be wantin' to go off to the medicine tree for, girl? You think you'll find magic to attract Jerosh?" The old woman chuckled and broke into a knee-slapping, cackling laugh. The elder joined her.

An-ee gave the elder a withering look. *Who is boss here, anyway?* He interpreted her expression accurately and whispered in an undertone to his mate.

She stopped her cackling but smiled snidely at An-ee. "You can try, girl, you can try. But no one else has kept his interest."

An-ee drew herself up, fighting the impulse to flee this old woman's scrutiny. "Obviously, you forget that I am here at the Master Dreamer's request. It is his wish I am fulfilling, not mine." She was gratified to see their embarrassed faces. "If I have your permission, Elder, I will continue my journey." She didn't wait to see if she had permission but rounded sharply and headed down the path through the bush.

It wasn't until she was out of sight of the elder's hut that she drew a deep breath to slow her fast-beating heart. *Old shark! The old woman is jealous.*

It wasn't as though An-ee hadn't been up against that before. It had been a long, long time ago, though. She would have to hone her people skills if she stayed in this camp long.

Taking her time, An-ee trod softly along the path. The medicine trees emitted their pungent aroma, and a plant she couldn't identify lent its sweet scent to the forest. Mixed in was the smell of the saltwater ocean. She kept to the trail, not wanting to venture too far into the thick masses of vines and leaves. The air was humid, and the mosquitoes attacked her. Even so, they weren't as bad as those flies back at the canyon. She walked quietly along the path. As quiet as she was, however, there was one who was quieter.

He came up behind her and blew on the back of her neck. A deep, masculine laughter broke out, which both startled and entranced her. Turning, she felt her breath catch in her throat.

He was handsome with his broad nose and merry, deep brown eyes. His hair was lighter than that of the other tribe members, and his skin was lighter too. But there was a hard, ruthless expression on his face that the other members of his clan lacked. An-ee wondered what caused it. "You must be Jerosh."

"That I am. You don't have to tell me who you are. I can tell from your lack of clothing. Two moons ago, I had a dream in which the Master Dreamer told me he would send a woman to help me. You must be An-ee."

"Yes. At first, I looked forward to finding you and your clan, but now I'm beginning to have doubts. There are undertones of fear here, but I haven't put my finger on the problem."

"You don't have to figure it out; I can tell you. There are many in our clan who want to follow the old ways, but the more enlightened want to do away with many of our rituals. This has divided the clan and could lead to internal warfare. We can't afford the strife or loss of life."

"Tell me why you need my help and what you think I can do."

"I don't know. To tell you the truth, even though I expected the Master Dreamer to send help, you are somewhat of a surprise."

She frowned. "In what way?"

"For one thing, you're beautiful. For another, you are much older than I expected."

And what? You'll turn me down for a younger woman? She wanted to smack him across his handsome, arrogant face and walk away. What was the consequence if she chose not to help him? Shabar had given her the consequence if he shunned her, but was there one for the possibility that *she* might deny *him*?

Looking at him, she wasn't sure she could do it. He was attractive and seemed to have integrity. She could see why he distanced himself from his clan, especially that old harridan, the elder's wife. An-ee told him this, leaving out the fact that she found him good-looking.

"Hadn't thought of her in those terms, but you're right. My mother is an *old harridan*," he said, mimicking her words.

Leave it to me to blunder at the first moment, she thought, blushing hotly. *No wonder the Master Dreamer keeps sending me back on these errands.*

"But I cannot take you as my mate," he went on. "I cannot do that to any woman. I must mate, but I do not want to. Do you see a solution? We must try to find one before this evening's ceremony."

She was confused. "What is the problem, Jerosh? I may be thickheaded, but I cannot see your dilemma."

"I cannot be a man to any woman. I tried with two women, but I could not. That is why my mate took another."

The problem became clear. *What was it Shabar told me? Jerosh was against the rites of passage in their clan. Had his initiation rite injured him? How can I go about asking my chosen mate this?*

Hesitating briefly, she plunged ahead. "Is it that you cannot penetrate a woman? If so, I'm sure there are many remedies for this. You must ask the shaman."

She paused, waiting for him to answer. This was no time for him to be embarrassed. Her life was at stake. *I've only been on earth a few days, and I'm hoping to stay longer in this land.*

"That is not my problem, An-ee." He wouldn't look at her directly but cast his eyes downward to her feet. "I don't know how to say this without causing you to resent me. I do not like women that way."

"Aah. Your mother knows this, does she?"

"She suspects, I think. I'm not sure that she truly knows. I have not said anything to anyone. Only my former mate knew, and now her life has been taken. I do not want the same thing to happen to you. Yet I know my body will not let me be with a woman."

An-ee scuffed her feet in the red soil, stirring up puffs of dust. She gave it careful thought. *Do I need a man?* She hadn't even thought of it in the short time she had been here. Her body was not awakened in that way. But what would she feel in the days to come, providing she was still alive? She did not think the Master Dreamer would send her here for such short duration. She wished she could talk to the MD. *What is he thinking? What right does he have to play with me this way?* She knew, of course, that he had every right. She was part of his dream.

She looked from the swirling pattern in the red dust to Jerosh's downcast face. "This evening at the special meal, I want you to tell your people I am your chosen mate. No," she held up a hand to forestall his outburst. "I won't ask you to bed me. No one has to know our agreement."

"But what happens when you long for a man to bed you? What happens when we do not produce a new soul? Everyone will know."

"No, they do not have to know. When the time comes that I need a man, we can devise a plan. What must I do besides be your mate to stop the village from suspecting that you prefer men?"

"I don't care if the village suspects that I prefer to bed men. No one will say anything."

"Aren't there other men with the same problem?"

"The ones I know like both men and women, so they do not stand out. They have female mates and have dispersed their seed. That's all the village asks of people. I just cannot think of bedding a woman without becoming ill."

Does he have to keep stressing how much he dislikes women? "You have made your point. You are like the chattering galahs, harping on one note until the whole world notices. If you want to keep things quiet, do not say another word about it. Now, how else do you need my help?"

"It is with the rites of passage. I want to stop them. I am sure that is the reason I am this way, and I don't want others to suffer. Shabar tells me the women suffer more than the men, even when all goes well with the rites."

She doubted the rites were responsible for his dislike of women, but didn't say so. She did know that Shabar was anxious about her son's upcoming initiation rite, though. An-ee intended to pursue the matter, but not just now. "Can I count on you to choose me this evening?"

"Yes, I will choose you. I am so happy I found you."

Arrogant male! Has he already forgotten that I found him? She smiled with confidence. Turning away, she said over her shoulder, "I'll see you at the evening meal."

He looked less than happy at the prospect, but she ignored her uneasiness. The thought of finding water held no appeal to her now, but she might as well go ahead as planned. If Jerosh liked washed and perfumed women, she would give him what he wanted so he wouldn't be too displeased at the evening's ritual.

CHAPTER 3

When she returned to Shabar's hut, An-ee found that Wil-Wil was still with the rest of the adult males on the beach.

"Shabar, what is this problem with your clan, anyway?" she asked.

Shabar pretended ignorance. "What do you mean? Surely there is nothing to hide from you. You were sent by the Master Dreamer. Nobody can dispute that, not even Riva, the elder's wife."

"Why should anyone think to dispute it? I have not asked for special treatment. It is your clan that has put me in this position. To tell you the truth, I would be happy to have a skirt to wear and go on my way."

"Don't say such things!" The shrillness of her voice revealed Shabar's deep shock. "Please, stay and help us abolish these outdated rites of passage. As long as Riva is here, she has control and insists on keeping our rites."

"Riva has more control than the elder? How can that be? Isn't he the head of this clan?"

"He's supposed to be, yes. But Riva has much influence over him. And the men don't see female initiation in a negative way. They have their foreskins cut in the old way, and the medicine man gives them a potion to make them forget the pain. Yet the girls get nothing for the pain."

"Why would the girls need medicine to forget the pain? What must the girls endure?"

"Oh, An-ee, we all have our clitorises removed." Shabar was near tears, thinking of the ordeal ahead of her girls.

"Did that happen to you?"

"Yes. It happened to all the village women. We want to know if Riva has had it done. I cannot think that one who has undergone the initiation can sit by and watch it done to others. An-ee was deep in thought. She didn't like Riva either, but another emotion flowed unbidden into her soul. She found herself feeling sorry for the old woman. The old shark was nastiness itself, but An-ee found herself groping for a thought that wouldn't quite form. There was an air of innate stubbornness about her. Why did she hold to her beliefs when the majority was clearly against the rite? With Shabar's children running in and out of the hut, however, An-ee was unable to give the matter much thought.

"If you want me to help abolish this ritual, where does Jerosh fit in? Why must I mate with him?"

Shabar was about to answer when her eyes moved to the doorway. Rach, a senior woman of the clan, stood at the entrance. She had an austere presence compared to the exuberant Shabar, but already An-ee saw a loving heart underneath her glowering exterior. Rach answered for Shabar. "If Jerosh keeps you as his mate, you will have the place of honor in our clan. Riva will lose a great deal of influence. Do not mistake me. She will still try to wield her authority, but if you have the backing of both Jerosh and the elder, you will succeed in her place."

"I cannot see Riva losing the backing of the elder, but I'm sure Jerosh will side with me. He appears to bear an animosity toward his mother." An-ee was flustered. She had told no one that she had met Jerosh on the path. She thought she'd better explain. "No one else need know," she told the two women.

"Yes. It is better this way," Rach acknowledged. "No one knows why Riva is as she is. But we all think she is a nasty one. Still, one's seeds usually have a strong bond with those who gave them life. Jerosh and Riva don't seem to have that bond."

"You must forgive me. I am new to this. Does this rite cause the girls distress?"

"Oh!" Both Rach and Shabar spoke at once. It was obvious that they felt their girls underwent a painful experience.

Rach continued, "It is not only the young who suffer. Women must carry the consequences for the rest of our lives. I can see that you do not understand. If you were born of woman, you would. If Jerosh chooses you for his mate, you will find out."

The two women assumed a distant expression, recalling their initiation rites. They seemed to forget An-ee was in the hut.

Standing up, An-ee said, "I think I will walk to the beach and watch the men preparing the feast."

"No!" The two women and the older children joined their voices in admonition. Obviously, this was also taboo. *Are women allowed to do anything in this encampment?* An-ee wondered. She walked off, leaving the two friends alone, with their eight children close by. *Where am I to go if I can't go to the beach?* She didn't want to return to the forest path where she had met Jerosh. She spotted a path leading in another direction in the forest and decided to follow that.

"Do you really think she was sent by the Master Dreamer, Shabar?" Rach remained just outside Shabar's hut, watching An-ee choose the path to the women's washing spring. Rach had doubts about An-ee, but as Shabar pointed out, they *had* found her naked in the desert. Even in clans that were led by males they doubted An-ee would be exiled with no clothing.

The two women continued to linger. Shabar grabbed her youngest and held him to her. She wouldn't have to worry about him for a while. Her two older souls worried her at the moment. Both would soon be initiated into the rites of adulthood. The older daughter had already begun her blood flow, though she was just ten seasons old. The younger boy was nine seasons and would undergo the male ritual. Wil-Wil had already accepted them as adults and was searching for suitable mates. Shabar had approached him about the female rites, but he had seemed unconcerned. "There is nothing to worry about, Shabar. We men soon forget the pain, and the rite does not prevent us from fathering children. By the looks of you," he said fondly, "our rites haven't prevented you from producing children either."

Shabar had to admit she was the most prolific tribal woman. Most other family units had two or three children. She was amazed that she and Wil-Wil had produced five, especially as she didn't particularly delight in the joining. Wil-Wil had no such problem, but she often wondered whether women could enjoy the joining too.

She couldn't deny that she loved the closeness of Wil-Wil's body when he came to her, his male scent surrounding her. She was intrigued by his pleasant, broad face with its faraway look as he deposited his child in her belly. She had asked him once what he felt when that happened, but he had looked at her with a puzzled frown. It was unthinkable for a woman to question a man as she had just questioned him, but he and Shabar had a closer relationship than other mated pairs of the village. He had learned this when the men got together for their corroborees, at which they sang and danced and tried to interact with the Dreamtime. In fact, he was nudged and winked at more often than he cared to admit. Could he help it if he loved to get close to Shabar?

He loved it when she beckoned to him, and he knew she had been to the washing spring, rubbing her body with the sweet-smelling plant that grew nearby. Sometimes it was all he could do to hold onto his seed until he entered her. Many times, he spilled it onto her fragrant belly too soon. She would laugh and say it was a wonder she produced any children, but he saw the disappointment in her eyes. He had seen the same disappointment at those times when he caressed her breasts until her nipples stiffened and beckoned him to suck them. He never told Shabar he felt sharp stabs of jealousy when one of his seeds suckled at her Breast. He wanted her breasts to be his alone. Shabar understood this need. After one of the babies had suckled and she had put the young soul aside for a nap, she would call to Wil-Wil and place his mouth on her nipple. He was always overwhelmed when the warm milk trickled down his throat, feeling ashamed and thinking he had stolen food from his seed, but Shabar would smile and say there was plenty.

At such times, she would undulate against him until he was fully aroused, and they would end in the darkness of the hut with him depositing more seed inside her soft, warm belly. But still Wil-Wil was mystified. Shabar wasn't aware that he knew she cried after mating. She would stifle her sobs in the crook of her arm so the children or neighbors wouldn't hear, but he knew, and he wanted to cry too. Was it fair that he should enjoy the experience so much but she should not?

Was it only between him and Shabar that such a feeling existed? She hadn't said anything to him but chose to keep her frustrations inside. Despite everything, however, he had still produced the most children, and that gave him a feeling of pride. He could accept the nudging and the winks. He was a loved one of the Master Dreamer. Otherwise, the Master Dreamer would not have given him and Shabar five souls to nurture and continue the Master Dreamer's dream.

Wil-Wil watched the two women after An-ee left. He knew they were plotting and scheming, but whatever it was, it was benign fun for the women. Let them have their little play. They deserved it for the long hours they worked.

True, the men went hunting for the clan with their throwing sticks or boomerangs, depending on where they hunted their prey. They often went to the great saltwater sea and found sharks, sea turtles, or crocodiles, carrying home prey on their shoulders. Sometimes they grabbed their waddies and fought off another clan that wanted their territory, but none of this was as hard as the women's work. If it were not for the women, they would not have woven baskets to carry their food. They would not have dishes or mats woven from boiled pandanus leaves. The women also carried digging sticks to unearth termites and witchetty grubs. Even Wil-Wil admitted these were more often food than the occasional kangaroo or saltwater meat.

Their clan had a good life. Why should they expend energy on hunting large animals when the forest provided an abundance of food? The flying squirrels were often targets of their throwing sticks, and occasionally they ate one of the larger snakes. There were so many fruit-producing trees that their diet could consist of only plants. But they needed the meat. Hadn't the Master Dreamer said this at the beginning of time? Kalbins down through the centuries had repeated the Master Dreamer's dictates, or thought they had. Wil-Wil looked forward to the night's feast of giant sea turtle. The men would enact the Dreamtime story, and the elder would tell them how fortunate they were to play their part in the Master Dreamer's dream. He would have believed it, too, if he didn't hear Shabar's quiet sobs when she thought no one could hear.

CHAPTER 4

Rach and Shabar settled with their backs against Shabar's hut and watched An-ee disappear around a bend in the path. The two were as different as possible, and yet there was a deep bond drawing them together. Shabar regarded Rach quietly. She was tall and slim, much slimmer and taller than the average clan woman. Her nose was as broad as any other, and her eyes were as dark. But Rach's eyes gave Shabar a sense of unease. Most of Rach's people, the Pitjantjatjara, carried a hint of merriment in their eyes. It was the knowledge that they were the Master Dreamer's chosen people. Rach's eyes held that same elation, but they also held a farseeing quality that the people of the Sea-turtle lacked.

Shabar often felt if she could experience satisfaction from mating, all would be well with her world. But she knew that wasn't entirely true. She worried for her seeds and their future rites of passage. For all their dissimilarities, Shabar knew that she and Rach held the same view about the rites. Shabar didn't know, however, if Rach suffered the same dissatisfaction from mating with Tolo. At that moment, Tolo was with the senior men preparing the sea turtle for the evening ritual. He would take up the Dreamtime story after the elder at the evening's feast. Shabar wondered if it was a good time to approach Rach with her question. Being the older and more self-contained, Rach would not bring up the subject. Shabar was sure of that. She wondered whether Rach was even interested in mating.

Rach appeared to be thinking beyond the daily concerns of the clan, but she never discussed her thoughts. Rach hadn't said anything the day many seasons ago when Shabar came across her sitting in the red mud after the wet season. Rach had gathered a clump of red clay in her hands, shaping it into a vessel like a woven basket used to carry food after a hunt. Shabar had laughingly pointed out how Rach looked like the small children. Rach had simply looked at her, seeming to see her for the first time. She had continued to smooth out the clay but eventually tossed it aside. Shabar had asked her what she was doing, but Rach had replied only, "Thinking." Shabar never saw Rach playing with the red clay again.

Shabar could constrain her curiosity no longer. If she wanted an answer, she asked and was not afraid of rebuff. "Rach, may I ask you a question? A question you may not want to answer?"

"Yes." Rach turned to the younger woman, a smile on her face.

"I mate with Wil-Wil and I know he is satisfied, yet I am not. Do you ever have feelings like that with Tolo?"

"I used to feel as you do about mating, but I'm past that now. I never felt satisfaction with Tolo, but he didn't notice. Not like Wil-Wil. I know he cares about you. Tolo cares about me, too, I guess. At least as much as he cares about anything. But Tolo isn't about to ask for change, especially in the female rites of passage. It's not high in his thoughts." Rach looked off in the distance with a sigh. "Tolo is happy with the clan and our life here. He doesn't notice when anyone is unhappy. I learned long ago that if I wanted to be content, I had to accept him as he is. Not all of us are born to fight against the way things are. I doubt you are, either." She turned to look at Shabar and noticed she was about to deny this. "Think about it for a moment. You want change, yes. You don't want your girl-souls to suffer like you, but are you strong enough to bring that change?"

"I don't agree with your opinion of me." Shabar's voice showed no resentment. It was a simple statement. Her personality did not lend itself to resentment. "But I do know that there is one person strong enough to fight for change. We have to make her understand that."

"She will find out after mating with Jerosh. I wonder if we can do anything to make sure he accepts her."

Shabar doubted it and said as much. "You know Jerosh is not about to be influenced by anyone in the village, especially a woman. I doubt he will accept An-ee tonight. I feel sorry for her. She's like a newborn babe. I wonder why the Master Dreamer sent her to us as a grown woman?"

A flash of disgust appeared on Rach's face. "Rach? What are you thinking? You're so quiet that sometimes I find you frightening. No one can ever tell what you're thinking, only that you often scowl," Shabar said, but she received only a tolerant look in exchange.

Rach wondered if Shabar was carrying Wil-Wil's seed again. What would the senior members of the tribe say about another soul? Food was plentiful. They did not have to worry about feeding it, but there was an unspoken tradition that a brood of four children or fewer was ideal. Was she jealous of Shabar? Maybe. Yet she knew that she didn't want to bear Tolo's seed again. If the Master Dreamer wished her to birth another soul, she supposed she would. But she wasn't even sure about the Master Dreamer. She couldn't tell Shabar that, though. She knew Shabar believed deeply in the Master Dreamer and would look at Rach in disbelief if she spoke otherwise.

Rach thought about An-ee. There was nothing about the young woman to cause envy or jealousy. She had a gentle way of speaking so that people knew she would not intentionally hurt them. An-ee showed an interest in the clan affairs and in the young souls. She had not done anything to hurt Rach, but deep down, Rach felt An-ee would precipitate a catastrophe in her adopted clan. There was nothing she could do about it, nor would she say anything to Shabar or anyone else in the village. She looked at Shabar and said, "I look forward to the feasting tonight."

The two women watched their children play for a few minutes then parted company. Shabar went into her hut, and Rach decided to visit Una, who lived with her mate Hamar and their three children in the hut at the outer edge of the encampment.

"Holla, Una. Do you have time to chat before the feasting tonight?" Rach spoke loudly as she approached the hut.

Una's curly, light brown head peeped through the hut doorway. The same stature as Shabar, she had a lighter complexion and hair than the other clan members. Rach remembered that she had come to them from a tribe farther south in the desert. All the younger women were latecomers to the clan. Fathers and uncles would approach other tribes, offering their girls to the tribe elder. Depending on the tribe, the women would integrate into the new clan, or she'd return to her original tribe with a new mate. Rach's clan was led by the eldest male member. Therefore, the men of the tribe brought women back to their clan, and their own women would move to their new mate's tribe. The Sea-turtle clan was Rach's tribe now and had been for the past twelve seasons. Una had been in the clan for only five.

Una's three youngsters were clustered around her, hanging onto her skirt of pandanus leaves. Although the lighter woman was almost the same age as Rach, she had mated later in life. Rach wondered if Una's limp, caused by a difficult birth, was a drawback. How much, Rach wondered, had Una's father paid to Hamar's family to take her as Hamar's mate? The limp didn't delay them when they went on trading missions or when they sought food amongst the rocks and trees. She wasn't as quick when she ran after her brood, but there were many women and men in the clan to help watch the youngsters.

Una's cheery *holla* answered her. "I see you were talking to Shabar. Is everything ready for the feast? I'm quite looking forward to it. It's many seasons since we had sea turtle. But I grow a little weary of listening to the elder spin his Dreamtime tales." She looked about her, afraid she was overheard.

"You must be careful, Una. Your offspring may be as noisy as the bees in the forest, but they hear everything they are not supposed to." All they needed, Rach thought, was for the traditionalists to hear dissent. The rite of passage controversy was enough for now. Let the elder weave his tales. They would approach one thing at a time.

"You're right. Did you wish to see me about something special? If not, I'm finishing a new skirt for this evening's feast. Mine is getting too small."

Rach gave her a discerning look. Was Una carrying seed, too? Una intercepted Rach's look. "You are too polite to ask, but I will answer anyway. No, I don't think so. I've just been eating more in the last few months. I don't know why, but I have been more uneasy in this camp than before."

Rach nodded. Una didn't have to worry about the female rites of passage. She was already a woman when she came into the camp, and the souls she had borne were all males. Deciding she had nothing more to say, Rach let Una get on with her skirt and returned to her own hut to prepare for the evening.

An-ee sang softly to herself as she skipped along the forest path. Trees ablaze with red flowers showered her with pollen as she passed under them. Watching her step more carefully, she spied a python in the underbrush and knew immediately that she had lost the ability to talk with animals. She had been warned. The Master Dreamer had given her lessons himself. Not all people were so favored. He often delegated others to do this work for him. But ever since she had seen him sobbing into the pouch of Wallaby, he had been extra nice to her. Now it was clear that she could not speak with animals, and she would gradually forget the Dreamtime.

An-ee was not overly concerned. This was a beautiful place. She watched as red and green parrots squawked and darted overhead. Cockatoos added their voices to the din. Their white feathers were a stark contrast to the dark leaves and the colorful plumage of the parrots. She didn't mind that she couldn't understand what they were saying. Part of her was still asleep. She was between two worlds. And it would take adjustments to become wholly of this world, but she knew she would. She had gone through this before. She couldn't remember, however, exactly where or when.

The red path led to the cold, crystal clear water of the spring. She dove in, reveling in the freshness. There had been nothing like this on their trek from the desert to the Sea-turtle encampment. Any water the group had found in the desert had been scarce. This water's coolness soothed her hot skin. If she couldn't be clothed for the evening's feast, at least she could be clean. She reached intuitively for the plant growing beside the water hole and crushed the leaves in her hands, rubbing the crushed leaves over her drying body. Sniffing the new fragrance, she knew she smelled of forest and flowers. She found the dirt path and followed it back to Shabar's hut—the only place she called home at the moment. No other spot had been designated for her. *If Jerosh denies me, what will I do?* An-ee wondered. She rejoined Shabar's family and waited. In the evening sky the Master Dreamer's lights were brightening when men, women, and children began wending their way along the path to the beach.

An-ee helped shepherd the young souls of Shabar and Wil-Wil along the well-marked path. There were a few bad moments when they entered the swampland where crocodiles and many poisonous snakes lived. Three of the younger males walked ahead, making noises and splashing at the water. They all crossed where the swamp was most shallow and narrow and were soon on the beach. The moon cast its silver threads upon the great sea, and the red embers of a beach fire added their glow to the sand and rocks. Tantalizing aromas wafted toward them.

The older men had caught a mammoth sea turtle. Fascinated, An-ee looked on as Wil-Wil told her how they had prepared it. He explained how they had built a fire and heated several small stones while the kalbin killed the turtle by slitting its throat with a sharpened stick. Then the men had placed several heated stones down its throat into the stomach. The slit had been sealed with bunches of reed grass, and the turtle had been left to cook slowly over the remaining fire. It had been roasting for the better part of the day and would be well cooked when the people were ready for the feast.

Most of the people sat on the sand, but being unclothed, An-ee chose to sit on a sun-warmed rock. The children, infected by the elders' excitement, sat impatiently waiting for the momentous event. The trumpeting of a didgeridoo pierced the night sky. Women and men took up clapsticks and clacked in rhythm with the lead man. She gazed with admiration at the beautiful didgeridoo, painted in geometric designs in red, ecru, and black.

When the elder took his position amidst the settled group, the didgeridoo player stopped his trumpeting, and only the rhythm of the sticks remained.

"In the Dreamtime," the elder began, "Waugal, the great rainbow snake, made mountains and freshwater springs. He sent us animals to hunt and eat. He sent us Thunder Man, so we would know fear and awe ..."

How the clan has mixed up the history! Does the Master Dreamer know how they have corrupted the beginning of earth time? An-ee wondered but was in no position to say anything. She knew she was fast forgetting the beginning herself. She was sure, however, that Waugal hadn't made the mountains. The elder passed something around to the men. "Pituri." The word was whispered in her ear. She turned and found Shabar sitting beside her. An-ee had been so engrossed in the scene she hadn't heard the other woman come to the rock. "Now the stories will become really good," Shabar whispered impishly. "The pituri allows our men to see into the Dreamtime. Women are not allowed into this realm. The men say we would defile it."

The young men were dancing in a frenzy, shaking their throwing sticks at imaginary animals in the dramatization of a hunt. The older men took their turn, showing how they had twisted a vine into a pliable lasso and captured the giant sea turtle. When the elder led them all in a prayer of thanks to the sea turtle, An-ee realized that the sea turtle was the tribal totem. They prayed for the sea turtle's forgiveness for taking its life, but explained how the sea turtle's longevity, instincts, and fertility were now part of each tribe member. The elder and several male members turned the turtle so that its shell was against the hot rocks. The kalbin strolled to the fire, pierced the leathery stomach with a pair of cuts in the shape of a cross, folded back the skin, and helped himself to the turtle's heart. As he bit into the source of the turtle's strength, the didgeridoo sounded, and the clapsticks took up the rhythm.

"Great Master Dreamer," the kalbin intoned, "Give us your blessing for this important ceremony. We thank you for sending this girl to be Jerosh's mate. We know you will allow Jerosh to refuse her if it is his wish, and we know you will allow us to send the girl's spirit back to you."

Do I detect a hopeful note in the kalbin's voice? An-ee wondered. *Is he hoping Jerosh and I will mate or that I will be sent back to the Dreamtime?* Several pairs of eyes were upon her. *Where is Jerosh anyway?* She hadn't seen him since coming to the beach. In fact, she was sure he hadn't been with everyone when they made their way across the swampy ground. She recognized hunger pangs in her stomach. Even if she was about to go back to the Dreamtime, she would like to go having a full stomach. She turned to Shabar. "Is it permitted for me to eat part of the great turtle?"

Shabar wasn't sure. She asked Rach, but Rach did not know either. They saw Riva eyeing them with a malicious look. As the eldest, Rach asked Riva's permission for An-ee to have a piece of the great sea turtle.

"Why you be asking me? I am just old woman. You must be asking the elder," she said snidely.

The women suspected that she took immense delight in An-ee's discomfort. Almost as one, they felt sympathy for the girl the Master Dreamer had sent into their midst. Sympathy aside, however, they were not about to ask the elder's permission for her to eat. They were unsure what to do, whispering amongst themselves. The kalbin finally noticed An-ee gazing longingly at the meat.

"In a moment, my child. We must first know whether Jerosh accepts you. If he does, then you must eat of our clan's totem. If he does not, we will dispatch you back to the Master Dreamer before you eat of it. I see the Namarakain nearby. But you are not sick so they cannot take your spirit. In fact, I would say you are quite strong." He was about to say more when an amethyst python slithered by, heading for the swampy ground. His eyes widened, and An-ee saw both fear and awe in his face. "Ah, I see. The Master Dreamer has sent a spirit to protect you. You must be an honored one."

She didn't feel honored. As time passed and Jerosh still failed to appear at the feasting, she felt apprehensive. *Does the elder take Jerosh's absence as a slight?* An-ee wondered. After all, Jerosh was his only son, and not showing up for the ceremony was a blatant disregard for tribal rites. As she was wondering about his motives and lack of respect for tribal customs, Jerosh walked over to the clustered group. He didn't look happy, she noticed. The kalbin passed him a piece of pituri to chew. The didgeridoo resumed its mournful sound, and the clapsticks slowed their rhythm. All eyes were on Jerosh and the high priest.

"Welcome, Jerosh. You know why you are here. As the elder's only son, you must produce an heir to carry on your line. The Master Dreamer has sent this woman to you ..."

Jerosh glanced in her direction. With the exception of Shabar and Rach, she was sure no one knew of their meeting. An-ee was certain Riva expected Jerosh to avoid her, given his experiences with women.

So he prefers the beds of males, An-ee thought. *He can have his preference. But if he expects me to help with his tribe, he better at least put up a good front.* Several moments passed before the priest came, lifted An-ee's hand, and led her to the fire where Jerosh stood. It was then that she noticed Jerosh carried something draped over one arm. "Jerosh, do you accept this woman the Master Dreamer sent you?"

An-ee was keenly aware of the muffled sounds around her. The didgeridoo and the clapsticks were silent. The voices of the birds were stilled. Only the lapping waves against the shore and the hissing fire's steam dared to intrude. She looked at Jerosh with his handsome face, receding forehead, heavy brow, and broad nose. She knew that she was much like him. They were of the same height. He had abundant hair on his chest and arms, although his legs were smooth. She felt quivering in her stomach and put the feeling down to hunger, but it was different from the feeling a few moments before.

"High Priest, I accept this woman as my helpmate. Does she accept me?"

Gasps assaulted her ears. Obviously Jerosh's words were a first for the encampment.

The kalbin's voice held censure. "The woman has no choice. You must know that. If you choose her, she is yours."

"I want her answer, High Priest." Both turned to look at An-ee. Jerosh had an odd look in his eyes she could not discern. The high priest's face showed consternation.

"I accept you." She figured she'd better bring his little charade to a close. Shouts of *holla, holla* rang out over the steaming sea turtle. Jerosh opened his arm to shake out the skirt he had made for her in the forest. It was made of the same pandanus strips that the clan used for utensils and mats, but he had adorned it with the red blooms from the fire tree.

He opened the skirt and put it around her waist. Pulling the cord and straightening the skirt, he tied the cord in a knot. "You are my mate. We must now eat of our totem." He reached into the sea turtle and withdrew a handful of eggs. With a slight shock, she realized the turtle was female. He put one in her mouth and then another. He ate the liver. "I eat of the liver to give me strength. You eat of the eggs to make you fertile. May our clan flourish in this land for many seasons."

The high priest retreated to stand by the elder. Jerosh took An-ee by the hand and led her to the elder's group. "Elder, I present to you my mate, An-ee. Riva, I present to you my mate, An-ee." Both Jerosh and An-ee ignored the piercing gaze of Riva.

After the solemn ceremony, everyone seemed in high spirits, and the corroboree continued into the night. No one returned to camp, and the whole group watched the sun rise to the Master Dreamer's realm and cast its golden light on the serene water. An-ee felt it was a good omen.

"Today, An-ee, you go to the caves. Jerosh must leave his handprint on the walls." It was Shabar speaking. Her easy camaraderie was gone, and in its place was a touch of aloofness.

"You treat me differently today. What has changed you toward me? Are you jealous that Jerosh and I are mated?"

"It is not that. You are moving toward being the leader of our clan. We must honor you."

"But don't you honor Riva?"

"Yes, but now she will slowly lose her standing. The elder will step down gradually as the high priest indoctrinates Jerosh into the clan rites. They start with his handprint on the cave walls, but to learn more of the teachings, Jerosh must produce a child, preferably a male."

How on earth did Jerosh and I get ourselves into this position? An-ee wondered. "What if that doesn't happen? What then?"

Shabar and Rach, who had joined them, looked away from her. "Shabar? Tell me."

"I believe you are sent back to the Master Dreamer."

An-ee had no time to think, for Jerosh came to her after sitting with the males all night and chewing pituri. "It's time, An-ee. We will go to the caves far toward the setting sun. I must leave my handprint to protect our clan from evil spirits."

"Do women go with you?" She saw the women exiting the beach, leaving behind the sea turtle remains.

"Only you come with us. The rest of the women and the older males must stay to protect our encampment."

An-ee didn't know why the camp needed protection but refrained from asking. She was learning that it didn't help having too much to say in this male-dominated camp. She did, however, call Shabar back to the beach. "Does no one take the turtle shell to use as a cooking utensil? Your tribe can also use it to trade. I'm sure others will find it useful."

When Shabar laughed uproariously, several of the women and men turned back. Shabar called to them. "An-ee thinks we should keep the great turtle's shell as a cooking pot or for trade." With one exception, the people joined in laughter. The exception walked to the fire and retrieved the shell. Taking it under her arm, Rach said, "I believe you are right. Our totem would be pleased if we made use of all her parts and wasted nothing. This will make an excellent communal cooking pot." She turned calmly and hastened after the departing group.

"Come. We must hurry, An-ee." Jerosh watched the scene but said nothing in the presence of the others. When they were alone, he said, "You have a friend in Rach. I know you and Shabar are friends, but Shabar sees only surfaces and has much to learn. Rach already thinks beyond the confines of this clan. She will help us in the future."

As he turned to follow the males on their westward journey, An-ee couldn't help but ask, "Why hasn't the clan ever thought of using the shell before this?"

"You have seen us, An-ee. We have all survived without the turtle shell. Even I had not thought of such a use for it." He didn't take her arm. That would have been a show of courtesy that was beyond the clan's thinking. After all, the women were strong and could travel well without the men's help. As they progressed along the path, An-ee saw what resembled a digging stick used by the camp women. She picked it up and dug in the sand as they walked. Carrying a woven basket Una had given her, she stopped every few paces to dig burrowing crabs from the sand. When the group turned inland from the great saltwater sea, she had enough to feed the five males and herself at their evening meal.

As one of the men made a small fire, she gathered nardoo shoots and kneaded them with pollen from the fire tree. From some deep recess within, she recalled how to forage and prepare a meal. She mixed in honey that one of the men found in a forest tree. She placed a large palm leaf on the ground and put the fern cakes in the center. Taking the crabs, she shoved sticks through them and placed them over the fire. Within a short time, they had their meal. It was much later that Rach's mate, Tolo, said to her, "That was one of the best meals I have had." She smiled her thanks to him, knowing what it cost him in male pride to cross the encampment and compliment her.

They slept on the open ground, keeping the small fire burning throughout the dark hours. There was no intimacy between her and Jerosh. *Knowing Jerosh,* An-ee thought, *he is probably heaving quiet sighs of relief he won't have to bed me.* She was glad of the skirt, though, for the forest floor was cool and damp. Her bare breasts felt cold against the earth, but the rest of her was warm as she thought of Jerosh sleeping beside her. Half asleep herself, she turned to him and saw a look of longing on his face. When he realized she was looking at him, he pretended to sleep. Bewildered, she turned her back to him and slept throughout the night.

CHAPTER 5

The next day, one after the other, the men left the camp to relieve themselves in the bush. Then An-ee took her turn. Being thirsty, she searched the nearby ground until she found a fresh-water spring. She wondered if the men knew of its existence. She decided they probably did, as they had been that way before. No one mentioned it to her, so she refrained from bringing it to their attention.

As they journeyed on, the males licked dew from the leaves of certain trees. Jerosh was in the lead with his father, so An-ee turned to ask the high priest about their conduct. "They are getting water. You must keep drinking if you are to keep well in this heat."

"But did the men not drink at the spring close by our encampment?" she asked.

The high priest's eyes widened in surprise. "I did not know there was a spring there. I'm sure the others do not know, either. You should have told us that you found a spring."

"I thought they came this way often, and they must know about it."

"I do not think so. But I must caution you not to say anything now. As you know, there are already a few people in the tribe who do not take kindly to your coming."

"Yes. Are you one of them, Kalbin?"

"I believe the Master Dreamer had his reasons for sending you. I must accept what he says and does. If I do not, I am not fit to be the high priest of this clan." He turned from her.

That certainly doesn't answer my question! An-ee thought.

An-ee knew that the kalbin had many questions about her and Jerosh. He had been dumbfounded at the sea turtle ceremony when Jerosh had presented her with that skirt—and not just an ordinary skirt but one with red flowers woven in it. Jerosh had told her that the kalbin had remarked that the decoration would have been a touch only women would have added. Never had he seen a man do that. "Further than that," *Jerosh* said now, "is that *I* gave you the skirt. It should have been my mother's place to present it to you. I've upset the kalbin. Already he sees that I'm rejecting the rules of our clan."

As the kalbin hastened his steps to keep up with the clan, his walking became mechanical. Annie's question consumed his thoughts. Did he believe in the Master Dreamer as he had told her he did? He couldn't say with any certainty. He was the high priest. He, above all others, should remember the Dreamtime, but he didn't.

From a woven pouch about his neck, he took a piece of pituri. Maybe if he chewed it while they walked, the answers would come to him. He concentrated on the birds and the smaller animals scuffling about his feet, barely noticing when An-ee broke from the line to dig about the tree roots. Soon he saw her placing witchetty grubs in her basket.

He had to admit she was beautiful. Was that why Jerosh had reacted as he had? But when had Jerosh seen her? The clan thinking was that Jerosh preferred men in his bed. The high priest had broached the subject with the elder, who had evaded the question, telling the kalbin to talk to Riva about the matter. The kalbin wondered how much leading the elder actually did. The old man was very much under the thumb of the bitter old Riva.

The high priest pondered the extent of Riva's influence. He did not know the cause of her bitterness, but her animosity was evident from the beginning of his position as kalbin. He had heard she was against any revisions in the camp rites, and he agreed with her on that point. Once traditions began breaking down, it was only a matter of time before chaos followed. What was their problem with the circumcisions, anyway? The tribes had practiced them for many, many seasons. He had to admit, though, he knew many tribes that did not include the female circumcision.

He was sure Rach was from one of those tribes. He didn't have the nerve to ask Tolo whether Rach had undergone initiation. It wasn't Tolo's wrath he feared. It was Rach's. She held herself aloof from the rest of the people and seemed to see right through him. He resented what he saw as her superiority, but she did have an inventive mind that others in the village lacked.

The turtle shell from last night's feast was proof. Other than An-ee, would anyone have seen the possibilities as a utensil? Now that he thought about it, why didn't their people use the large shells that amassed on the beach? Why didn't they use the tree branches to make furrows in the ground to plant seed? He had seen another tribe do that, yet even he had not suggested it to the Sea-turtle clan. He stopped himself. The pituri was affecting his mind more this morning. If he wasn't careful, he would become a Rama-Rama, a crazy person running about and shouting his ideas.

The pituri was strong, but it was not bringing him closer to the Dreamtime as it had in the past. Could it be because he doubted? He quickened his steps. He could not afford to lose sight of the others. The vegetation was thick, and he refused to get lost. If he proved an encumbrance, the clan would consider electing another high priest. Tolo glanced back toward him, but said nothing.

Tolo had changed in the past few years, the kalbin noted. His mating with Rach would have caused that. After all, the women's ideas rubbed off on the men. The kalbin had met with clans that placed a female at the head of the encampment, and he could not see much difference between the two. Although the males *were* a little more subdued in the matriarchal clans than in the clans that had a male as leader. In tribes such as Rach's, the men still hunted, although the high priest noticed that most of their meals were gathered from nearby vegetation.

So much for the pituri. It wasn't helping this morning, and he spit the rest of it into the nearest bush.

Jerosh walked second in the group, behind his father. They didn't speak as they made their way toward the sacred site. He thought he hid his anxiety about his new mating quite well. At least his father had not said anything yet. No one would expect him to bed with An-ee on this journey. First they must go to the sacred site and receive the blessings of the spirits residing there. He wondered what would happen if they didn't give their blessing. Surely that would be no cause for alarm. After all, it was the Master Dreamer who had sent An-ee. Would the spirits dare to reject one of their Master's chosen ones? He wondered about meeting with An-ee on the path that day. Why had he felt so at home with her? He felt he had known her all his life.

What worried him at the moment was his lie. What had caused him to come up with that story about preferring men? He knew, of course, gossip in the camp was of the same opinion. Truthfully, he was hungry for a woman but terrified to mate with one. He had his reasons. An-ee would find out soon enough, and then what would happen? Would she leave him? That would not bode well for her. He could leave her, but the high priest would still put her to death, regardless of the Master Dreamer's wishes. No, he could not do that to her.

He knew if she laughed when she discovered his problem, he would be mortified. He held to one hope. After she found out, she would help him change the rites of passage. It was the only thing keeping him from thinking about her potential ridicule.

The elder kept the fast pace that would get them closer to the sacred site. They would spend two more nights in the bush before they arrived. He wished it could be more. The elder couldn't let Jerosh see the sympathy in his face. He knew what was wrong with Jerosh, but he didn't know how to help him. He couldn't tell anyone, even the high priest, who believed Jerosh preferred men. Riva was the only other person who knew the problem. That was the reason she had turned from a fun-loving and gentle person to the poisonous snake she was today.

Now and then, he could talk Riva out of her spiteful fits. Sometimes he would soothe her and try to make her happy. It was becoming more difficult. What he couldn't understand, though, was why Riva didn't condemn the rites of passage. Why did she take such perverse pleasure in seeing the rites carried out? Coming upon her quietly, he would see tears in her eyes and know that she was exhibiting great control in holding them back. Others could never see the elder's wife in tears. He knew the rest of the clan thought he was dominated by her, but they didn't know. They didn't know, and he couldn't tell them. He worried for Jerosh and his mating bed. He liked An-ee and didn't want to see her hurt by anyone, especially Riva.

Tolo kept pace behind Jerosh and ahead of Hamar. Rach had told him to keep an eye on the participants of the journey, but she wouldn't tell him why. The elder was quieter than usual, but Tolo attributed that to the seriousness of their pilgrimage. Not much bothered the old elder. Tolo suspected that if the old man were worried about anything, he would go to Riva to solve the problem. That aside, he was still the clan's elder and deserved the respect of his people. Also, he did come up with good suggestions at times. There was that day he and Rach had argued about putting plaited mats on the hut floor. Tolo had not seen the necessity, but Rach had insisted that they take the matter to the elder, who surprised Tolo by siding with Rach. "It helps to keep the dampness away from the body, Tolo. I'm surprised one of us hasn't thought of that before." They had put down the mat and it had worked so well that the elder put one down in his, and many of the clan members followed their lead. Yes, the old elder had his good points.

Tolo let his eyes glance over the back of Jerosh. Was the man a little bowed today? Was he wishing to be done with the journey so he could bed his mate? Tolo knew that would be his desire. But he too had heard the rumors about Jerosh. What would happen if the spirits didn't let him put his prints on the cave walls? Would that mean the next elder would be chosen from another of their clan? Tolo knew who would make a good elder. Unfortunately, it wasn't possible in their clan — or was it? They were begging for change. Would the clan go that far? Tolo had no ambitions for the position himself and was quite content to let others make decisions, but he knew Rach would make a great elder.

He looked back to see if the high priest was following. Tolo noticed the glazed look in the kalbin's eyes. Was he chewing pituri to prepare himself for meeting the cave spirits? It seemed too early, but Tolo didn't understand all that the priest had to do, so he kept quiet. He wouldn't dare question the high priest. He wished Rach were here so he could discuss it with her.

He shifted his gaze up through the tall trees to a small section of sky. Now he could speak out, for this was something he understood. "Elder, I think we must stop to find shelter. The sky tells me Thunder-man is upon us. And the galahs and parrots are quiet."

"We must keep going, Tolo. We are sheltered under these trees, even if Thunder-man decides to send wind and ice. A hut wouldn't provide any more shelter than these trees."

The rest of the men seemed to agree, so Tolo said no more. The elder was right, of course. If they were without the woman, he would have agreed also. As it was, he thought they should stop and seek shelter under an overhanging rock. They had found An-ee in the desert. She wouldn't be used to the fierce rains that could assail this bushland. It was the dry season, of course, but that didn't mean it didn't rain, especially if Thunder-man was bored and decided to tease them. They had been subjected to his mischievous behavior many times over the years. He was likely laughing at the group journeying its way along the bush path.

The wind suddenly shook the tree tops, pushing them out of the way so Thunder-man could drop icy pellets on the walking party. The men suffered little as their heads were thick with dark curly hair, and their arms and chests were covered with straighter hair. Their faces, too, wore the same brown curls. An-ee, however, felt the sting of the ice pellets on her face and breasts. She couldn't bring up her hands for protection, because she carried the basket with witchetty grubs and the nardoo fern.

The other men didn't notice her discomfort, but Tolo broke off a palm leaf and shielded her head with it. She smiled at him with the gentlest smile he had ever seen. In that moment, even though the eyes of the other men were upon him, he smiled back, and he knew there was a bond between them. It wasn't as though he wanted to mate with her, but he knew he could trust An-ee with his life. No words passed between them. He held the frond to protect her until Thunder-man tired of his game, and with one last gust, decided he had played with them enough for one day.

An-ee was going to save the witchetty grubs for their evening meal but decided to pass them around as they walked. Afterward, the men seemed a little cheerier. As they walked, they chanted a story about their land. An-ee knew it was for her benefit. They were giving her the history of their clan and land from the Dreamtime to present. She listened, entranced. Frequently, the tales were a repetition from the night of the sea turtle feast, but some were new to her. The clan had developed them over many moons of time. When they came to the end, she gave them a big smile and simply said, "Thank you." There was no need to say anything else. Even if the spirits at the sacred site didn't accept her, she knew she was accepted by these men. She was already a friend of three women. A warm glow filled her heart.

Her heart was an odd thing. She still wasn't accustomed to her body. Every time she thought she had it figured out, she discovered something new. For instance, this pump inside her thumped and banged at the most awkward times. She thought anyone close by must hear it too. There was the time she had walked into a low branch as they entered the rain forest from the desert. She had felt the stabbing pain in her eye, and the water wouldn't stop running. Then her heart had started hammering away. Only when Rach squeezed the juice of a plant into her eye had she felt comfortable again. She let her mind wander to how her heart had beaten erratically when she had met Jerosh and how it skipped and thumped every time he came near her. With these stimulating thoughts, her heart beat even harder as she followed the elder down the path.

CHAPTER 6

After four days of travel through the rain forest, the group came upon the sacred caves. Clans through hundreds of seasons had left their tales of successful hunting, mating, and meetings with the spirits. An-ee felt her skin prickle when she realized that her mating with Jerosh would be added to the stories.

The elder called a halt, and the men prepared a more elaborate camp than they had in the bush. Halfway between rain forest and desert, the trees were smaller and scarcer. An-ee helped find enough branches to build a large hut. Then, under the guidance of the men, she built a smaller one for herself. The elder and the kalbin chose to sleep outside under the overhanging rock, almost as though they guarded the sacred site. Knowing the men would stop her, An-ee did not bother trying to get closer to the caves. With the exception of the elder and the kalbin, the men all slept together, so Jerosh had another reprieve. She didn't dream of the Before Time. In fact, she could barely remember it. Instead, the image of Jerosh floated through her dreams.

The next day, the religious ceremonies began in earnest. The elder painted his face and body with white and yellow ocher. His markings told of past hunts and how the sea turtle had become their totem. "In the Long Ago," he intoned, "an intrepid clan member rescued the great sea turtle from a tangle of reeds in the salt swamps bordering the sea. In gratitude, the sea turtle blessed the people and gave permission for the clansmen to use it as their identification." An-ee wondered whether the sea turtle knew its descendants would be eaten at future feasts. She doubted it, but kept the doubts to herself.

The kalbin painted his face and body the same way, using the spiritually significant white ocher. His designs told of the Dreamtime and the Master Dreamer. He chanted in a sing-song voice that rose to a high pitch and lowered to a thundering bass. "The Master Dreamer dreamed this land in the time before time, when we were all asleep." As he sang the story, he passed out pieces of pituri to the men, and An-ee became lost in her own musings. As if from a distance, she noted that the others swayed as they listened to the tale. She could smell the soft scent of many flowers, the sweat of the men, and the aroma of Jerosh. He sat in his cloak of painted figures, emitting a soft, medicinal scent after his wash in the eucalyptus dew.

"He gave this land to us for safekeeping, and he gave all the animals and plants to us for our use. He taught us how to hunt for meat, and he taught our women how to dig for plants and grubs. This is our land for now and into the coming seasons. The Master Dreamer has told us that others will come from across the sea to this land. Then the land will not be our land. We will have to share with these men of pale skin and light-colored hair."

An-ee couldn't remember the Master Dreamer ever saying anything like that. If he told the people so many seasons ago, he might have decided once was enough. She wondered whether it was important and thought not. She wouldn't be here in the distant seasons and neither would these people with her.

"We must look after this land for our Master Dreamer. We must not let the evil spirits keep us from our task. Look upon the sacred site of the spirits, and I will show you the story of our land and people."

The kalbin was not chewing the pituri plant. She saw Jerosh placing another leaf in his mouth and watched as he swayed in a trance. The rest of the men did the same. She was swaying also, but her mind was elsewhere. *What was it the kalbin said?* She had lost track of his story. *If I want to do the Master Dreamer's work,* Annie thought, *I better pay attention.*

"This is a picture of the fierce crocodile. Two of our ancestors went to the Dream Land on this hunt. Their story is told

here for all to know how brave our people were. We must keep
that bravery."

The high priest pointed out two red and white figures on the
cave walls. They were tall and thin. "These are the Namarakain,
waiting to steal the souls of the sick. They wait in this wall until
their chance. They are thin, because we give them little opportunity to seize our people. We are strong. We are powerful. We
are the Master Dreamer's dreams."

The men agreed in a chorus of "Ah-yes," slurred by the effects
of the pituri. An-ee wasn't sure if she was supposed to join the
chorus or not, so she kept quiet. If she spoke up wrongly, she
wasn't sure what her punishment would entail. If she violated
their ceremonial rites, she was sure that no one would come to
her rescue.

"This figure here," intoned the kalbin, pointing his finger at
an elongated, white figure on the wall, "is not a painting but
the shadow of Mimi. Mimi can blow on the rock, and it will
open and let her in. We do not know whether she dwells within
the rock, or whether she seeks temporary shelter there from the
Namarakain."

The kalbin was winding down. An-ee began to feel isolated
from the group, even though she swayed in unison with the
men. It was all she could do not to hum the tune lilting through
her mind. Where was her mind, anyway? She seemed to float
above the men who looked at the kalbin with reverence. She
knew she wasn't in the Dreamtime. There was land below her.
Red land. Her land. The land that she came back to time after
time.

The kalbin took a step toward Jerosh and her body. How
was she to get back? At this thought, she was back in her body,
swaying in rhythm. She became aware of the flies again and
the hot sun. The kalbin held his right hand out to her and his
left to Jerosh. He raised them both from the ground and led
them closer to the paintings on the wall. She hadn't noticed
the elder mixing ground powders. He passed a scoopful to the
kalbin, who held it above his head and intoned a chant to the
Master Dreamer. Then he placed the bark scoop before Jerosh,

who took a handful of powder into his mouth. Jerosh placed his hand on a bare spot on the red rock wall and blew the white powder over his hand. After a second, he lifted his hand away, and she saw that he left his hand's outline on the rock wall. In long seasons to come in the red land, tales would be told of Jerosh and An-ee.

Left standing while Jerosh performed his artistic work, she began to wonder what part she played in this. She wondered why she was here with the group at all. After Jerosh blew the white ocher onto the wall, the elder gave him a drink of water from a bark scoop. Jerosh swished the water around his mouth and spit it out. Then the kalbin lifted An-ee's hand and joined it with Jerosh's. "These two people are united at the sacred site of the Master Dreamer. We have seen no evil spirits about. This tells us this union is blessed. Today we will stay at the sacred site and feast. Tomorrow we return to the Sea-turtle clan. When Jerosh and An-ee bring forth their first child, Jerosh will begin instruction from his father. If no child is produced, Jerosh will begin instruction under me to become the next kalbin. This will be decided after twelve moons. If An-ee has given life, or she is carrying a new spirit, Jerosh will become your next elder. If not, An-ee must go into exile, and Jerosh will assume my title. Now An-ee knew what the tribe expected of her. She would be in a dilemma, however, until she spoke with Jerosh alone. She didn't want to run afoul of his plans. Did he want to be the next elder of the clan or the next kalbin?

The ceremony over, the men spent a half hour debating the merits of a kangaroo hunt. It was obvious to An-ee the debate was a show for her benefit. For this hunt, they brought their boomerangs, and as Tolo was the master boomerang thrower, he was elected the group leader. It was clear that An-ee was to stay behind to prepare the rest of the meal.

She didn't mind and began to forage for nardoo ferns. As the men left, she retraced her steps into the bush where she had seen bees earlier. When she found the spot, she shinnied up the tree and grabbed a chunk of honeycomb. She eased down the smooth bark of the trunk until she felt the ground. When she arrived back at the encampment, she looked at the comb and noticed several cells of grubs among the honey. That would be a bonus.

She left the comb submerged in a basket of cool water, ensuring the scent didn't attract a swarm to camp. Picking up another basket, she went looking for low hanging branches bearing blossoms. When she found several, she shook the pollen into a bark cup, wrapped it in a large leaf, and placed it in the basket.

As she turned to leave, she spotted a male emu on a large nest under a bush. She had to be careful. She recalled from some deep and almost-forgotten experience that one hard push from his leg could cause serious harm. She backed away, and when she was out of sight, she imitated the female emu in distress. When she peeked around a branch, she saw the male lift its head with his quandary evident in his eyes. Should he go to his mate, or should he protect the nest? She waited several minutes and then imitated the distress call again. This time, the male made up his mind. He rose from the nest, and An-ee crawled on her belly, lifting four of the large green eggs and leaving six. The emu, not hearing any more distress calls, sat down again upon his depleted brood, and she retreated backward, clutching the treasure.

Relaxed in the men's absence and successful in her food gathering, An-ee was in a euphoric mood as she crept back to the cave site. Gathering small twigs, she made a fire from the coal she had kept alive in a green leaf. The first night on the trail, the men were surprised when she pulled it out of her basket. There had been looks of admiration, but not one of them gave her a word of praise. She had been particularly disappointed that Jerosh didn't say anything, especially after he had made such a display of giving her the skirt.

There were large pieces of sandstone at the outer edges of the cave, and she placed them in a ring around the twigs and grass fire. She placed the eggs close to the hot sandstones where they would cook as she prepared the rest of the meal. With the kangaroo meat, they would eat well this night—maybe even enough to go without food for a day or two.

An-ee was beginning to feel uncomfortable from all the food she had eaten over the past few days. She wanted to feel light again, like she felt when the kalbin was giving his rendition of their history. She thought of that recent experience while she mixed nardoo fern with the pollen and honeycomb. Did the kalbin speak the truth? Did it matter? She saw their history as nothing more than a means to keep the people together. People were so afraid of drifting outside the life they knew, and what they knew was handed down season after season in a serpentine strand. Looking back, all they could see of the strand were the outer curves. The inner stretches remained hidden. At the moment, An-ee had no earth history to believe, so she thought she might as well accept what the kalbin said.

The men returned to camp without a kangaroo, or honey ants, or even termites. As she looked at them, Tolo and Jerosh spoke as one.

"An-ee! You should have seen the big red kangaroo we saw."

"It was too fast. Tolo couldn't get close enough to throw his boomerang, and our throwing sticks were useless. It was the only one we saw." Jerosh seemed to have been appointed the one to explain. She wondered why they thought she needed an explanation.

She said, "Well, it doesn't matter. I have nardoo fern cakes with honeycomb and pollen. Emu eggs and witchetty grubs are cooking over the fire. I also found sweet water and have added honey to it. We can have a good meal from that." She smiled at the men's astonished faces. *If they think I'm going to be helpless, they're in for a shock. No wonder the Master Dreamer sent me to Jerosh. Between the two of us, we should be able to expand the awareness of the clan.* She noticed the elder was looking at her with admiration and humor. The kalbin was not. She didn't know why, but he was extremely wary of her. He tried to hide it during the sacred cave ceremony, but she could feel the intense emotion emanating from him. She decided to ask Jerosh what caused the kalbin's intense negativity around her.

They feasted on her prepared meal and listened to Tolo trumpet the didgeridoo while the men clacked their sticks in rhythm. The elder told a story of the Dreamtime, and they withdrew into the huts to sleep. The next day they would return to the village.

She awakened when someone nestled against her back. Lying quietly, she let Jerosh's hand caress her breast and send shivers into her stomach. She felt his full organ at her back, engorged with the seed that he would plant in her this night. *Will it grow?* An-ee's mind raced. *Will Jerosh be the next clan elder?* She wanted to speak to him about these questions first. She needed to know what he wanted before he planted his seed. She turned onto her back to whisper to him. Her eyes widened. It was the kalbin. He tried to place his hand over her mouth, but she anticipated his movement and bit him on the wrist. He muffled his grunt of pain and outrage with his hand and slipped out of the black hut into the star-laden night.

For the rest of the night, An-ee stayed awake. This was not supposed to be this way. Did the kalbin put his seed in all the women? Was that part of his role? Was he supposed to do it before the mate had a chance? She made up her mind to ask Jerosh in the morning. She wanted to talk to him alone, but it looked as though it would be impossible before they returned to their encampment.

Should she ask the elder about it? She felt that he was on her side. In fact, all of the men except the kalbin seemed to like her. For the remaining hours, she thought about this world into which she had been thrust. It was harder when she had nothing with which to compare her journey. Her head was a confusion of many thoughts as well as faded and distorted memories. She wanted Jerosh there with her. Why wasn't he? They had been joined at the feast of the sea turtle in front of the whole encampment. They had been presented at the sacred site. What more did this clan require? She knew it wasn't the Master Dreamer who made these rules. He more or less dreamed the outline, and the clans filled in the rest. Like the outline of Mimi on the cave walls or the outline of Jerosh's hand, outlines didn't tell the whole story. They left a lot to one's imagination.

CHAPTER 7

Seven full rising moons had passed. Jerosh and An-ee had finished construction of their hut and were occupying it as a mated couple, assuming their roles as clan members. They had not yet coupled. When An-ee had told Jerosh about the kalbin, he had frowned and expressed bewilderment and disbelief at the actions of the high priest. Other than that, he said nothing about the incident. She didn't think any of the women would believe her story, unless the same thing had happened to them. She rather thought it hadn't.

"You and I will have to mate soon. Shabar was questioning me today if I carried your seed. This clan is too small to keep such things secret. Also, Shabar said I do not have the look of a woman who has coupled."

"I know how it is for you. And Shabar is right. You still have the look of an unmated woman." Jerosh looked embarrassed.

"Is it that you wish to become the high priest?"

"No!" Jerosh's violent response shocked her. "I do not respect the kalbin, and I wouldn't want to be in his position."

"Why do you think he came to me?"

"I don't know. I have been trying to decide whether I should speak to the elder."

"If you do that, you must realize the kalbin will deny his action."

He turned to her with a soft look. Her insides were doing funny things. "I know, yet I can't help but think it would have been a good thing if he completed what he set out to do. At least then you would have given life to a new member of the clan. You might even have enjoyed the coupling."

"How can you say that? I am mated with you."

56

"You don't even know what it is like to be mated, and I cannot do that with you. We must think of what to do." He bowed his head into his hands.

She went over to him and began running her hands over his chest and stomach. She was new to this, but the feelings that were inside her urged her on. She noticed the bulge in Jerosh's loincloth. She knew it was from here that the seed for the new life would come.

"Am I so ugly, Jerosh? Could you not once put your seed inside me? I do not care that you prefer men, but if you want to be the next elder of the Sea-turtle clan, you know you must give life to a new soul from the Dreamtime."

Jerosh was breathing heavily, and deep emotions played across his face. Lowering her onto a mat on the floor of the hut, he removed the skirt he had made for her. "This is not as good a skirt as the one Shabar owns. They take ages to make."

"I love this skirt, Jerosh. The red flowers are gone now, but I can get more to weave into the fronds. You must want me more than you know to have made it."

"In many ways you are like a child. You do not understand the ways of my clan."

"Then explain them." First he looked at her nub of flesh that seemed to make women happy with mating. He took the nub and gently rubbed it with his fingers. She groaned and undulated against his hand. If this was mating, she loved it. Without willing it, she shuddered, and with a soft moan relaxed into the earth floor. "You gave me your seed. I know it will grow in me."

"No. I have not given you my seed. I have given you pleasure. Our women have a difficult time achieving this. That is why I am against the rites of our village. Our women lose their nub of pleasure as soon as they reach the age of initiation."

She frowned. "You mean the little nub is taken from them?"
"Yes."

"I wish to give life to your seed. You are a good and intelligent man. Of course, Tolo is too," she added teasingly. "I should ask him to give me his seed."

He glowered at her. "You are my woman. If Tolo even came near you, both you and he would be killed. That is why I am surprised the kalbin came to you." It astonished him that he found An-ee so appealing and wanted to protect her. He knew that An-ee found him attractive too, and this thought humbled him even more. He lifted her and held her in his arms. Her sweet scent intoxicated him. "I feel as if we've known each other since the beginning of time." When he pressed her breasts against his chest, a tear escaped the corner of his eye, and a small sad smile softened his lips.

She noticed that the bulge under his loincloth was gone. Reaching under the woven leaves, she massaged his organ until it was engorged. Before he had time to react, she removed his cloth. She was sure what she saw was not normal. The pouch hanging between his thighs was huge and held his many seeds, but his organ was mutilated so the end was thick with fleshy nodules that traveled to the middle of his organ. He was embarrassed, and his organ shrank again. When it shrunk, it looked like one of the warty melons she had seen growing close to the pathway to the river.

"I do not think this is as it should be. What is wrong?" He did not prefer men to women. "This is why you cannot give me your seed, isn't it? This is why you are against the rites of your clan." The revelation cleared up many questions in her mind. "Who else knows about this?"

"The elder, of course, and Riva. Perhaps the high priest, but I am not sure."

"But have they not gone to your medicine man for help?"

"I think not. After all, he takes part in the ritual. No one else has this problem."

She took his hand away from where he shielded his shrunken organ and examined it closely, understanding why the initiation rites had to be amended. "They can't be abandoned entirely. That is too much to ask. But if we can prevent this from happening again, I will do all I can to help. In the meantime, I wonder if there is anything we can do to help you."

"Please don't do anything to bring the wrath of the village down on you. I thank the Master Dreamer every day for giving you to me. I would not like to lose you. Now that you've seen my problem, I do not have to worry anymore. You see that I cannot bed you or give you my seed, but I can pleasure you in other ways."

She could find no words to reply. Compassion welled in her, and she put her hand to his face. Her mind worked to find a solution. When she could think of none, she left him to go to Shabar's hut, where Shabar was showing her how to make a more permanent skirt.

As they worked the leaves, she remarked to Shabar about her swollen belly. Shabar laughed. "You won't believe this, but I say Wil-Wil only has to look at me, and I carry his seed."

"What?"

"I'm joking, but it is possible. You do not know yet with Jerosh, but Wil-Wil can plant his seed without putting his organ in me. He often takes his finger and puts it inside of me. When we are both in the mood, he spills his seed on his finger before he puts it in my belly, and I'm sure the Master Dreamer sometimes lets a woman carry seed this way." Shabar gave a laugh of embarrassment. "I shouldn't be telling you these things. I'm sure they would not be accepted by the elder or the kalbin."

"You know I wouldn't tell anyone. What you and I say is between us. I wouldn't even tell Rach."

"I wouldn't mind you saying anything to Rach. She is not from this clan, and she understands a great many things. Perhaps you're right, though. The fewer people who know our personal life, the better." She placed her hand on her swollen belly and moaned. "Just thinking about it makes me want Wil-Wil. Oh, An-ee, am I evil to have these thoughts?"

"Not evil, no. But you *have* given life to more souls than anyone else in this clan. You can ask the shaman for an herb so you do not give life so often."

Shabar looked as though the thought appealed to her. "After I thrust this life into the world, I may take your advice. The shaman will know what to do. Wil-Wil may not be pleased, though. For all his protestations, I know he is proud that he has given me so much seed." The youngest of Wil-Wil's seeds interrupted them, and An-ee took her leave.

The women were preparing the communal meal, and An-ee took her place with the others around the fire to help. Rach was there with her three children preparing roots to steam in the green leaves. The people exhibited unusual restlessness. She asked Rach about it.

"It is time for us to go hunting and gathering again. Our clan cannot sit still in this encampment for much longer. Except for the mission when we found you, the camp has been here for a longer time than usual. We are not used to staying in one spot for so long. I've spoken with Tolo, and he agrees we should visit my Lizard clan. I'm taking your advice and gathering shells and the turtle shell to take with us."

"What does this clan trade that your tribe does not have?"

"The women of my Lizard clan do not have the skirts of the Sea-turtle clan, for one thing. They also do not have medicines such as we have from the many plants here. We can also give them woven mats and baskets."

"What do we get in return?"

"They give us tools made from hard stone. We use these for preparing the leaves for weaving. They also give us many honey ants, which we like to eat."

"I've tasted the honey ants and enjoy them, but it seems that the Turtle clan gives more than it gets."

"Not so. We also get medicine from the death snake and the tiger snake. The adders do not live here, but their medicine helps cure many illnesses. Even if it were not for the ants, tools, and medicines, the Pitjantjatjara allow us to visit the most holy of holy sites. They tend Uluru and Kata Tjuta. Oh, An-ee, you will love it when we visit. I know you will."

Intense longing filled Rach's voice. Her eyes had a sparkle that was generally missing, even when she spoke of Tolo or her children.

"When do we go?"

"Not till after the older boys go through their rites. They will be doing so soon. My Luk, Shabar's boy, Jub, and Raja's boy, Shak. They start tomorrow with the older men and the kalbin cutting their organs, and then they must live alone in the bush for two moon cycles. When they return, there will be a feast like at your mating. But we will have large fish and not a sea turtle."

An-ee was alerted. "Must the boys have their organs cut? It seems like a horrendously painful rite. And perhaps they will not be able to sow their seed afterwards." She was thinking of Jerosh's badly mutilated organ and did not wish that on any boy or man.

She was not prepared for Rach's answer. "The boys look forward to it. Oh, not the actual cutting, but they do not feel anything."

"How do you know? Even if you ask them, they would deny it. Can you honestly see any of the boys protesting? It would not seem manly for them to complain."

"No, An-ee. It is the rite of this clan. They must go through it." Rach was determined An-ee understand her position. When An-ee let her gaze wander from Rach, she realized everyone was looking at them and listening to their conversation. Determined to speak with Rach when they were alone, An-ee let the matter drop and helped in the food preparation.

Throughout the meal, laughter and talk flowed. The older men regaled the clan with their feats in the bush during their own initiation periods. She suspected that much of their talk was building their egos and letting the younger men know they had ideals to live up to. No one seemed to mind, and the past hunts grew more fierce and perilous as the evening progressed.

Even after all the food was eaten, members of the clan continued to sit around the communal fire until the Master Dreamer's lights were dimming in the sky. She noticed the four boys were included in the group, and the men were teasing them about the upcoming ceremony. The boys, all about eight seasons old, were putting up a brave front. She glanced at Jerosh and saw anxiety on his face. She longed to allay his fears.

An-ee's glance happened to fall on Riva, and An-ee started in surprise. *Is that sorrow I see in the old woman's face?* Riva was the most ardent advocate for the ceremonial rites. Her gaze went to the kalbin, and she discovered him looking at her with haughty aloofness and wariness. She decided to ignore him and turned back to Jerosh, placing her hand on his arm as she did so.

Gradually, the couples broke apart and went to their huts. She wanted to tell Jerosh of the plan she'd been devising since the afternoon he had pleasured her, but she knew now was not the time. Inside their hut, she smiled at him. "Come down to the pool with me. The moon is giving out much light tonight." She wanted to get him alone, without his loincloth, in the cooling spring waters. But he turned from her and pretended to sleep.

She overheard the kalbin return to a discussion with the senior tribe members. They were making sure everything was ready for the morrow. The high priest knew her thoughts on the rites, but if the camp was to remain united, they must continue the ceremonies. He wouldn't let traditional rites be thrown away.

Rach returned with Tolo to their hut. She shouldn't have been so harsh with An-ee, but she hadn't wanted the rest of the camp to hear. It was one thing to voice an opinion to a friend and another to stand in front of the whole camp and say what was wrong. The time would come, though. And she wasn't sure whether she or Tolo had the strength for it.

Tolo, who had been quietly working close to the center of the camp, knew what happened at the meal preparation. "You were severe with An-ee. Was that necessary? After all, she doesn't know our rites."

He was glad Rach wasn't jealous of his friendship with An-ee. He wouldn't be jealous if Rach wanted a friendship with Jerosh, but she didn't. Jerosh was a funny fellow, though. Very aloof. He never went to the pool with the men. He had heard that Jerosh preferred to bed men, but he didn't know if that was true or not. He had never seen Jerosh make any advances toward any man. And all the men had given their seeds to women except Jerosh.

He hoped An-ee would give life to Jerosh's seed soon. That would put all the rumors to rest. Maybe it would even make old Riva happy. With that thought in his mind, he turned away from Rach without waiting for her answer. Besides, he knew Rach's answer. They thought the same. He was glad they had gone to the Lizard clan for his woman, and although he would never say so, he thought he had the best mate in the camp. He went to sleep with a smile on his face, not seeing the answering smile on Rach's face.

CHAPTER 8

When An-ee went into the forest to pick fruit for their morning meal, she passed the initiates. The three men-to-be were drinking a liquid the shaman gave them. Two of the older men, uncles to the young males, were down on all fours in the center of the camp. The sound of the didgeridoo blasted through the bush, making the gliders shiver in the treetops. The cockatoos and parrots squawked loudly, trying to outdo the didgeridoo.

One of the men took an initiate and bent him backwards across the backs of the two kneeling men. As the kalbin intoned a chant to the Master Dreamer, the women cheered on the luckless young men. Taking a sharp cutting stone, the kalbin cut the foreskin of the organ of the boy. He appeared not to feel it. In fact, he was near giggling. *What potent mixture*, An-ee wondered, *has he been given?*

After the piece of skin was removed, the kalbin rubbed a mixture of honey and a plant leaf into the wound, and the boy was allowed up. The elder removed him into the bush where he urinated quietly, his back turned to the camp. Everyone pretended not to notice, and he returned with a confident grin.

After the same ritual was followed with the three remaining boys, the older men, the kalbin, and the elder led each boy in a different direction into the bush where they would live alone for two moon cycles. They would have to hunt their own food, but they must not hunt the larger animals such as the emu or the kangaroo. Besides being dangerous, these animals deserved a worthy opponent, according to tradition. And the boys must not hunt the sea turtle. It was too soon. To be hunted by a mere initiate would turn the clan's totem against them.

When the ceremony was over, An-ee looked for Jerosh. Finding him nowhere, she decided to visit Riva. If she talked to the old woman, she might understand her better. It was a good time, as the elder was still taking one of the boys down an easterly path. She prayed to the Master Dreamer to watch over the youngsters. They weren't Jerosh's seed, but they were some other man's, and she knew all the men felt both pride and concern.

The old woman was not in her hut. Knowing of Jerosh's problem, An-ee felt she understood Riva's emotional turmoil and guilt. She followed the path to the pool. The woman was in the water scrubbing herself with an abrasive plant that grew nearby. Not wanting to intrude, An-ee crept quietly backward before Riva could see her. When Riva came out of the pool and was putting her skirt back on, An-ee retraced her steps noisily to the pool. Riva looked up. "You don't have to pretend you be just getting here. I saw you coming the first time. But I do thank you for your consideration of an old woman's feelings."

They were the first pleasant words she had heard from Riva, and for a moment An-ee was too amazed to reply. Gathering herself, she asked permission to speak. "I think you know what it is about."

Riva seemed reluctant, but An-ee divined the old woman needed to talk. She wouldn't come to the pool for such a scrubbing if she didn't have misgivings about the rituals. Besides bathing, the pool was used as a place for spiritual cleansing and rebirth, and it seemed to have worked a miracle on Riva. An-ee took advantage of Riva's more amenable mood. "Riva, you must tell me what happened to Jerosh." The old woman withdrew into herself, but An-ee persisted. "I know you feel sad it happened. I think that is why you cover up with your nastiness and don't let people get close to you. You feel you're to blame, don't you?"

Refusing to look in An-ee's eyes, the old woman gazed at a nearby tree and whispered *yes*.

"Does the elder blame you?"

"He blames himself as much as he blames me. You must understand. Jerosh be the only soul we gave life to." Riva paused and looked at the sky. She looked everywhere but at An-ee. "Because Jerosh be the elder's child, we asked the kalbin to cut the flesh around his organ. Because Jerosh be the elder's son, he was given nothing for the pain, but he didn't cry out. I be so proud of him. But something went wrong. He didn't heal as he should have. For a long time I blamed the shaman, accusing him of putting the wrong plant and honey on the boy's organ, but he has always denied this."

An-ee felt sympathy, both for Jerosh and the woman who bore him "So you don't know what went wrong? Why Jerosh has those horrible bumps all over his organ?"

"No. No one knows. We told no one except the kalbin. We could not make Jerosh a joke for our clan. It be enough that he cannot plant his seed." She gave An-ee a look of pity and guilt. "And I also feel it be my fault the kalbin will either exile or kill you. He does not truly believe the Master Dreamer sent you. He knows you and Jerosh will not give life, and he won't tolerate any defilement of our clan, nor does he want Jerosh as the next kalbin."

"The kalbin who is here now, was he at Jerosh's ceremony?"

Riva shook her head. "No. He knows Jerosh be wanting the circumcision rites abolished. And I believe he thinks Jerosh prefers men. He wants to get rid of Jerosh, but he doesn't know how."

An-ee considered for a moment and decided to tell Riva about the kalbin's attempt to put his seed in her. Riva's shock was palpable.

"I think he wants to make sure Jerosh be not the next kalbin," Riva pointed out. An-ee had a plan she had been formulating since the early hours of the day before. She told it to Riva, trusting the old woman to accept the idea.

"You think it will work?" The old woman gave An-ee a look saying she hoped An-ee wasn't a Rama-Rama.

"Yes."

Riva nodded her head. She was glad Ann-ee hadn't asked about the ceremonial rites. What could she say? Part of Riva wanted another to suffer as she suffered. Part of her wanted the ceremonies to continue, because she felt the same as the kalbin. Riva hoped An-ee would begin to understand her position. If tradition came to a halt, what would follow? Riva couldn't explain any of this to An-ee. She turned and followed a different path back to her hut and left An-ee to follow the original path.

An-ee looked after her for a few minutes, feeling certain Jerosh's mother regretted telling her so much. But she was glad she had sought out the old woman. At least An-ee had her blessing for what would happen next. Retracing her steps back to the clan camp, she met Una.

"You have been to the pool? I am going there and was hoping to find a companion to bathe with me. Shabar is busy with her eldest girl, and Rach is holding tightly to her younger son, who will be going through the initiation rites in a few years. I think the rites this morning hurt them more than the boys." Agreeing, An-ee left her to travel to the pool alone. She did not feel like Una's company. And from what Una had said, neither Shabar nor Rach would be good company, either. She sought out Jerosh, who was playing a game of throwing sticks into a circle with several other clan men. She placed her hand on his shoulder.

"I need you for a moment." He flushed with embarrassment. A woman never went to her mate in front of the others in the clan.

"Holla. Your woman does not come from a clan that removes the nub, huh?" Hamar nudged the man next to him, and they all broke into ribald laughter. If she continued making these social errors, Jerosh would not be as happy with her as he was now. Pretending she didn't care whether Jerosh followed her, she turned away. The remark about her nub brought back memories of the other night, and all at once she did want Jerosh for that.

Jerosh continued with his game for a little while longer to save face with his fellow males. She knew he was nervous about getting close to her. He wanted to spill his seed into her and knew he could not. She didn't even know if he could release his seed. He could relieve himself of water, so there was nothing wrong with his organ that way. *Yes*, Annie thought. *I will offer my idea.*

Jerosh entered their hut, glowering and muttering about women in general. She held back her laughter, believing his voluble expletives were for the benefit of his fellow males. But she soon found she was wrong. She had not seen her mate this angry before. "You made a fool of me. I did not expect that of you."

"I didn't mean to. You know I would not make you a fool in front of your fellow males." Jerosh wasn't listening. He was too agitated.

"I made you a skirt and gave it to you. I was willing to make a fool of myself for you, but I did not expect *you* to make a fool of *me*."

When he was in this foul mood, he wouldn't be romantically inclined. "Go back to your fellows. I will tell you what I want later." To her consternation, he went.

She thought about following him and apologizing, but that would make the situation worse. The other men would take sides, either for or against Jerosh. She stayed where she was, but she felt uncomfortable. These people had learned their social customs over hundreds of years, yet they expected her to know everything in a few short months.

The MD had much to answer for. When she returned from this journey, she would tell the old man what she thought of his methods. Why he sent some as infants and others fully grown was beyond her. He probably devised the method in one of his moods after too much wine. She couldn't remember too much about that time, anyway. In fact, she would swear *she* was dreaming this whole thing.

She stayed in their hut alone for most of the afternoon and then joined the rest of the women in preparing food for their evening meal. It was a much-subdued group with Shabar and Rach feeling the absence of their sons. Shabar kept her hand possessively over her stomach. Wil-Wil gave his mate a solicitous look. An-ee liked him. She truly liked most of the mates of her women friends. They all had one thing in common. They looked more protectively on their mates than the older men did. Were customs changing on their own? Was a quiet revolution taking place within the Sea-turtle clan? An-ee knew that the women of this clan couldn't wait that long.

As the Master Dreamer's moon rose over the treetops, the couples drifted off to their huts. There was none of the laughter and play that normally followed the evening meal. "The men are going to need to console their mates tonight, it seems," Jerosh said, with a small mocking smile playing about his mouth. "It is not as bad as you women think, An-ee."

"What do you mean? The women are thinking of their young men out in the bush alone, not to mention the ritual cutting of their organ, which must be quite painful." She hoped to lead into her plan.

"Do not say anything to the other women, but the boys are not completely alone in the bush. The kalbin and some of the senior men check periodically on the initiates. The boys are not supposed to know this."

"You mean they aren't out there alone?"

"Yes, they are. But somebody always knows how they are doing.

"I think it must still be frightening." A shudder went through her at the thought of being in the rain forest with the poisonous snakes and spiders.

Jerosh looked at her. "I remember one or two nights when I felt fright, but not as often or as long as you think. After all, the rain forest is our home. How could they feel frightened in their home? The boys learned quite early how to take care of themselves in the forest. The rite just reinforces their ability to rely on their own resources. There can't always be another person to depend on, An-ee. This rite makes the boy strong and alert to the sounds of the bush."

She went over to him again. He seemed to be in a better mood than before. She didn't know what would heal his organ. Perhaps there was nothing that could be done. The damage had been many seasons ago.

About to speak and coax him, she noticed that Jerosh caught her mood. "So, you want to be pleasured again, do you? It's a good thing I cannot give you my seed. You would be giving life every nine moons."

She smiled. The thought wasn't so bad. They were lying on the woven mat on the earth floor. "I talked to Shabar last noon meal." Jerosh stiffened beside her. "I didn't say anything about you," she assured him. "But I was teasing her about giving life again so soon after she birthed her last one, and she said something that made me think we might try to implant your seed in me."

When she revealed her plan, he was startled and reluctant, but she persisted. "We can try it. Please!"

He relaxed and began caressing her as he had before, letting his hand glide over her eager body, from her slender throat to her dark brown arms and legs. When he went over her entire form, he concentrated on her center of pleasure. At the same time, she massaged his organ and willed him to orgasm. When he at last spilled his seed, she took some on her finger and inserted it inside her body. He rubbed her until she moaned and undulated with rapture.

Finding the whole procedure exciting, he became aroused again. Once more, she brought him to orgasm, and he took the spilled seed in his hand and inserted it inside her, bringing her once again to ecstasy. When they were calm, they chanted a prayer to the Master Dreamer to bless them with a new life.

For the two moon cycles while the boys were away in the bush, An-ee and Jerosh continued their experiment. The clan wasn't paying much attention to them these days. Their focus was on the great kunapipi ceremony following the boys' return.

On the day of their return, the clan gathered on the beach, with a large fish roasting over the fire. Eggs from many birds and the female fish were gathered in a woven basket and set to one side. Each of the boys presented a male animal to the clan, and the elder and the kalbin ceremoniously accepted each one. These were the boys' first kills for the community.

The young men stood in a circle around the basket of eggs, their backs to the females. The men formed a circle around them, effectively shutting them off from view. Then the young initiates were given a plant to chew. After chewing, there was much laughing as the boys took their organs in their hands. When the boys pretended to spill their seed onto the eggs, the kalbin raised the basket above his head and showed it to the clan. "These initiates are now members of the Sea-turtle clan. On our next mission to another tribe, we will negotiate women for them."

"Jerosh—"

"Shush. I know what you wish to know. I will tell you later."

Shabar and Rach went from worried mothers to proud mothers. An-ee couldn't help but feel a little resentment at being excluded from this group. Even though many other women were excluded, this was temporary. They either had sons who had gone through the ceremony, or they had sons who would go through the ceremony. As yet, An-ee had neither.

CHAPTER 9

The large trading party left at dawn, taking the same path An-ee and the men had traveled to the sacred site. This time, she was not the lone woman. All the Sea-turtle clan women were on the trek, even Riva. The young children were left in the care of older siblings and three men who were too aged for the journey. Amid chagrined laughing from some of the older members, Rach and An-ee carried four turtle shells and several seashells to trade. Three kilometers down the path, they turned and headed southward. As they traveled farther, they left the bush behind and came upon the desert where An-ee had awoken from the Before Time. The hot, dry air greedily sucked their bodies' moisture. Still, the desert was more comfortable for An-ee than the bush land. In the bush, it was humid, and the heat pierced the body like tiny darts.

The flies were more numerous and persistent here than in the rain forest where water was more abundant. As the flies landed on their bodies and searched for moisture, the people brushed at them with the palm fronds they brought from the forest or with goose wing fans, which they had acquired on earlier trips. Una walked a short distance from the others and began digging with her stick. An-ee saw nothing but the ever-present red sand, but soon, several women were gathering honey ants into their baskets. An-ee, whose tongue was thick with dust, recognized the bloated toad. She was the first to grab one and disgorge its water into her mouth. She was also excessively hungry but didn't say anything. Her idea had worked. In her belly was the growing soul of Jerosh's seed. For three rising moons, the soul had made its presence known, but she told no one.

She wanted to take Riva aside on this trek to tell her, but it was impossible. When they stopped at night, they all huddled together on the desert floor under the Master Dreamer's hanging lamps. The men slept on the outside of the circle to guard against snakes, scorpions, and spiders. It was doubtful that they were efficient at their job, for the bellowing snores were a good indication they were sleeping deeply. Possibly, their noise traveled through the ground and kept the poisonous invaders away. At any rate, no one had been bitten. They made their way quickly, despite the heat, to the sacred site of Uluru. Rach's people had been born here, into this red sandstone land of the lizard and the snake.

As they approached the series of hills, Rach hurried her steps to greet her people in their tongue. An-ee found it difficult to decipher their language, although she rather liked the cadence of the words. It was terse and less melodic than the Sea-turtle language. The people were friendlier, though.

After a feast and ceremony, the two clans settled down to business. Wil-Wil presented his woven baskets. Tolo presented the clan elder with a new didgeridoo, and Rach presented her tribe with the shells, explaining how An-ee had suggested their use. Other turtle women gave out skirts, prompting An-ee to ask, "Will your people wear these skirts? It is so hot here."

Rach replied, "It gets quite cold at night in this desert, especially in the winter. They will be glad of clothing then." Just then, the elder of the Sea-turtle clan came and took An-ee by the hand, presenting her to the Pitjantjatjara clan. It did not take An-ee long to realize they were showing her off. She, who was of the Dream Land, was given to their tribe to help Jerosh. Wasn't this a sign that the Sea-turtle clan was favored by the Master Dreamer? An-ee had a hard time hiding her smile. She couldn't follow all that was said, but she saw the elder of the Sea-turtle clan frown. He turned a look of amazement upon her. "The elder of the Pitjantjatjara clan has many special powers. He says you carry Jerosh's seed. How can that be?" His voice carried to the kalbin, who hurried over.

"She cannot carry Jerosh's seed." The kalbin was furious. "It must be another man's. She has defiled our clan."

"It is Jerosh's. After all, was I not sent by the Master Dreamer? Jerosh is quite capable of giving seed."

"No! She lies."

"She does not lie, Kalbin. I know it be true." Riva's voice spoke softly, and her face held a look of happiness. "Why do you have such hatred toward An-ee and Jerosh?"

"I do not have hatred toward them, Riva." He spoke hesitantly. "I know they are strong and powerful. I know others look to them for leadership. I worry that they will bring disaster to our clan." An-ee could not comprehend his reasoning. She walked away from them toward Jerosh.

"You heard?"

"Yes. It is true, then? What you say? You carry my seed?"

She wanted to laugh, but he had such a look of wonder and disbelief that she could not. "I tell you as I told the kalbin, I come from the Master Dreamer. I can do these things."

They were interrupted by the Pitjantjatjara's shaman, who walked over to An-ee and presented her with an amulet stone. "You must keep this and hand it down to your young soul. It gives protection. It is from the Master Dreamer."

Thanking the man, An-ee took the proffered brown stone wrapped with a leather thong and put it around her neck. She turned to Jerosh, who was at her side.

"I wish to be alone for a while. I must go to the sacred mountain and give thanks to the Master Dreamer."

"Why would you go there?" It wasn't just Jerosh looking at her quizzically. Several members of the group voiced the same question.

"Because this is the sacred mountain for all our clans, not just the Pitjantjatjara. They tend the sacred sites, but it is for all our nations." She was annoyed that the kalbin's outburst had robbed her of the contentment she felt on the trip. She needed to get away and make friends with the land. She loved this land that they were visiting. It lacked the lushness of the rain forest, the freshness of the sea, and even basic shelter. But the land beckoned her soul. She longed to stay in the red land until she delivered her child. She yearned to listen to the tales of this clan, whose language was so different from that of the Sea-turtle.

These desert dwellers spoke laconically. They didn't need the long, convoluted tales of their past deeds and glories. It was enough to be the keepers of the sacred sites.

She turned from the group and walked purposively toward Kata Tjuta, the sacred mountain, aware that both clans watched her. The journey would be a half-day's walk. The groups had met halfway between Uluru and Kata Tjuta on the flat land where little could hide. They did not need her for bartering young females. She would have told the young women to stay with their clan, knowing what a future with the Sea-turtles held. Yet, its initiation rites aside, the Sea-turtle clan offered much. She knew little of the Pitjantjatjara or their customs, but she knew they did not practice female mutilation. Generally, they seemed more mild mannered than Jerosh's clan. Rach was the epitome of their temperaments, and An-ee liked Rach immensely.

The sand was hot underfoot, but she forced herself to think of other things than the heat. She avoided the desert rose wherever its brilliant pink flower lit the red sand. Half the time she watched her path, and the other half she kept her eyes on the distant monoliths. She kept a straighter line that way. She hadn't thought of visiting the site before the kalbin's outburst. Now it was as though the Master Dreamer took her by the hand and led her there.

Once she had made up her mind to go, she did not hesitate. Riva had given her a strange look but did not say anything. Nor had the kalbin said a word after his brief venting of fury. Although she found the kalbin's reasoning hard to understand, she did relate to his fear. He didn't hate her or Jerosh so much as he feared what was coming. Perhaps if she got in touch with the Master Dreamer, *she* would know what was in the future, because the MD sure wasn't letting her in on his scheming and planning.

By nightfall, she arrived at Kata Tjuta. The flies came out in droves to suck the moisture from her body. She carried a goose-wing fan for brushing them away, and as she lay down to rest, she used it to cover her face and breasts. Her skirt covered her from the waist to the ankles, and she drew her feet up inside its protection. Only her arms were exposed to the insects.

Jerosh watched as An-ee walked with a determined step away from the meeting place. He felt a loss at her leaving. Still, a part of him was ecstatic that she carried his seed. He didn't have to seek out his mother. Turning, he saw Riva watching him with an excited glow in her eyes. He walked casually to her, not wanting to cause a further stir among the clan. "What do you think about An-ee's announcement?"

"She be good for you. Her method for transferring your seed worked. You could have gone your whole life and not given your seed. The Master Dreamer chose you to carry out his plan."

"I don't know his plan. What do you know about it? Does the elder know anything of the plan?" Jerosh couldn't stem the spate of questions tumbling from his lips. "What does the kalbin know about it?"

"The kalbin knows nothing. Trust me. That be part of his animosity toward you. He thinks you know secret and high things that he should know. That worries him. He fears he will lose his place in the clan. He fears the changes that will take place."

"You have changed also. At the beginning, you were against An-ee too."

"No. You be wrong. I be not against An-ee. I be afraid. Afraid *of* her and afraid *for* her. I also feared what she would do to our clan. And I am still afraid of that. I am afraid of the kalbin's reaction to her."

"If the Master Dreamer's plan is good, why should you worry?"

"I'm not so sure the Master Dreamer controls our destiny. At times I think we use him to put our own plans into place." She held up her hand to forestall any more questions. "I be happy she carries your seed. The elder be happy too."

"You do not doubt that it is my seed?"

"No. An-ee came to me many rising moons ago and told me of her plan. I believe her. I know I be nasty when she first came to us. I be worried for how she would treat you. Now I know she be loving you and wanting your happiness. Because of that, I be loving her too. Now, I must go and help the kalbin, the elder, and Rach select the young women for our young men. Many whom we would choose be refusing to come to the Sea-turtle clan."

Jerosh wanted to talk more with her, but she turned abruptly and left. He wasn't surprised that the girls refused to enter his clan. The Sea-turtle clan would put them through the old rites, unless he could change the rites so newly mated women wouldn't have their center of delight mutilated. He wondered if he dare ask Rach why she didn't have to go through the ceremony.

The elders of both clans came to an agreement. Jerosh noticed the chosen females were all quite young and not yet entered into womanhood. He looked at Riva, who refused to acknowledge his unspoken question.

"Now we feast on kangaroo. The girls will return with you to your clan at daylight." The elder of the desert clan spoke in a falsely cheerful voice, but he refused to look at any of his clan women. Jerosh understood. By the elder's unease, Jerosh didn't think the Pitjantjatjara elder had an easy decision this time. The elders and their mates chose the youngest acceptable girls without resorting to babes at their mother's breast.

Jerosh's appetite for the desired kangaroo meat vanished with his thoughts. If An-ee carried a girl, he would not want his woman-child to endure the ritual. Was this what the Master Dreamer had in mind when he sent An-ee? Jerosh felt himself become hotter than the desert sand he was sitting on. He knew he was right. He may not be able to help these new young women, but when it came time for his female seed to go through the ritual, he hoped to have garnered support to prevent further mutilation of any young woman in their tribe. Through An-ee, he had learned to honor all women, something that had been lacking in his life to that point. Yes, he would be strong enough to defy the kalbin and others. He owed this to An-ee and to his own mother.

An-ee felt the cold desert air seeping into her body. She wasn't able to reach the Master Dreamer. Where was he when she needed him? It was fine sending her here with orders to help, but at least give her an idea what she was supposed to help with. She removed the goose wing fan from her face and saw the sandstone hills, the Master Dreamer's sacred mount. She couldn't even see the outlines of Mimi in the walls. Not that she could see much in the darkness. The cursory glance she had given them when she first arrived revealed nothing either, and she was too exhausted to look further. As she lay on the sand, she thought about her life. The kalbin and Riva's reservations aside, it was a good life. Jerosh was much more sensitive to her needs than the other men seemed with their mates. Of course, she didn't know how they acted when they were alone. Even Jerosh was embarrassed to act lovingly in the presence of others.

When people realized she meant no harm, much of their earlier resentment disappeared. But there were still others who wanted her out of the clan. Even so, with the birth of the new soul, her place in the clan was assured. How would the new women fit into their clan? Would the kalbin and elder force them through the maturation rites? Could she enlist the help of Rach to ensure that they didn't go through the ceremony? Rach would know what to do. If An-ee carried Jerosh's female seed, she would not want her daughter to undergo the ceremony. She didn't want her man seed to go through his ceremony either.

As he was growing up, Jerosh had been looked on by the kalbin as an evil spirit or as one in disfavor with the Master Dreamer. It took Jerosh many talks with Riva to settle the question. She swore he was not in disfavor with the Master Dreamer but did not receive the right curing leaf to his wound. An-ee questioned this when Jerosh had told her. Didn't all the boys have the same leaf applied to their organ? Then how could his be wrong? As a boy, Jerosh had wondered the same thing. But in his manhood, he concluded that there was nothing to be done. The one important aspect was resolved by the Master Dreamer and An-ee. He had fathered a child.

She waved the goose wing across her body to stir up a breeze. Just thinking about their intimate encounters made her hot. She turned her head to the side and looked at the black hills. There was no answer there. Countless fires shone from the black sky, and she let her eyes go out of focus and her mind go blank. *"You are doing the right thing, An-ee."*

Was that the answer she needed? The inner voice in her head gave such an enigmatic response to her plea. The Master Dreamer could be annoying. In the meantime, she let her thoughts wander to Jerosh. She couldn't wait to return to him and the rest of the clan tomorrow. There was no sense in going all the way back to the other sacred rock. She would join them as they returned north from Uluru, meeting them at the hidden spring on the track home. She felt peaceful. The next thing she knew, the morning sun was rising in the sky, and she hurried to rejoin the Sea-turtle clan before the day became too hot.

By the time An-ee arrived at the spring, the clan had moved on, leaving Jerosh behind to wait for her. His smile sent shivers coursing through her. She had a hard time getting the words out. "Was this planned?"

He grinned and embraced her, running his hand over her face and breasts. "I love you."

Under the warming sun, he pleasured her and she felt the stirring of the life within. Taking his hand, she placed it over her womb so that he could feel the new soul also. And they both knew they were following the Master Dreamer's dream.

CHAPTER 10

Over the years, An-ee's gentle spirit developed an inner core as strong as the eucalyptus tree. "I will win, Kalbin. I will win. You cannot continue to initiate women the way it is done in this clan."

"You may think you are strong, An-ee, but you need the agreement of the people. And I know that most don't want change."

Jerosh was nowhere to be found. She didn't think it likely that he disappeared when he saw the kalbin coming. He was stronger than that, but his was more a passive strength that she could quite understand. Jerosh would not argue for his cause. He would simply live his life according to his beliefs and hope others would follow. He was probably with the shaman learning more about herbs and healing. An-ee recognized his talent for this, and she knew he was searching for medicines to guard against complications of circumcision.

Using their impregnating technique, she and Jerosh gave three new souls life. Their eldest neared her maturation rites, and An-ee was adamant her girl-soul would not undergo the circumcision. The kalbin was just as insistent that she would.

"Do you know what you're doing when you rob the young women of their pleasure zones Kalbin? Does it give you satisfaction to see women mutilated?"

Just as the women dug beneath the soil for witchetty grubs and ants, she was determined to dig into the kalbin and unearth his motives. It was much easier to dig for witchetty grubs. Following the Master Dreamer's design, the grubs at least recognized their role in life. An-ee wasn't so sure about the haughty kalbin.

"You will have a struggle with the rites this season. We weren't strong enough to stop them several seasons ago when the young Pitjantjatjara women mated with our young men, but this time is different. The new direction can come from you or the clan. You decide which is better."

"You don't understand what you're asking. You are asking for major amendments to the rituals of the Sea-turtle clan. I cannot allow that to happen."

"*You* cannot *allow* that to happen?" She echoed his words. She saw his sense of power and smugness in his beliefs. "You hold your place, because the people of this clan respect you. If you continue with your practices, the people will call for your replacement."

Unconcerned with her assessment of him, he replied to her allegations. "For all your supposed connections to the Master Dreamer, you are naïve. You would not have your center of pleasure if you had arrived earlier in the camp. The same for Rach. But taking the pleasure bud from the younger women saves them anguish later in life when they may feel dissatisfied with their mates. With their center of pleasure, they could look elsewhere for satisfaction. With it removed, this would not be the case."

"Kalbin ..." She hesitated, wondering how to continue. "The pleasure bud is only part of a woman. It does not take the place of the woman's insides where she feels when she wants her mate."

"If that's true, why are you so troubled over the rites?" He laughed at her look of discouragement, certain she had no answer for him.

"I am troubled because you are violating these young women. You seem to devalue women and view them as chattels. Yet, you gain a great sense of power keeping these women subjugated. *Women!* Is that the extent of your power? Keeping women under your control?" The kalbin looked embarrassed.

Giving him a respectful nod, she turned away. Whether he was wrong or right, she still acknowledged and respected his position. At this point, anything less would antagonize him more.

When she returned to the center of the village compound, she found many women sitting about the central fire discussing the forthcoming female rituals. Shabar sat with her two daughters, both of whom were already betrothed to members of the Pitjantjatjara clan. They had already undergone the mutilation. Now Shabar prepared her third daughter for the ritual. Wil-Wil had overseen her betrothal to a member of the Kamilaroi clan. Her worth would soar after the initiation custom.

"Good day, Shabar. Have you seen Jerosh?" An-ee wanted to speak with Shabar but knew she could not do so openly. Away from the other members, she could count on Shabar's support. But in front of the other villagers, Shabar would denounce her, as would each of the anti-circumcision supporters in the clan. An-ee could not fault them. Their customs were deep-rooted, and although they wished to see reform in their rites, not one of them was strong enough to go against the kalbin or what might be the Master Dreamer's plan. The latter was more firmly entrenched. Kalbins came and went, but the Master Dreamer's design had been since the Time-Before-Time.

Jerosh sat with his friends in a corner of the campground. Few were inside their huts in the daytime. The women gathered leaves for food and medicine, and they dug for grubs in the soil or rotted sections of trees. There was no need to plant seeds, for the Master Dreamer had given them abundant food in the tropical forest. It interested An-ee that the Sea-turtle tribe had such a variety of foods. The ocean gave them fish and turtles, and the forest gave them roots and fruits. They knew of no other tribes with so much excess. The Pitjantjatjara thought they were the Chosen Ones, but the Sea-turtle clan thought differently.

Unmated adults worked outside their huts, making baskets or weaving palm fronds into new roofing material. Children stayed outside practicing hunting skills or meal preparation. The mated women were at a communal fire. The souls she had given Jerosh were with the other children in the campground.

An urge to hug them overwhelmed her. Why couldn't she and Jerosh prevent the maturation ritual alone? Did they need the backing of the group? Thinking about it, the best course was sabotaging the ritual. But how? Catching Jerosh's eye, An-ee walked to their hut, signaling him to follow at a distance.

Her arms longed for Wyn, their eldest soul. Surely Jerosh would help her. The clan would support Jerosh in all his endeavors, but it was not enough to say they supported him. They had to show their support. With Riva's resurgence of youth, An-ee saw her attempt to rectify what had happened to her son. Riva would stand behind them. Would the elder do the same? It was not a question of whether he supported their point of view regarding the rituals. It was more basic than that, and at the same time more complex, for it involved their deep-seated beliefs.

An-ee didn't wish to disturb the old man who had planted the seed of Jerosh in Riva's belly. He had defended An-ee when she first came to the tribe many seasons ago, and he had sided with her even when his mate seemed to resent her presence. It came down to which of the two men, the elder or the kalbin, wielded the most power over the people. The elder exercised his rights over the daily matters of the village and ruled with a fair hand. The people would remember that. But the kalbin held their souls, and with his fear of change, she knew he would use his power to sway the people to his cause.

Jerosh had not followed her into the hut. She was glad now that he hadn't. For a few more moments she stayed in the darkness, her hand resting on her belly. Was she again carrying Jerosh's seed? Leaving the hut, she wandered to the fire and met Una. "I think I'll go to the river to bathe. Would you mind my little ones for a while?"

"Surely. But do you go to the river alone? Shouldn't one of the other women go with you?"

"No. That's not necessary. You women are discussing the forthcoming maturation ritual, and you know my feelings on the matter. I think you will all feel better if I leave for a short time, so you don't have to mind your words in front of me."

"I wish I could say differently. You know that we feel in our hearts what you say is right, but we are not as strong as you. And our men will not stand behind us as Jerosh stands behind you. You were wise to give him two daughters and one son. For that I am sure Jerosh honors you almost as much as he reveres the Master Dreamer."

An-ee turned away from the group of women. To have Jerosh revere her as he revered the Master Dreamer? For a brief moment she was frightened. Although the moist heat penetrated her skin with a thousand hot darts, chills overtook her. She understood more keenly how the other women felt. Being afraid hadn't even appeared in her realm of experience. Frustrated, annoyed, or befuddled perhaps, but never afraid. For the first time in her life, she felt real fear, and spasms racked her body. If the kalbin noticed her fear, and she had no doubt he would, his sense of victory would be complete. She would not give him that victory. She was determined to succeed. She took slow, deep breaths, keeping her mind on the Master Dreamer's plan. Jerosh was still avoiding her eyes. She turned to the river path and walked away from the encampment. Her deep breathing had calmed her fears, and she felt a sense of peace. The MD would not be angry with her if Jerosh revered her. Hadn't he sent her on this errand to help Jerosh? He must have foreseen what would happen. Even if he had been in his cups when he had devised this dream, he was sufficiently fair-minded not to take his errors in judgment out on his dream-people.

Veering from the path, An-ee stood for a moment looking back at the groups. Her eldest daughter was with the women's group, and An-ee restrained herself from running back and holding her. She wanted to protect her child against the mutilation and ease the fear that flashed across her face. Jerosh couldn't be there for her at the maturation ritual. The men were only allowed afterward for the feasting. *They don't even see the contradiction in having a male kalbin for the female circumcision,* An-ee thought. *How was the kalbin assigned this role?*

In other clans, a woman performed the operation on the maturing girl-souls. An-ee would ask Jerosh about it when she returned. Perhaps Riva could explain why the kalbin performed the mutilation on both the males and the females.

Sheltered from the eyes of the camp, An-ee stood for another few moments. She longed for Jerosh to hold her and tell her how much she meant to him. Forget the Master Dreamer. She wanted Jerosh to give *her* the credit for his beautiful seed. After a length of time, when the sun climbed higher in the sky, she knew Jerosh was not coming after her on the path. She should have known. It was forbidden for males to bathe in the river at the same time as females, even if they were mated, although there were many times when mated couples disregarded this rule, An-ee and Jerosh among them.

She walked slowly, gazing at a pohutukawa tree. Its blossoms were a brilliant scarlet with yellow anthers. A bush kangaroo jostled a nearby bush as it leaped out of her way. Even when she noticed a poisonous snake slither across her path, she felt no fear. A pygmy glider soared in the high treetops. The smell of eucalyptus was pungent. This world was so beautiful. The Master Dreamer had dreamed a work of art.

As she strolled toward the river, she fingered the small sea turtle totem Jerosh had carved from a branch. He had burned a hole through the neck of the totem, threaded it with a strip of kangaroo hide, and presented it to her on the birth of their first child. How proud he had been — how ecstatic. He had assumed he would never father a young soul, and he had been given this miracle. Even after the birth of their third seed, his wonderment never ceased.

The birth of the first secured An-ee a place in the Sea-turtle clan. Jerosh's gift reinforced her position. She had seen Riva glance at the totem and nod her silent agreement. Riva had taken the girl from An-ee's body and lifted her toward the sunlight, giving the child her blessing. An-ee had removed the sacred amulet stone that was given to her by the Pitjantjatjara and placed it around the child's neck where it remained. As the girl grew, they told her the story of the sacred stone, and she knew she was the one blessed to pass it on. Jerosh had been welcomed into the group of men and plied with fermented milk until the singing had ended with manly snores and grunts. He was now one of them.

An-ee saw a movement in her peripheral vision and thought of Wil-Wil. She wondered if he were coming along the parallel path back to the village. The people had made it this way so that the two groups would not meet. When she reached the river, she removed her skirt and stuck a toe in the water. Finding the water warm, she waded farther in until she was midstream, and the softly flowing water was just past her waist. Lying on her back, she felt herself relax, and she gazed at the small portion of blue sky visible through the overhanging trees. The sky looked different at Uluru, but in the rain forest it was serene nonetheless.

Although the tropical forest had its beauty, including the river, the desert of the Pitjantjatjara was closer to her soul. Fresh flowing water like this river would be rare in the red center. The sun was harsher there, sand burnt the feet, and flies sucked the body. Yet there was a majesty that even this lush forest lacked. She and Jerosh had only returned once since they went on the trek to barter for female mates. But he had seen how the desert beckoned her.

Once she birthed this new seed, she would ask Jerosh about returning to the red center. She doubted there would be more souls after this one. Even Shabar, the most prolific of their village, had sought advice from the shaman to halt at five. There was not the need to be extra productive, and no one minded if a couple had one or two children. For all the tribe's annoying laws and customs, mated couples were allowed many freedoms and choices. Yes, she was content the Master Dreamer had sent her to the Sea-turtle clan, and she knew she had made a good start in getting them to change their views about the initiation rites.

There had been moments when she doubted the MD's decision, but she knew that she loved Jerosh with a love that flowed as quietly and smoothly as the river. Her love had deep, secret places where no one could ever intrude. Thinking of him, she closed her eyes and relaxed into the water. Once she had gathered her strength, she would oppose the kalbin and make herself heard. As she floated with the current, she thought of how she had encouraged Jerosh's love for plants and medicines. She thought of the knowledge he had gained talking with the older tribal members and the shaman. If they could do nothing about the imminent maturation rites, at least Jerosh had a store of information about cures, and she had secured his promise that he would pass on his knowledge to their seeds. She also had given Jerosh more confidence in his own abilities. Already there were many in the clan who were willing to take a stand against old traditions. The river took her around a bend, a short distance from the village. Suddenly, she was startled when a strong arm grasped her neck and pulled her head under. She knew it was the kalbin. She struggled and gasped for breath, feeling the warm water flow down her throat. The arm continued to hold her head underwater.

CHAPTER 11

Hey ho, heel and toe,
Lifetimes come, and lifetimes go.
Heel and toe, heel and toe,
Each of us has a need to grow.

Wallaby sang and pranced, its silky coat gleaming in the soft light of the Dreamtime. Annie laughed. It was a deep laugh, filled with a joy she hadn't felt in a long time. Her gentleness was back, but it carried sorrow. "Wallaby, I don't know how I can be so happy when I should be repentant for not completing my last assignment."

"Oh, but you did complete it." Wallaby looked at her with a quizzical grin. "Hasn't the Master Dreamer spoken with you yet?"

"No. I haven't seen or even heard anything of him. If he wants to talk to me, he certainly hasn't made his presence known."

"He will be with you soon. From what he said earlier, I gather he's busy. But he is overjoyed with your latest accomplishments."

She didn't know how that could be. Her latest odyssey to earth hadn't been that successful. The last thing she remembered was swimming in the river, trying to relax and letting her thoughts flow along with the current. It wasn't a bad trip that last time. She liked Jerosh in his last dreaming. And she adored the souls that she and Jerosh had brought forth. A sudden thought struck her. "Wallaby, what about the soul I carried? Where is it?"

You were not pregnant. You shouldn't be worrying, anyway. You're in the Dreamtime."

"I'm not worrying, Wallaby. I'm curious."

Heel and toe, heel and toe
Round and round the sun we go
To the stars, to the moon.
To the earth very soon.

"Annie ... Annie!" His voice reverberated through the Dreamtime land, bounced from the misty hills, slid along the green grass, and buried itself in Annie's soul. Soon she saw him. He looked in much better form than the last time she'd seen him "Annie. Hello, girl. You had a hard time of it this last excursion."

"Excursion? That's what you call my trying time down there?"

"Never mind, Annie. You'll forget."

She was forgetting already. But there was one thing she couldn't forget. She hadn't completed her task. "Master Dreamer, you must know I didn't do a good job this time. What should I do about it?"

"You did a good job, Annie." He looked at her sternly. "I wouldn't have sent you, otherwise. In fact, you did such a good job I think you will have to go back only once or twice more."

She barely heard the "good job." She was too concerned with the "once or twice more."

"Again?" she squeaked.

"Annie, Annie, Annie. You can be stubborn and very obtuse. Do you want to see what happened after you left the Sea-turtle clan?"

His beard had grown longer since she'd last seen him. His eyes looked clearer and more serene. They were no longer red from his bouts of crying and drinking. In all, he was quite an authoritative, benign figure. She thought she could respect him after all.

"Yes. I'd like to see the souls Jerosh and I helped into the world."

He passed his hand over the mist, and a window opened. Her girls were women now, going about the bush village much as she had. There was the village fire pit, and there on the beach was another ceremonial fire. She could see the sea turtle steaming on the hot coals. Her seeds were preparing their girls for the coming-of-age ceremony.

Goodness! Annie thought. *Has it been that long?*

She identified an older Wil-Wil and a graying Shabar. She wouldn't have recognized many of the people, but she intuitively knew them.

The kalbin was a stooped old man, but it wasn't the kalbin she had known. It was Tolo. A twinge went through her as she witnessed him in his role in the ceremony. The Master Dreamer noticed.

"Don't fear, Annie. Yes, the old kalbin killed you, but if it hadn't been the kalbin, it would have been one of the others who were afraid of your powers. The people suspected him and forced him to admit his guilt. He resigned his position and left their camp. Watch. I'm pleased with what you did."

She watched as the women of the Sea-turtle clan prepared the meal. The men kept the fire fed with driftwood from the beach. A few played musical instruments that she didn't recognize. They had progressed in that direction, anyway. The women-to-be were dressed in short grass skirts, bleached almost white. Garlands of red and white flowers from the pohutukawa trees adorned their heads. They danced in a circle around the fire, laughing as they went. Young men danced in a wider circle about the girls. As one group went one way, the other group reversed.

The ceremony had lost much of its pseudo-religious quality. She turned to the Master Dreamer with a question. "Were the circumcision rites for women abolished?"

"Yes. Thanks to your efforts."

Then she saw the shaman in his ceremonial garb. It was Jerosh.

She looked inquiringly at the Master Dreamer, who nodded. "When Jerosh's father came back to us, Jerosh turned down the position of elder to be a shaman. Wil-Wil became the new elder."

She turned back to the picture below. She was fascinated by the young women. At a signal from the elder, both circles stopped, and each young woman was paired with a young man. As each pair seemed exuberant and happy, she concluded the partners had selected each other. The kalbin went to stand beside Elder Wil-Wil, and the couples were pronounced mated. After that, the feasting of the sea turtle took place. They hadn't done away with all the ceremonies, then. The sea turtle feast ensured that each pair was fertile. The scene changed. She watched Jerosh drift away from the ceremonies. No one commented on his leaving. He trod a serene woodland path, and stopping beside a red pohutukawa tree, he leaned against its trunk. His lips moved, and she became aware of his thoughts. "I loved you, An-ee. More than life itself. Will we meet again, I wonder?" Through the reddish earth she could see the bones of a woman buried beneath the tree. They were red from the ocher rubbed into her lifeless body. She knew they were her bones but felt no emotion.

"You would be proud, An-ee, to see how our village turned out. The souls we birthed are beautiful. I miss you." She saw the tears gather in his eyes and spill down his cheeks. He was still in the land where emotions ruled. But he wouldn't be for long.

> Time is fleeting.
> Time is fast.
> There is no time.
> There is no past.
> All things exist in the here-time.
> All things exist in the near-time.
> There is no time.

She lost interest in the scene below. The people in the village would tread their paths as she walked hers.

The Master Dreamer waved a hand again, and the scene disappeared. "Jerosh, Riva, Rach, Wil-Wil, Shabar, and a few others forced the village to do away with the circumcision of the young women. Good work, Annie."

He disappeared, and she was back in the garden with dancing all around her.

Heel and toe, heel and toe,
Back we go and to and fro.
Seeds of love we must sow.
Blossoms bud and blossoms grow.
Go Annie, go and sow.

"No." She didn't feel like returning yet. Couldn't she just play here for a while? Wasn't she entitled to rest? Where was he so she could ask him about it? How long had she been here, anyway?

Time flows on, Annie; time flows free,
Like a river to the sea.
But you can
Lock time.
Rock time.
Mock time.
Stop time.

CHAPTER 12

Start time ...

Once the proud keepers of the red center, the Pitjantjatjara were losing ground to the newcomers. Eleven-year-old An-ee stood before her parents and waited as her mother slipped the amulet over An-ee's head and tucked it beneath her ragged dress.

"You must find the white people, An-ee. You must learn their ways."

"Why can't I stay here, Mama? I don't want to go." Tears slid down her cheeks.

"Our ways are dying. We want the best for you. Now go."

An-ee kissed each of her parents in turn, and without another word, she started her journey into the white man's world. She had no idea where she was going or what she would do, but from hidden depths within her, she found the courage to look ahead.

The amulet was lucky for her in her quest. Several days later, she arrived in the early morning to Coober Pedy and found work as a housekeeper to one of the white miners. Her luck held. She had witnessed the brutalities her people had suffered at the hands of the newcomers, but her employer was mild-mannered and courteous. He gave her a small salary and room and board. The only thing he asked her to do, aside from keeping a clean house and preparing meals, was to listen as he read from his white man's Bible. Although she understood very little of what he read, she did enlarge her English vocabulary by listening. With her improved language skills, she became familiar with the community around her.

At the very moment of her arrival in Coober Pedy, newly-weds arrived by ship to Sydney Harbor. The steamer had made its way from England's soft, green fields to the harsh, strange land in the southern hemisphere. In the Hare and Hound Pub, Daniel had listened, wide-eyed, as the red-bearded man regaled his fellows with tales of Australia. Opals! It was what Daniel had waited for all his young life. He didn't want to follow in his father's footsteps as a clerical worker. How insufferably boring! There wasn't once he remembered his father coming home with an exciting or interesting story to share. Daniel knew his mother was satisfied, or at least she pretended to be. He, however, could not accept the same routine.

Even while courting Jenny, his wanderlust manifested itself. How could he convince her to travel to Australia with him? What was it the man in the pub had said? The people were free in Australia. They weren't restricted by the customs of a genteel society. Daniel had exited the pub as fast as he could. He could hardly wait to impart his newfound information to Jenny.

Jenny was less than enthusiastic about Daniel's latest venture. What had finally persuaded her was her mother's enthusiasm when Jenny mentioned Daniel's latest madcap scheme. "Darling, you can always come home if you don't like it. Wire us, and we'll send you the return passage."

The more Daniel's spirits lifted as the steamship neared home port in Sydney Harbor, the more Jenny's plummeted. Although she and Daniel had courted for several months before their marriage, she found she knew nothing about him. Where would he find the perseverance to make his life in this mostly uncharted southern continent?

She looked at him from under her lashes. His skin was fair and tended to freckle in the sun. She'd heard the Australian sun could spell disaster for fair-skinned people like Daniel. She, too, was fair-skinned. She felt another frisson of fear when she pictured them in the unknown land. They had no friends there to welcome them, and no one to whom they could turn. She knew that Daniel had his heart set on finding opals. He had not even entertained the idea of homesteading. She wondered if she would feel differently if she had a home. She was good at adapting, and she was a good household manager, even surpassing her mother's formidable talent. But scrubbing for opals in the hot, dry land did not appeal to her.

Sydney teemed with rough-looking men who frightened Jenny. She knew that England shipped convicts to Australia, and these men seemed the worst of the lot. She timidly descended the gangplank. Daniel had no such fear. His face was alight with excitement as he looked around. Jenny wished she felt the same keen sense of exhilaration. The air was humid and hot. Even before landing on the quay, she felt sweat trickling under her long velvet dress.

The only contact they'd had on the ship was a grizzled old miner heading back to Coober Pedy. He had taken one look at them and advised that they return to England. They couldn't. Their money did not stretch to return passage. Jenny wanted to cry. Daniel's attention had strayed to a few masculine-looking women. One had taken his arm, but Jenny glared at the woman and promptly took Daniel's other arm. He removed the woman's hand from his arm and gave her a friendly smile. "Could you point us to the nearest lodging?"

They were directed to a ramshackle house where a weary woman took in travelers. "Came out with me husband, I did. He had these big plans to make money, but never did. Then he got sick and died and left me to manage on me own."

"That won't happen to us." Daniel grinned at her. "Jenny and I are going to make a good team and find enough opals so we can return to England rich." He ignored the woman's tightened lips as he and Jenny climbed the stairs to a sparse but clean bedroom. They stayed for two days and nights. Jenny was happy to be on land and wanted to stay longer in the town before they traveled northwest to fulfill Daniel's dream, but Daniel, the tales of the man in the pub still ringing in his ears, was eager to begin their new life in the desert. As Jenny had not heard the stories, she was more inclined to take the advice of the grizzled miner on the ship to return to England.

The hot dust filled Jenny's lungs, and the burning sun pierced the muslin covering her arms. In the two years since she and Daniel had come by camel to Coober Pedy, Jenny had wilted and withered like the gardens she had tried to plant. She clutched a crumpled telegraph wire in her fist. Her frustration caused her to hiccup as she tried to stem the tears threatening to overflow. She smoothed the yellow paper and reread the message: Bad turn of events here stop Unable to send money as requested stop Have faith in your new life stop Give regards to Daniel stop Your loving father stop.

Jenny knew her parents could not understand her predicament. If anyone asked, she would swear she still loved Daniel, but she didn't feel like being a wife to him. She was always so tired. She held her head over a bowl of steaming water as another fit of coughing took hold.

Contrary to all her thoughts otherwise, Daniel had adjusted better to this godforsaken land than Jenny had. He thrived on the constant hope of finding a large opal and retiring to the more temperate southern coast. He had no desire to return to England, nor did he want Jenny to return. She was his wife, and that meant "till death do us part," as he quoted to her almost daily.

Others at Coober Pedy used their mine shafts for shelter from the blazing sun, but Jenny could not. Although the temperature underground remained a constant twenty to thirty degrees cooler than the daytime average, the dampness underground sent chills through her. It was neither the dampness of the early morning English mists across the hills at Bishop's Cleeve, nor the dewdrops on the daisy-dotted fields. This damp was insidious; it was a rotting damp like the grave. She was uncomfortable underground and above ground in the heat. Jenny's spirits continued to plunge, and her body began a downward slide.

Since they had come to Coober Pedy, they had seen others find large opals and return to their homes, fulfilling their quests to strike it rich. Opals from Coober Pedy lacked the fiery brilliance of other opals, and they did not hold the mystique of sapphires and rubies. But it was clear that Jenny was not going to get Daniel to shelve his boyish dream of striking it rich. Opals simply held an allure for him that other gems did not. Gradually, as more men returned to England and showed off the pastel radiance of the Coober Pedy opals, the market, once closed in favor of fierier gems, opened up. There was now a great demand for Coober Pedy opals. Wealthy people increasingly wanted the stone, and Daniel's hopes that he would find the one big opal that would make him a rich man rose ever higher.

Neophytes came to stake their claim, leading camels and pushing wheelbarrows. Many of the newcomers had struck it rich while Daniel still chipped away and found only inferior gems. One day, Jenny faced Daniel as he came from the mine beside their one-room shack.

"I must find a way to return to England. Just for a visit. Please!" But Daniel, having tasted freedom in the new land, could not bring himself to return with Jenny, nor did he even have the money for a single passage. He was not oblivious to Jenny's ill health, but he was sure she would rally quickly. Jenny had always been robust.

Some weeks after the telegram, the weather turned cooler, and Jenny felt better than she had in a long while. Her tiredness from the past several months was still bone deep, but the nausea abated. She hoped she'd finally adjusted to this new land.

Drifting in and out of the area were many Aborigines, who were deemed fair game for snide remarks and cruelty by the white immigrants. They didn't even look like the few Negroes one saw in England. These creatures had broad faces, large noses, wore little or no clothing, and looked fierce. Neither Daniel nor Jenny understood their language, and they didn't try to understand the indigenous people either. They chose to ignore this unpleasant aspect of their Australian life.

One day, Daniel entered the door of their dirt-floor shack with a young Aborigine girl. "Old Sven Pedersen's returning to

Norway. He gave us his gin to help out." Daniel did not notice Jenny wince at the derogatory term and continued. "She should be good for something around here. Even if it's just keeping you company." He had given up hope of Jenny working in the mines. Other women mined, and in many instances they were-better at finding gems than the men were. But Jenny showed no interest.

Now they both looked at the young girl, who they guessed was about thirteen, although they weren't good at estimating the age of Aborigines. Her large, brown eyes held fear and resignation, and Jenny's heart contracted like it did when her father killed the Christmas goose. "She can help until I feel bet-ter." She turned to the young girl. "What's your name? Do you have one?"

The girl, still frightened, whispered her Aboriginal name, but neither Daniel nor Jenny could repeat the terse syllables. When the girl understood, she ducked her head. "Mr. Pedersen, him call me Annie."

"Well, Annie, what did you do for Mr. Pedersen?" Jenny lowered her voice to match the young girl's whisper.

"Me cook Mr. Pedersen food, and me clean him house."

Jenny knew Mr. Pedersen had a four-room shack, which was kept spotless. They had learned that Mr. Pedersen wanted to bring his family to Australia, but they refused to come. Now he was returning to Norway a wealthier man than when he left, though still not a rich man. Daniel had another surprise. "Mr. Pedersen also left us his house. He says he doesn't want any-thing for it."

Jenny's heart lifted. If she weren't so tired, she would have run to Daniel and hugged him. His hair, bleached almost white by the onslaught of sun, set off the reddened, freckled skin. He had lost weight since he came to Australia, but in its place were a determination and strength not present when she married him. She willed herself to smile. "When can we move in?"

"He's leaving tomorrow morning. Going north to meet the train when it comes into town. He says we can move in any-time. Tonight if we like."

"We should wait until he leaves. He might feel uncomfortable if we move in before he goes. Thank you, Daniel. I know
I've been a frustration to you, but I didn't know I would feel ill
and so tired."

"You're not, love. I wish I could make things better for you."
Daniel couldn't fully hide his disappointment. He berated himself for not taking Jenny back to England, but the idea of returning without anything to show for this impulsive scheme galled
him. He hoped she understood and silently begged her to say
so. "In the meantime, what are we going to do with this gin?"

Jenny cringed at the slur, but there was no sense saying anything. She didn't want to disturb their newfound happiness.
"She can sleep outside for tonight." She turned to the girl to see
if she understood.

"Me sleep outside tonight, ma'am. Annie see Master
Dreamer's lamps."

Annie understood much more than they knew. Because she
was quiet and did her work well, the whites tended to ignore
her. She wasn't a slave. She had more freedom than the white
folk in chains. If she took it into her head to leave the whites
and go back to her own people, her parents would give her
a harder time than the whites ever did because they would
believe she was throwing away a good future. The worst that
could happen with the whites was that they would say she was
unreliable. Somehow, she didn't think she would be beaten,
especially when she was with Mr. Pedersen.

She missed Mr. Pedersen already. He asked nothing of her
but to cook his meals and clean his house. She had heard stories of whites mounting black women whenever they wanted,
but that had not happened to her.

She remembered the time Mr. Pedersen had asked a friend
in for a meal. "Sven, you old son of a gun, ya didn't tell me ya
had a bed partner. No wonder you're so calm all the time."

"She cooks for me, and a good cook she is, but that's all. She's
a child." Neither man said anything more, but Annie knew Bill
didn't believe Mr. Pedersen. Now with another family, she
looked at the Master Dreamer's lights, wondering where her

journey would lead. There had been a time when she recalled the Master Dreamer dimly, but that memory faded as she grew older.

Breathing deeply, she felt the apprehension leave her. She hadn't wanted to come to Mr. Daniel and Miz Jenny. Mr. Daniel had the same fierce independence as Mr. Pedersen. She wasn't sure he had the same firmness, but he would be focused on finding the iridescent stones they so revered. As long as she did her job, he would be easy with her. This wasn't so with all her people. She had seen the broken arms and missing teeth, but she knew Mr. Daniel wouldn't be like that. No, she was more afraid of Miz Jenny.

CHAPTER 13

Annie lay under the Master Dreamer's lights and thought of Jenny. It was not that Miz Jenny was mean. Deep down, she cared for all things. Annie thought there was a feeling, though, that she was better than Annie's people. But Jenny was not any different from the other white folk who came to Annie's land. They looked on her people as they looked on horses and camels. Maybe they even had more feeling for their horses and camels. That's the way things were, and the white people were probably right. After all, they had come to her land in a big boat from far away, where the people were not black. Her people did not have boats like that. Her people did not even have big huts like the whites.

Miz Jenny scared her because Annie knew she was leaving the Master Dreamer's dream. People like that always scared her. It was as if they were on a higher, secret journey.

Was the Master Dreamer looking at them? He must expect Miz Jenny soon. That made her special. His lamps were bright that night. They hung in the black sky like miners' lamps in their shacks. The MD must have a very big shack, but she couldn't remember. The whole Dreamtime was vague now. If she was back with her people, they would have feasts and storytelling to remember, but blacks often forgot with the whites.

In the morning, the Master Dreamer's lamps dimmed. It was time to move Miz Jenny and Mr. Daniel to Mr. Pedersen's hut. Annie knew that hut. The shack of Mr. Daniel and Miz Jenny didn't mean anything to her. Mr. Daniel woke her up and said to help the missus move into Mr. Pedersen's. Annie had to pee first. She nodded and moved away to a bottlebrush to pee. He watched her, fascinated. She wanted a drink of water but was afraid to ask. At Mr. Pedersen's, she never had to ask. Whenever she wanted food or drink, Mr. Pedersen said to help herself. She found Jenny inside. She looked better than she had yesterday, and Annie wondered if she had been wrong about the woman. She helped them move into Mr. Pedersen's. Miz Jenny told her to take a room for herself, so Annie took the one she used when Mr. Pedersen owned the house. The window looked south, and a cool breeze came in at night. Of course, all the flies came in too, but she was used to that. Back in her Pitjantjatjara clan, there were more flies than people. She wanted to go back but knew her people thought she was better here. *Go,* they said, *and learn the ways of the white people. Learn to speak like them. We see no future for us here. It is what the Master Dreamer has planned.*

She helped Jenny put their meager items in the big new hut. They did not have as much as Mr. Pedersen, but Mr. Pedersen had left most of his white man's goods in the hut. He said he wouldn't need them in Norway. If Annie went back to her people, would she leave what she had acquired? She was becoming accustomed to wearing a cloth covering. It was soft, and she liked the cover it provided. She wondered why she had thoughts of leaving. There were no such thoughts when she was with Mr. Pedersen.

As she worked, Jenny asked, "How old are you, Annie?"

"I not know, Miz Jenny." Annie did not know how old she was in the white man's words. Jenny said she looked thirteen or fourteen. Annie couldn't say.

Her people did not practice the coming-of-age ritual anymore. In fact, many of her people did nothing now that the white men came. The men lay around and drank the white men's intoxicating brew. They smoked and coughed. Some even coughed like Miz Jenny was coughing. Soon Annie's people would be gone. Was that the Master Dreamer's plan?

Her people were not better or worse than the white people. Like the white man's liquor, her people had pituri that made them happy and drunk. With the white man's liquor, her people got drunk, but they were not happy anymore. Now they were drunk and sad.

After they were in the house for several days and Daniel saw that Jenny was better, he decided to try his luck at a mine farther north. "You'll be all right, Jenny. Annie is here with you. You can teach her more English while I'm gone. You would like that."

No one asked Annie what she wanted, but she had come to learn the white man's language and ways. Annie was sure, though, that Miz Jenny was too tired to teach her anything. Jenny smiled at Mr. Daniel. "You go ahead. The faster you find a good opal, the faster we can go back to Bishop's Cleeve."

Daniel's smile widened across his face. Annie decided he was like a hungry little boy who finds honey ants. She guessed Mr. Daniel had a hunger like that. He did not seem to notice that there was little food in the house, but Annie did not go hungry. She could eat the larvae of the many termite hills or squeeze the toad for water. But she never showed any of these things to Daniel and Jenny. They would look on them with horror. She also refrained from telling them honey ants were tastier than that awful gluey porridge they wanted her to make with the whitish-brown grains, the brown stuff they called sugar, and the dried pieces of toad skin they called raisins. She could hardly get it down her throat, but the honey ant burst with sun-warmed honey and a slight tang.

The next morning, Daniel, his skin now permanently red, headed north with a borrowed camel. After he left, Jenny's strength ebbed further. She mostly slept, and Annie kept her cool with cloths dipped in cool water. She also found pieces of light cloth to put over her room's window to allow a little breeze but keep the flies out. The flies got into the rest of the house, though, so she took more cloth until she covered every window.

"Miz Jenny, you be all right? Me go find gum trees," Annie said one day. The gum trees grew at a distance, but she did not tell Jenny that.

"Yes. I'll be fine." Jenny did not ask why Annie wanted the gum trees, but Annie heard fear in the Englishwoman's voice.

She left before the sun came up, for she knew she had a long walk ahead of her. It took her almost a whole day to come to the river gums that grew in a great canyon to the west. She gathered the leaves in a pillowcase sack and retraced her steps. She walked at night and arrived home at midday the next day. Jenny was still coughing, and Annie wiped the woman's forehead with a cool cloth.

After she gave Miz Jenny a drink of water, she took the rest and boiled it over a small fire outside. When the water bubbled, she dropped in gum leaves and took the steaming pot into Jenny's room. The woman coughed harder and spit up blood. Annie gave her a small sip of the cooling liquid. She seemed much better after that, and she put her hand on Annie's head, smoothing out the matted hairs. "You know, don't you? You know I'm dying. I'm afraid your medicine is too late. Maybe if I had taken it sooner ..."

Annie knew Miz Jenny wasn't blaming her. All Annie could hope now was that Jenny's passing to the Master Dreamer would be easier after taking the gum broth. Annie let her sleep and was happy her breathing seemed easier. She crushed more gum leaves into hot water until the air was pungent. She found a rag and washed the whole house with the medicine. The house smelled clean. She had done the same for Mr. Pedersen when he fell ill. He swore it had saved his life. Mr. Pedersen had recovered and had returned to his real home, but Annie knew that would not happen this time.

She went out while Jenny was sleeping and found a snake lying in the shade of a low saltbush. "Mr. Snake, Miz Jenny need you." After breaking its neck, skinning it, and cutting it into pieces, she put it in a pot of boiling water and added pepper leaves and salt. It remained boiling until the meat was soft. She poured off the broth into a cup, careful that no remnants of snake meat fell in the cup.

If Jenny asked where she had found the meat, Annie would tell her, and she knew Jenny would not touch it. With broth, she would think Annie made it from plants. She heard Jenny stir in her bed and took her the broth to drink. The woman was quite pleased, and after drinking the whole cup, she fell asleep again.

Annie tried to keep busy and not think too much about Miz Jenny dying. If the Master Dreamer wanted her to live, he would do something about it. She wondered whether she was sent to help the woman get over this illness. If so, the Master Dreamer had sent her too late. She could see that Miz Jenny would not last much longer in this world. Annie fretted that Jenny would die before Mr. Daniel returned, and she wondered whether he would blame her. She thought it quite likely. He was a man who could not accept responsibility for his actions.

She kept busy by washing the walls, ceilings, and floors with gum leaves. When she finished, the house no longer smelled like a dying house. As she was on her hands and knees scrubbing the kitchen floor, she heard yelling and saw Mr. Daniel running and leading the camel. He looked like a man who had at last found his dream.

"Jenny! Jenny!"

Annie went to the door and took the reins of the camel to hobble it outside the house. "Shush! Mr. Daniel, shush!" She grabbed his arm and saw the look of understanding in his eyes. She had not warned him because Jenny was ill. If he let the other miners know that he had found opals, he would be robbed of his treasure, or he would be joining Miz Jenny in the Dreamtime. There was much jealousy among the miners, and his neighbors wouldn't be happy about Daniel's new wealth when they had none. When men saw their dreams slipping away, they did harsh things. He lifted his bag from the camel's back and entered the house. Other than from his first outburst, no one would know whether or not he had been successful in the mines.

"Jenny?" Annie saw that he was bursting to tell his woman of his find. Annie pointed toward the bedroom. "Is she still sickly?" He walked quietly but hopefully toward their room. He took in the pale face of his wife on the bed, the smell of the river gums, and the cloth across the window. His woman was laboring for breath. For fifteen minutes he looked down at her with a mixture of tenderness, guilt, and disappointment. "You've looked after her well. Do you think she'll get better?"

Annie shook her head. She was not a shaman or even a kalbin, but she did know when a person was ready to return to the Dreamtime. Since the white people had come to her country, her people were used to death.

Sensing Daniel's presence, Jenny opened her eyes. She took in his features and said weakly, "You look happy. Did you find your opals, then?" Tears gathered in his eyes. He opened his fist, which had been clenched at his side.

Annie stood frozen. In Mr. Daniel's hand was the biggest black opal she had ever seen. Jenny said, "I'm glad."

Jenny's smile weakened. Daniel said, "Darling, you can visit England." There was no answer. Jenny had passed to the Dreamtime with her praise for Daniel still lingering on her lips.

"Jenny! Jenny!" Daniel shook her, trying to make her wake. Annie touched his arm. "Mr. Daniel, she gone to Dreamtime." He looked with wild eyes at the black girl. She had seen eyes like that before in both white and black men. It was the shock of discovering there were things they couldn't control. How they reacted depended on how much control they thought they had. It takes time to learn that one must live with the world and not against it. Annie's people knew that, and young as she was, Annie knew some people never realized that, whether black or white. Mr. Daniel had lived his dream, but he tried to drag his woman into the dream with him. Miz Jenny had had dreams too, but no one would ever know that now.

Annie touched him again. "I get help, Mr. Daniel. I get somebody help." He held her back. "No, Jenny. No." It took Annie a moment to realize that he called her by his woman's name. She left him there and returned to the kitchen. She had noticed that when the people from that land called England were upset, they liked to have a cup of tea. She set about to boil water over a small outdoor fire, noticing as she did that several men were gazing at her. Thinking she might save Mr. Daniel from speaking to his neighbors, she approached them. "Miz Jenny go to Dreamtime. Mr. Daniel with her now."

"Did he get opals, Annie?" The question was echoed by all four men. They were more interested in the stone than another human's life. She had seen that in whites before. They treated their women as her tribe's men dared not treat theirs. The women of the Pitjantjatjara were special. There was a legend in her tribe that long ago they practiced female mutilation as a rite of passage. The men still underwent such a rite, but the women did not. They had their own beautiful ceremony, which Annie had seen often before she left her tribe. It was said that Rach, an ancestress, had fought to bring about change, and then she fought to help An-ee of the Sea-turtle Clan have the rite of passage abolished from that tribe. Yes, their women were better treated than the women from across the sea.

She answered them as they deserved. "No. I not think so. Mr. Daniel upset about Miz Jenny. I go help." She picked up the pot of boiling water and dropped in the tea leaves, taking it into the house.

Mr. Daniel was leaning over his woman, stroking her face and talking to her. Annie brought him a cup of tea. He looked at her with eyes that were crazed by guilt and grief. "Thank you, Jenny. I loved you, you know. I know you didn't think I would make it out here. I know you didn't believe in me. That made me work that much harder. I didn't want you returning to England thinking I was a failure. Forgive me. Please forgive me." He grabbed Annie's arm. The tea sat forgotten on a chair beside the bed. "Jenny, please forgive me." He gulped in breaths of air. He drew Annie to him. She pulled away.

"Drink your tea, Mr. Daniel. You feel better." She left him in the room and sat on a wooden bench in the living room. She would have left that house of death, but she did not want to meet up with the miners again. As she sat wondering what to do, Daniel came out. His face still bore an anguished look. There was nothing she could do. He had to live with his woman's death for the rest of his life, questioning whether their lives would have been different in England. Wiser than her years, Annie recognized all this. She felt older than Mr. Daniel.

With a set look on his face, he came to where she sat. She was too inexperienced to interpret it at that time. "Please say you forgive me." He was beside her. Thinking it would ease him, Annie took a cloth dipped in the gum leaf solution and soothed his sweating and tearstained face. He grabbed her hand and kissed the palm. Soon he was kissing her mouth as she had never been kissed before. She wasn't sure she liked it. His tongue was touching hers. His hand slid under her cotton dress and stroked her breast. Then the dress was off, and he was molding her breasts hard in his hands. "I love you. I love you. How could you leave me now?"

She watched as he unbuttoned his trousers and pulled out his male organ. She had never been with a man before and was terrified. His hand continued to mold her breasts and stomach. He was hurting her. He pushed her to the floor and spread her legs apart with his knee, plunging his male organ into her. It felt like he was shoving a handful of hot desert sand into her body. He kept crying and calling her Jenny and moving faster and faster. All she could feel was sand rubbing against her as though he were trying to scour them both clean. Then it was over, and he lay on her, shaking and crying. "Oh God. Oh God."

It was a long time before he noticed the tears running down Annie's face as she lay on the floor. Never again would she feel the same way about him. It did not bother her that he had entered her while Jenny was dead in the next room. Somehow she understood his need and anguish. It did not bother her that he had caused her a great deal of pain. It bothered Annie that he was not thinking of her as a person at all.

CHAPTER 14

Annie's world had changed. No longer was she a young girl. She was hurting, and she felt a deep need to return to her own people. Daniel had buried Jenny in a small graveyard on the outskirts of the small town. It was not a place of beauty or a spiritual place like her tribal burial sites. It was no different from the red soil covering the rest of the desert. To mark it as a final resting place, a small, white, wooden cross was placed at the gateway to the grounds. As people died from various causes — starvation, disease, murder — each was buried with a cross of sticks. Mr. Pedersen had told her it had to do with their belief in God. Annie didn't understand it then or now. The Master Dreamer did not require a symbol from his people. And she didn't know much about the white man's God. Some of the crossed sticks had names, but many did not. Miz Jenny's did not. Annie knew Mr. Daniel could not bring himself to place her name there. He had not yet admitted that she was gone. Annie felt sad that Miz Jenny was far away from her home and tribe. It made her realize her isolation.

In his grief, Daniel turned to Annie. At first, she wanted to run away. How could she make him understand that she was not his woman? Her curly, brown hair was not like Miz Jenny's straight, blond hair. Her brown eyes were nothing like Jenny's blue eyes. Annie was not an English rose trying to bloom where the desert rose should flourish. Annie *was* that desert rose.

He hid the black opal in a hole under his bed. Annie did not know enough English to explain what she thought he should do. She thought he should go back to England. With the rare black opal, he could return as a wealthy man. But his eyes held a look like some of the other miners' eyes did. It was the look of greed. One opal was not enough. Mr. Daniel would work and search until he realized that if he remained in this place, where he was unused to the harsh sun, there would be no use in having an opal of any size or color. If the Master Dreamer willed it, he would eventually homestead in a milder part of Australia or return to his faraway land.

It was a week after Miz Jenny had been buried, and Daniel sought her out again. This time, he was gentler, apologizing for how he took her before. Annie knew that she was nothing more than a convenience for him to exorcise his guilt and frustration. He continued to search for opals. She continued to clean his home, cook his meals, and lie still as he mounted her. Truthfully, at times she enjoyed his mounting. When she let herself feel, she experienced a physical release that she didn't really comprehend.

They continued this way for several months. All the while, she listened to his speech. He taught her to read the few books that they received from others. Every three weeks or so, Daniel would go to the nearest town and trade one of his smaller milky opals for food and other supplies, including newspapers. It was a way to pass the time while he adjusted to his new life. For Annie, it was a way to learn.

What if she did let him mount her? Was that so terrible? She had feelings too, although she doubted Mr. Daniel realized that, especially not at first. After the first few months, he stopped calling her Jenny. He started to use *Annie*. And sometimes *gin*. Although *gin* and *boong* hurt, they were less painful than "Jenny." When he called her Jenny, Annie felt that he wanted to replace his wife. A full year passed, and one day she noticed that her woman's flow had stopped, and her belly was thickening. She knew she carried his child.

One day, Daniel came in from his mine and found her lying on the floor. "Annie, Annie, what are you doing? My God, please don't die. Not again." She knew then he was not over Jenny's death. In his mind, she still replaced Jenny.

"Mr. Daniel, I got your baby in me. What I do?"

"Why ..., why ask me, Annie?" His sun-bleached brows creased in a frown. "Wha ..., what do you boongs do in a case like this? Do you get rid of it? If you want to have it, okay. But I will not be its father. Am I its father? My God, what will people think if they see a black baby calling me *father*?"

"Mr. Daniel, there lots of black babies calling white man *father*." She was angry. She already saw her child's future, and she knew its life would be hard. She saw Daniel for the first time. "I leave. Go back to my people."

"That would be best." She could see he was still adjusting to her, a black gin, carrying his seed. All the time he had been mounting her, he did not think that he would father a child.

With that, he made as if to leave but turned back. She was already lying on the floor, so again he mounted her and released his seed. With it, he released the demons that were bedeviling him. When he finished, he left. Where he went, she didn't know. He came back much later when the Master Dreamer's lamps hung in the sky. He came to her as she lay in her bed. "I'm sorry. I really am. I've been out in the desert all day thinking about things. If you want to stay here until the baby is born, that's all right with me. After that, we'll see." He looked at her for a long time. She could see that he wanted to mount her, but for the first time, his conscience made him pull away.

Their lives carried on as before, except he didn't try to mount her again. On the day she gave birth to their son, Daniel left to go to his mine. She had to decide whether to give birth in the white man's house or in the desert in her own way. She had lived with the white man so long that she had not prepared for a desert birth, so she decided to give birth in the house. She didn't dare ask him to stay, knowing he would say no. Although this was her first birth, she had seen many babies born in her desert tribe. She forced herself to relax between the gripping pains. She would not cry out. There were few women around this camp, and the few were not about to help a black woman give birth. She could not trust them with her child or herself. It was hard enough for them to bear one of their own cohabiting with a gin. It was a denial of their white attractiveness.

She walked around the rooms as long as she could stand. When the baby's head began to emerge, she squatted over a heaped pile of sand that she had placed in the middle of the room. It absorbed the birth fluids and represented her desert home. Joshua was born quickly. Annie caught him in her hands, and after clearing his mouth, she cut the cord with a knife and wrapped him in a soft, white cloth. He had his father's look about him. His nose wasn't as flat or broad as hers, but his hair was black. Anyone looking at him would have seen a resemblance to his father. She wondered how Mr. Daniel would react.

When he came back in from the mines, Daniel said nothing. As she prepared his supper, he looked at Annie. Then he looked at Joshua asleep in Annie's bed. He must have noticed the boy's resemblance to him, because she heard him leave the house and retch in the backyard. It was dark, and she wondered if any of their neighbors heard him. Annie knew what she had to do.

As he sat for his meal, she sat across from him at the table. He pushed his food around his plate, and she knew he was too upset to eat. "Mr. Daniel. Mr. Daniel!" She called his name more firmly. He was older than she, but at that moment she was more ancient. "I think you go back to your England. I make you bag for your black opal. You wear it always until you get back. Many people kill for that opal. You go back. You do not belong here."

She didn't know what she hoped he would say, but she expected his response. "You're right. But you know I can't take you with me. You wouldn't fit in. You understand, don't you?"

"Yes. I take Joshua and go back my people. They accept him better than your people."

"Joshua. That's what you call him, then?"

"Yes." He did not ask why, and she didn't tell him. It was from a story Mr. Pedersen had told her once from the white man's Bible. As he read from that Bible each evening, he had stopped every so often and asked, "Do you understand what this means?" She had nodded, but she didn't understand or care. It meant nothing to her. Their God was no different from her Master Dreamer, yet her Master Dreamer had a softer quality. He didn't point a finger and accuse like Mr. Daniel's God did.

Some of the stories Mr. Pedersen had read appealed to her more than others. Annie liked the one about Joshua and the battle of Jericho. She could picture the men from her tribe blowing their didgeridoos and the woven fence around their compound toppling over.

She said nothing of this to Mr. Daniel. She had learned a lot from Mr. Pedersen, and Annie had to admit she respected Mr. Pedersen more than she ever respected Miz Jenny or Mr. Daniel. What she had gained from Mr. Daniel was a child that belonged to neither race, and one that he refused to accept. It would be better if Mr. Daniel returned home and forgot Annie and Joshua, as she hoped to forget him.

As he sat at the table, she went to his room and brought out the black opal. From a piece of canvas that he used to carry his mining tools, she stitched a pouch that he could wear around his neck. He didn't look at her or say anything. He went to the child and stood for many minutes gazing down at him. There were many like Mr. Daniel in the world, even in her own Pitjantjatjara tribe. She hoped there were fewer in her tribe than in his.

As she picked up the opal to place in the bag, she remembered something Mr. Pedersen had said. "The white man has a saying, Annie, that opals mean tears." She believed it. That black opal meant the black tears she would shed in the days to come, and it meant the tears her people had shed since the white man came. She didn't love Mr. Daniel, and he did not love her. She had replaced his wife. The baby started to cry, and Annie took him to her breast. At the same time, she handed Mr. Daniel the pouch.

"Thank you. I will leave tomorrow morning, before it gets too hot. I will get to Sydney in a couple of days if all goes well. Uh … you likely won't hear from me again. I want to give you these small opals. You can buy what you need with these." He took a handful of opalescent stones and pressed them into her palm.

"What about house, Mr. Daniel?" She looked about the four rooms.

"Leave it. Somebody will want it, I'm sure. There is nothing I want here."

"You must take things belong your woman."

"Yes. There must be something I can take back to her parents. Oh, yes. Jenny had a hairbrush. Her mum will like that. If there is anything you want, please take it."

She knew he was trying to ease his guilt, but she wondered if she did want anything from the house. "I think."

"Good. And please continue to learn English. It will help, you know."

She knew that, and she also knew that he wanted the boy to learn his language. She had every intention of learning more of the white man's tongue and teaching her son, but she wasn't about to say anything to Mr. Daniel.

Daniel left early the next day. After he left, Annie went through the house and chose a few useful things such as the muslin from the windows, which could be traded. She had already decided what to do. First, she would go to her tribe and remain until the boy was a little older. After that, she would get a job with another white family. She understood that it would be her responsibility to her boy. As she set out to leave, she went to the nearest neighbor and called, "We leave house. If anybody want, they take."

A man came to the door of his shack. "Thank you, Annie. You're leaving then?"

She nodded and noticed him look down at her boy cradled against her breast. "Mr. Daniel leave. I go my people." His woman didn't even emerge from the house to wish her well. Annie didn't care but tucked the memory away in case she ever wished she were white. Annie turned and left Coober Pedy, making her way across the hot, burning sands in a northwest direction. She headed for the sacred lands of Uluru and Kata Tjuta.

Her people had walked this land since the Dreamtime. She knew she could survive, but she fretted about her boy. Over the centuries, her people had adjusted to the harsh climate. But her boy was half-European, and she worried how he would fare. She brought water in a kangaroo hide pouch. She knew she had to keep milk in her breasts for her boy, who slept in a sling-like carrying cradle and suckled as she walked. Feeling warm liquid on her arm, she knew Joshua was excreting his first meal. She held him away from her, and the dung dropped to the ground. Soon, bugs and worms would slake their thirst on the droppings. Nothing was wasted in this hot, dry land.

Under the burning sun and across the red sands, carrying her few belongings on her back, she trekked toward her destination. The baby was cradled securely in his muslin sling, so her hands were free to dig into termite hills for larvae. When she came across a desert oak, she looked for honey ants but found none.

There was no lingering twilight in this land. One minute the sun burned hot, and the next, the sky darkened, and the Master Dreamer hung his lamps. The air cooled, but the flies persisted, trying to suck fluids from anywhere they could. She wrapped another layer of muslin around Joshua and draped a piece over herself as protection. Before she lived with the Europeans, she wasn't bothered by flies. She supposed one could get used to anything if there was no other way.

Covering herself in the muslin canopy, she dozed on the still-warm sand. She made sure she was far away from plants that might harbor snakes that fed at night. She wasn't afraid for herself, but Joshua still carried the scent of a feeble newborn. She dozed fitfully, waking enough to help Joshua find her breast. The dark night passed. The morning sun rose over the horizon, its fingers of brilliant orange flicking streaks of blue night across the sky. Was her predicament part of the Master Dreamer's plan? If so, how would she proceed? She wondered about Mr. Daniel. She doubted he had reached Sydney yet.

And if he had, he would have to wait for a steamer to take him home.

Years earlier, when she had gone with her clan to trade near the port city, she had seen people come off the steamer in chains. The women prisoners fared the worst. If they survived the voyage, they were tossed onto the loading pier like garbage. Men, having been nowhere near a woman for years, whooped and shouted and picked out the ones they fancied. Annie felt sorry for the women. She learned many years later from both Mr. Pedersen and Mr. Daniel that some had families at home. They were sent to her country for stealing a loaf of bread to feed their families or for some other trifle. When Mr. Daniel told her, she was shocked. "That not happen my people. My people no steal to fill their bellies." Her people were the Pitjantjatjara, keepers of the sacred hills of the Master Dreamer. They would not lower themselves to treat their women so harshly.

Mr. Daniel was returning to England, but he wouldn't be one to grab a poor woman. She chuckled mockingly to herself. He didn't have to trek to a steamship to find a woman after his wife died. No. He had a willing woman living with him. She looked at her boy, asleep at her breast. Right then, as the sun's orange flame burst into yellow in the morning sky, she promised herself that she would raise this boy to be the best he could, for he carried the seeds of two worlds — one ancient and one new.

CHAPTER 15

Annie drank water from the kangaroo pouch and folded the muslin canopy into her pack. Joshua continued to suckle in his sleep. He didn't cry, and she was thankful. As the sun rose higher, she continued trekking. It would take three days to reach her tribe. She hoped they were still in the area. There had been so many changes in her life and in the tribes that she wasn't certain her family would be in the compound where she left them. Possibly the men had formed a hunting party with another tribe and were looking for a kangaroo, or tribal members were away on a trading mission. There didn't seem any particular time for hunting or trading. She guessed that whenever the people grew tired of camp, they sent word for a hunt or a trade.

Even if there were a hunt or a trade, there would be people around camp. As their bodies stiffened and became sore, the older men stayed close to home, rubbing the gum tree leaves into their limbs. In her tribe, the elders were revered. They would soon rejoin the Master Dreamer as their dreams finished. She felt she was just beginning whatever dreams the Master Dreamer had planned. She fingered the prized amulet around her neck. It hadn't protected her from Mr. Daniel, and she thought deeply about her beliefs as she walked.

Then she smiled. No, it hadn't protected her from Mr. Daniel, but it had brought her Joshua. She took the amulet and placed it about the neck of her son, asking the Master Dreamer to bless him. In the bright desert sun, there was no mistaking his heritage. His whiteness was well camouflaged. His skin was lighter, but she knew it would darken in the sun.

After drinking some water, she resumed her journey. She did not perceive this land like the whites did. The white man found the country monotonous. To see the land, you had to love it. What the European saw as one shade of red soil was actually an array of colors. What he saw as desolate and barren was filled with life. The white man did not see he was kin to the termites in their hills or the birds circling overhead seeking carrion. He did not recognize that he was a brother to the desert plants, honey ants, and snakes as surely as he was a brother to his family.

Not all white men devalued the land. She knew white men who came to this land and made it their own. They had a deep feeling for her land, while those that came and went did not. Even though her people knew the European made a mistake by pulling out all the trees, they could see he had feelings for the land. But he did not understand it.

Annie thought that the Master Dreamer must be disappointed with the white men, but he did not judge them, because he knew they did not know what they were doing. Annie's people were the keepers of the Master Dreamer's dream. They lived with the sparse trees, the bottlebrush, the flies, and the red sand in the hot country. The white man should have stayed on the coast if he wanted to live in this vast land. He was used to the coast. The white man felt he must conquer the land. Her people knew they must live with it. *That's our main difference,* Annie thought. *The white man says my people are lazy, because they do not conquer the land. My people think the white man is cruel, because he hurts the land. Because he hurts the land, he hurts the land's people. My people hurt.*

After three days, she carried Joshua into her people's camp, looking for those who had given her life. The kalbin emerged from his hut and looked at her for a long time. She knew he read her soul. "Good day, Kalbin. I look for those who gave me life." She spoke in the Pitjantjatjara dialect. He answered in the same.

"They are away on a trading mission." The man was tall and broad. His skin was darker than hers, and his hair was a deep black. He looked fierce, but she had known him since childhood and was not frightened. "You are carrying a child. A white man's child," he said, reverting to English There was no censure in his words. She was not the first to return with a white man's child. Each time, though, it was a humiliating experience for her people. If they were regarded as equals to the white man, there would be no hostility. But they were not.

Annie knew exceptions. A few white men enjoyed the black women as their own, but these were very few. The kalbin stood before her, looking her over. Although the Europeans had brought woven cloth to their land, he chose to wear a breechcloth of split leaves. He stood silently, waiting for her to move. It took her a few moments to realize he had spoken in English. She replied in the terse syllables of her language.

"How old is the child?" He asked in their native tongue.

"Four days, Kalbin."

"You should still be in the women's house resting, not walking on long journeys. Why do you return?"

"The man went back to England." She did not say more, but the kalbin understood. Joshua stirred at her breast, and the kalbin reached over and pulled aside the muslin covering. He looked for several seconds at her son's lighter skin, straighter hair, and slender nose. Touching the amulet around Joshua's neck, he took Joshua gently from her breast and laughed as the baby howled in protest. He held the crying baby up and murmured words that Annie could not hear. When he turned back to her, his expression was lighter.

"When the people return to camp, we will have a naming ceremony for this boy. He is the Master Dreamer's chosen one." The high priest returned the boy, and Joshua immediately found her nipple. With a smile, the kalbin walked away, leaving her to find her way about the camp.

She was about to enter her parents' hut when she remembered that as a woman with her own child, she wasn't allowed inside. From the corner of her eye, she saw the kalbin watching her. She turned and found the hut for new mothers. Alone, she had the cool darkness to herself. Weary from her arduous journey across the burning sand, she lay down on a rush mat and fell asleep. When she awoke, she found a bowl of gruel outside the doorway. Thinking the people had returned, she looked for the person who had left it, but the camp was still empty. Surely the kalbin hadn't put it there. It was unheard of for the high priest to cater to a woman's needs.

After eating the sweet gruel, she searched for the kalbin. Annie found him with two elderly men that she hadn't seen before. She knew not to say anything while he was with the men. "Kalbin, I was wondering whether any of our people had returned."

"Not yet, An-ee." He spoke in a mixture of Pitjantjatjara and English, giving her English name an odd pronunciation. Then she noticed that one of the older men had lesions on his skin and was missing several fingers. His nose, broad by birthright, was collapsed even more. She recognized the disease as leprosy.

"Does the man have any pituri to chew? I have a few leaves in my pouch. He is welcome to them." The kalbin looked at her in astonishment. She knew he wondered how she came by them. The pituri was chewed by the tribe farther north, the Sea-turtle clan, to enter the Dreamtime visions. Her people often traded honey ants for it. She expected the hunters and traders to bring pituri leaves when they returned, to ease the old man's pain. In the meantime, she could give him the pituri she had brought from Coober Pedy.

The kalbin looked pleased and nodded but said nothing. She didn't expect him to. Both men nodded to her. The kalbin must have told the men who she was, for it was doubtful that they remembered her. She did not remember them, but she had left the camp even before her woman's flow started. She returned to the hut and retrieved the few leaves.

Aware that she would offend the old man by offering him pituri a few days after giving birth, she handed the leaves to the kalbin. She thought men were so strange. The kalbin understood and took the leaves into his hut, nodding to her in dismissal. He returned a few minutes later and gave the man the leaves. It was obvious that he was in the last stages of the disease and was isolated from the rest of the camp. But her people did not leave him alone entirely. She did not know if the other man had leprosy. Although elderly, he exhibited no signs of disease. He may have been in camp simply because of age.

Joshua and she spent the first night in camp on their own. She did not mind, but there was a slight feeling of unease. She had been away too long, and although she still felt Aborigine, she knew she had absorbed many of the white man's customs. She could not return completely to her former life in camp.

Two days later, the people returned. "Look. It is An-ee." The voice was that of Annie's childhood friend. As the girl rushed forward to greet her, she saw that Annie carried a child and stopped short. Already Annie had surpassed her in experience, and that was enough to divide the once-close girls. She was not the only one to draw back. Annie's parents stopped and stared long moments at their daughter. They had sent her to the whites years before, but it wasn't because they didn't love her. They foresaw the way their world was going, and they thought she would have a better future. Their native land was disappearing under the onslaught of white people. Kangaroos, which the tribe needed for meat, were attacked by the white man's camels. Trees, which the tribe needed for foods and medicines, were clear-cut so the whites could homestead. Her people were not angry; they were frightened. Just as the Namarakain, the malignant spirits, waited to steal the soul of the leprosy-afflicted man, the white man waited to steal the sick souls of her people.

"Why have you come back?" Her mother voiced the question in their own tongue. "You do not belong here now."

"You are still my people. I wish to stay with you for a time. I brought my son home to learn the ways of his people."

"Our people do not have the old ways anymore. You do not have the old ways, either. You are not welcome here. Did you see anyone but a childhood friend welcome you back?" Her voice was harsh, and Annie knew she found it difficult to say what had to be said. Annie did not belong. She knew that even before she made the trek across the red sands to her people. But she did not belong to the white man's world, either.

"And what about your son?" her mother added. "Where does he belong?"

"I don't know, but I wish to stay a few days, anyway. The kalbin said we will have a naming ceremony for him." There were gasps throughout the group.

"The kalbin said this? Even though we were gone from camp?"

Annie knew the kalbin spoke without the people's consent, but he was the priest and had every right to do so. He was the one in touch with the wishes of the Master Dreamer. A man stepped forward to gaze at Joshua. He was taller than the other men in the tribe, but his features were the same.

He had the short, broad face, broad nose, and small chin of her people. Although her tribe's people were not tall, they had long legs to offset their short bodies. It seemed to her that although there were variances among the many tribes, they did not stand out like those of the white man. Mr. Pedersen, for instance, was tall and muscular, while Mr. Daniel was much shorter. Both men were fair, but she had seen others with hair as dark as tribal men. White men were every shade from light brown to pink to freckled. Few were white. Annie supposed her tribe's differences would be apparent as well if you studied them deeply. It was doubtful, however, the white man would study tribes thoroughly. They herded Aboriginal people into special areas where many died mysteriously. She was sure this was her parents' message. Just as her people were told in dreams that they would die out, Annie's mother had a dream as well. She dreamt her children would succeed in the new world.

The kalbin strolled into the center of the group. He had painted his face with white clay and red ocher. Annie thought he was preparing to bury the dying man, but it was not that at all. He held up his hand for silence. "Hear this, my people. Annie, whom you call An-ee, has returned for a short stay with her people." He made it sound as though he and Annie had already discussed this. "We are here to give a name to her child. Hear you this. This child is the future. He is the future of our people. He is the future of our land. This evening we give him a secret name of our tribe. But he will be known by his white man's name — Joshua." With that, he turned and strolled away. Annie wondered what he was planning. She would never mention the gruel. That would be a secret she kept from her family and friends.

As Joshua was six days old, she could still use the women's hut until she made her own. She left to prepare for the evening ceremony.

Custom stated that her family should supply the necessary food for the naming ceremony, but as the event was unexpected, several families brought food as their offering to the newborn. The kalbin seemed to play a more important role in this ritual naming than she remembered from previous times, but she guessed that was because he saw a special future for Joshua. The priest lifted his offering to the Master Dreamer and declared Joshua the special child, *Aruta*, to be known in both the Pitjantjatjara tribe and his future white man's tribe as *Joshua*. The kalbin foresaw that, regardless of his skin tone, the boy would go through many years of wanting to be more white than black. The ceremony continued with nardoo fern cakes, damper, and honey ants that Annie gathered from the desert oak just before she reached her people's camp.

As the days passed into months and years, Annie felt suspended in an in-between time. As the kalbin explained, she was needed to help assimilate her son into his first culture. It was necessary that Joshua learn as many of his people's customs as possible, because he would carry them into the future. Annie spent her days helping around the camp and staying on good terms with the people, but she was still an outsider.

In the dark of night, she sometimes lay in her new hut thinking of Mr. Daniel in his far-off home. Could he return to England unaffected by his experiences in Australia? Did he ever think of

Joshua? If he met an Englishwoman and had children, would he remember his Australian child?

Joshua did not lack a father figure. He thrived as each man taught him how to hunt, how to paint his body for the different ceremonies, and how to behave in camp. As winter set into the desert, and they moved into the Uluru caves for warmth, the elder decided it was time to take another gathering trip to the Sea-turtle clan. After his announcement, Annie shivered uncontrollably and continued shivering throughout the long night. She felt worse than when she had learned she was pregnant. She didn't know why and didn't want to say anything, because she had no rational explanation. She covered her fear and joined the tribe in the morning with an ecstatic Joshua beside her.

They left before the sun rose. Several days after setting out, carrying honey ants and termite larvae, they came upon the trees that the men used to make boomerangs. Their tribe had traded them until others became proficient in making their own. The Sea-turtle clan was the master in boomerang use, but the men of the Pitjantjatjara liked to make a few for their own use and trade. They stayed a few days while the men carved several weapons. They continued their journey with the new trading articles complete. The farther north they traveled, the hotter it became, until they reached the rain forest.

CHAPTER 16

Annie did not understand her apprehension about meeting the Sea-turtle clan. She recalled going on one of the trading parties when she was a little younger than Joshua, but she remembered nothing about the trip except a shadowy specter hovered around her in the rain forest.

Several days after her people traveled north, they came upon a small group of the Sea-turtle clan at the edge of their encampment. Their kalbin had dreamed the Pitjantjatjara would meet them soon, and they rushed to meet the desert tribe. Joshua ran ahead and greeted the clan's children. Pleased that he wasn't shy, Annie refrained from holding him back. She figured his assertiveness was due to the attention he received in his tribe, but there was more to it. The Sea-turtle children embraced him as their own. Annie was uncomfortable in the camp. A few of the women were friendly, but her unease caused them to withdraw. She did not like the Sea-turtle land at all. When the women suggested going to the river to bathe, images of drowning caused her to panic. She demurred, saying she was having her woman's flow. She could not show how terrified she was by their suggestion. As the younger women left to swim in the river, she lingered in the camp. There was a familiar feeling about it. It was sadness mixed with happiness and love.

Her mother prodded Annie's memory. "Do you remember coming here with us when you were very little?"

"Yes. But I don't like the rain forest, Mother. I don't think I'll feel safe until I am back in the desert, where it is open and you can see your enemies coming."

"Enemies? We haven't been enemies with the Sea-turtle clan for hundreds of years. Where did you get that idea?"

Annie couldn't say, because she didn't know herself. She was still reeling from her mother using her English name for the past few days. She wasn't sure if her mother accepted the name, or if it was her way of telling Annie that she no longer belonged to the clan family. Annie was sure if she went to the white man's world and left Joshua with his grandmother, her mother would be happy. She adored Joshua to the point of saying that his lighter skin, straighter hair, and narrower nose were an improvement. Yes, her mother would be delighted. Annie couldn't do that, though. Nor did she think the kalbin would permit it.

Of all her clan, the kalbin respected and honored her most. He revered her as the mother of the tribe's future, and as such, she commanded deference. He did nothing to suggest he wanted more. In the years since she had returned to her people, she had been with no male. This angered one or two of the men in the camp who wanted to bed her. She heard mutterings about preferring a white man's organ to theirs. But she wasn't interested in mating with any of them, because this would force her to stay in the tribe. She knew from the first few days she would not remain with them.

After the trading concluded, Annie's tribe was treated to cooked sea turtle on the beach. As a group, they walked to the water's edge. The Master Dreamer's lamps were strung in the sky, creating a feeling of gaiety. Annie didn't feel the cold chill on the beach as she had amidst the trees.

She felt almost happy near the ocean but couldn't place why. As the dances commenced around the steaming turtle, she laughed with the rest of the tribe. Their melodic tongue was more musical than the Pitjantjatjara. They also had a storyteller who held the audience spellbound with his tales of catching the sea turtle. The next story was about the way the tribal women were treated in the early years. A tingling sensation went through her. The woman next to her turned as she felt Annie shiver. "That does not happen now," she said. "That practice was stopped a thousand years ago by a tribe member sent to us by the Master Dreamer."

Annie didn't have time to think about the woman's words. She turned back to the storyteller who engaged in a story about an emu hunt. The whole tribe laughed, including men being teased by the story. The evening became pleasant. The woman who explained about the women's ritual turned toward Annie again as they picked themselves off the sandy beach. "They say your son was sent by the Master Dreamer, like that woman years ago."

Annie had trouble comprehending her language but managed to pick up a few words. Deep in her being, she understood what the woman said, but she could not remember who in her tribe spoke the Sea-turtle clan language. It was a good thing the woman of the Sea-turtle clan spoke a little Pitjantjatjara.

"Our kalbin seems to think so. At least he says Joshua is special, but I have seen nothing to indicate that he is a chosen one."

"He is a child. Even now he may see things differently than other children, but we do not know. You must be special too, for you are his mother. The Master Dreamer would not choose just any woman to give birth to this child."

Annie kept her misgivings to herself. She loved Joshua deeply, but at times, she was a little jealous of the attention he received. She did have a plan, however, to ensure Joshua went as far as possible in their world, which was fast becoming the land of the white man.

Annie remained in camp while Joshua learned the ways of his black ancestors. The years passed swiftly. Joshua grew into a delightful young man. He was still younger than Annie had been when her parents had introduced her to the white world. She went to the kalbin. "It is time," she said. He looked at her at length before replying.

"Are you certain it is time for Joshua to leave, or is it *your* wish to return to the white world?"

She had wanted to return for many years, but she wasn't thinking of herself. Joshua was idle like many of the males in her camp, and she did not want that for him. He was taller than the other boys his age. This made him seem older than he was, and because of this, she expected more from him. She said none of this to the kalbin, but she was sure he knew her heart. She said again, "It is time."

"We will miss you. I wonder if you will miss us as much. Your mother's grown close to Joshua. She will not take well to his leaving."

"My parents have other children and grandchildren. That will have to satisfy them."

"*I* will miss you, Annie. I did not tell you before, because I knew you had many hurts and thoughts. I also know you could never be happy with me in this camp. I am the kalbin, and I cannot leave. You cannot stay. That is the way of our lives. I wish you well, and I wish Joshua well. One day I will hear of the great things he is doing. The amulet stone you passed on belongs to him now. Put your faith in the amulet, and put your faith in Joshua. When he leaves you, give him your blessing." He stood for a few moments before turning and walking away. She thought of the amulet around Josh's neck. It was so much a part of her, she nearly forgot that her parents had given it to her when they sent her away. And the kalbin was right. The amulet had protected her. She came from Mr. Daniel's with her health and her son.

She knew the kalbin liked her. But that was the difference between the kalbin and Mr. Daniel. Joshua's father thought of himself. If he had felt anything for Joshua, it was fleeting, and he had only contempt for her. Back in England, she doubted he thought of them at all. The kalbin rose above his jealousies and lust to help her and Joshua. If anything happened to either Annie or Joshua, the kalbin would weep in silence, alone. She left him and stopped at her parents' hut.

"Where will you go?" her father asked.

She replied in his language. "The homesteading whites are the ones misusing our land, but that is where I must go. Joshua must have a chance to do whatever the Master Dreamer planned for him. I will cook and clean for these people and make a place for Joshua." Her son was her life; she had no other. Years before, her parents let her go, and although they had shed tears then, there were none now.

In the white man's year of 1875, Annie took her son and trekked again across the red desert to Mpartwe, a trading post for many tribes. Annie's clan could trade here instead of going far north to the Sea-turtle clan, but there was a special bond between the two peoples. One often visited the other and went nowhere near the trading post. The sun was hot. Years earlier, she was responsible for Joshua on their trek home to her people. Now he claimed responsibility for her. At least part of the time. He was still a young boy with many playful ways. One day, they found a bloated toad and squeezed it to disgorge its water. Afterwards, they placed it under a spinifex bush and scared a sleeping snake. Joshua picked up the snake and wrapped it around her neck, laughing at the necklace he had given her. "Jumpin' joey! Don't you ever do that again!" He knew she meant it, but at the same time, they both laughed. It was a long time since they had felt free enough to laugh.

Annie had never asked Joshua how he felt about living in or leaving the camp. She thought he was too young, but seeing the far-away look in his eyes, she knew he understood more deeply and saw more than she did. "You never said how you liked living with our people." She spoke to him in the Pitjantjatjara language, and Joshua answered with the same. His English was worse than hers, for he had only his mother's instruction in the language.

"These are my people; I know no others. Everyone was nice to me. I know they weren't always nice to you, but no one said a bad word to me."

"You say the tribe is your people, but do you know you are part of another people, who live across the great seas in a far-away land?"

"People in the camp told me that, but I didn't know what they meant."

"You are part white, and we're going to their world. I will work again for the white man, so you may learn his ways. I think the Master Dreamer chose you for a special life. I do not know what. But I do know that we must return to the white man."

"Will I see my father?"

She wished she could tell him *yes.* "No. Your father returned to his country. This land was not for him. The land where he lives is soft and green. It does not have the red sands. He does not have to squeeze Mr. Toad or find secret water holes to live. He does not have to eat snakes and plants."

"Why couldn't we go with him? I could show him how I throw the boomerang and how I dig for termites in the hills. I could show him how to dig for witchetty grubs under the trees like in the northern land."

She smiled. To Mr. Daniel, these were the ways of the boongs—the wild men living like animals in the land he left behind. No, Mr. Daniel would not be happy to learn that his son could perform tribal feats beyond his years. "He would love to know you do these things. And one day you can show him. But not yet."

He seemed satisfied and went about looking for honey ants for their evening meal. Afterwards, they curled together for warmth and watched the Master Dreamer hang his lamps in the sky. They tried to count them, but soon fell asleep. They awakened as the lamps went out and the sun rose above the horizon. For three days they traveled until they reached Mpartwe. She wondered how long she would have to wait before she found a white family willing to give an Aborigine woman and her half-breed son employment.

CHAPTER 17

Mpartwe was dirty and dismal. A few corrugated tin buildings stood haphazardly along a cleared red sand path. One building looked better than the rest, and Annie saw that it was some sort of trading post or white man's store. At once, Annie was accosted by a bearded white man covered with the ever-present fine, red dust. Through his russet facial hair, she saw his yellowed and rotting teeth. "You wanna earn a free meal, girlie?" His hand reached out and molded her breast. She would not be part of that again. Most of the whites treated Aboriginal women like slaves or worse. He would feed her his lumpy white gruel if she would share his bed, do his laundry, and slave for him. She much preferred searching for honey ants and witchetty grubs. She even preferred going hungry. What he wanted from her was not going to help Joshua.

The white men carried disease, which killed many of her people. She would not be one of his victims. Thank the Master Dreamer Mr. Daniel had not given her a disease. Her people could heal some illnesses with their medicines, but their medicine men could not cure the diseases they did not know. They tried the medicines at their disposal but with little success. Because of this, tribal people died in great numbers. Those who didn't die of disease were often hunted as her people hunted the kangaroo and the sea turtle.

Her people did not hunt animal for sport. True, they often made a sport of the hunt. But hunting was a serious affair. It could mean the difference between a satisfied belly and starving. And her people always gave thanks to the Master Dreamer for allowing the animal's capture. They respected the animals for their abilities, and they knew that the hunt was a covenant between the hunters and the animal. It was a covenant contracted in the years of the Dreamtime and fulfilled in this world.

No, she wanted no part of the white man's bed. She wanted the white man's employment and no more. She could clean and wash clothes. And by the disreputable dress of most of the men in the village, she could tell there would be plenty of opportunity. But she wouldn't work for just anyone. She had to work somewhere Josh could learn the white man's language and the best of the white man's ways. Joshua was her priority. He had an understanding beyond his years, and knowing what she sought, he quietly pulled at her elbow. About to admonish him for tugging, Annie gazed in the direction he looked.

The man looked more affluent than the others in the dusty village. That didn't mean too much, Annie knew. Some of the opal miners she had known looked scruffy and threadbare, but they had a fortune in stashed opals. This man's clothes were free of red dust. By his side was a white woman with a kind face. Her appearance reminded Annie of Mr. Daniel's wife, but this woman's face showed an inner strength that Miz Jenny had lacked. The man's coloring was similar to Mr. Daniel's, but there the similarity ended. This man's face showed integrity that had been lacking in Mr. Daniel's. He was not Mr. Daniel. Mr. Daniel would never return to this country. His time here held too many sad memories, but Annie knew she and Joshua were not included. They were nothing more than a passing moment during a short, unhappy period of his life. If he remembered his time at all, it would be for the loss of his wife. In time, even that would diminish. Annie doubted anyone in his faraway country would ever hear of Joshua from his father.

She glanced toward the man again. He had a commanding appearance. He seemed stern but not cruel. She tried to guess whether he was here to spread word of the white man's God. He did not look like the adventuresome type who was here for the gems or gold hidden in the land. She hesitated. To approach a white man and beg for a position in his household was putting oneself in danger. It was more perilous than teasing a poisonous snake. She didn't want to make a move. At the same time, she looked about the village and realized her prospects were slim. Joshua and she could wait a few days to see if any cattlemen came into the village, but she preferred to have employment as soon as possible. Sending a silent prayer to the Master Dreamer, she pulled Joshua toward the couple. "Me work for you."

They were startled. The man turned toward the woman with a question on his face. This was not what Annie had expected. The white man sometimes deferred to his mate but not often in this part of the world. He waited for his woman to eye Annie up and down. Her deep blue eyes searched Annie's soul. Annie hoped the Master Dreamer had put enough there to appeal to the woman. After looking at Annie for a long time in silence, the woman turned her gaze upon Joshua. He stood still and looked up at her.

"Me Joshua. Me good worker too." Josh gave her one of his open grins.

A smile tugged at the corner of her severe mouth. "Mr. Peart, I think we could find a place for them, don't you?" She may have phrased it as a question, but there was no mistaking the authority in her voice. Mr. Peart heard it too.

With another swift glance at Joshua and Annie, she said, "Can you cook and keep a house clean?"

Annie nodded vigorously. "And Joshua good much work."

Annie heard the man's whisper to his wife about Joshua's looking like a bastard. Turning to Annie, he ordered, "You are not to sleep with any of the white men in my employ. Is that understood?"

Annie had no such intention. She wanted Joshua to learn English, but she had her limits. She was sure that his wife had lots to say about the matter too. If she didn't need the job so badly, Annie would have walked off. But Joshua clinched the matter. With his wide grin and sparkling eyes, he informed them, "Good. Me work you. You teach me English. Me go to school. Me be doctor."

When Joshua had decided to be a doctor, Annie didn't know. He had said nothing to her about his dream.

"When can you start?" Mrs. Peart asked.

"Today." Annie wasn't about to let the opportunity slip from her hands. In front of the assayer's shop, the dirty man who had accosted her was still leering, holding up a pouch for her to see and shaking it. She turned away from him. He was one of the Europeans in search of gold. These men didn't realize that her people had lived with the gold, opals, rubies, and sapphires for thousands of years. The hot sun blazed down. The red dust lay in pockets around the small village, covering everything. Even in the short time the Pearts and she had talked, the dust settled onto Mrs. Peart's bonnet and into the creases of her blue gown. Sweat ran down her face. The dust, like the flies, gravitated to moisture. Realizing his wife's discomfort, Mr. Peart nodded toward the horse and cart and said to Annie, "You'll have to walk beside the carriage. I'm afraid the cart is only large enough to hold Mrs. Peart, our sack of flour, and other supplies."

Annie nodded. Walking was as natural to her as breathing, and she knew her place in the white man's world. Joshua didn't fear distance either. Mr. Peart helped his wife into the cart and took his place beside her. Joshua and Annie walked beside them as they set out for their new home. The familiar red dust oozed between Annie's toes, giving her a sense of security. The flies buzzed unremittingly, and she used her goose wing fan to keep them away. Joshua looked at Mrs. Peart and then his mother. Without a word, she gave him the fan, and for the rest of the journey, he waved flies away from the white woman in the cart. The journey didn't take long. It was barely an hour's walk from the small trading center. By the time they reached the house, Joshua had won his way into Mrs. Peart's heart. Annie still needed to prove herself.

The Peart house wasn't large by anyone's standards, and the area around the home was small. It was not a homesteading property. She had heard the tales from her people as the older members shook their heads in bewilderment. Finding lush forests, the Europeans methodically cut them down to plant their wheat and other crops. Why did the Master Dreamer allow such an atrocity in his land? Did he think it taught his people a lesson? The year after clearing, the crops thrived. Then there was devastation unlike anything Annie's people had ever seen. Under the soil was salt from ancient Dreamtime oceans. The trees had kept the salt confined well below the soil, but once the trees had been removed, the salt rose to the surface. Nothing grew. The dream of large, prosperous homesteads had been shattered. Many whites returned home. Others chose to stay but took up other trades. In many cases, they prospered in their new endeavors. The land, however, was ailing.

My people could have told them, Annie thought. Those who had lived on this land since the Dreamtime understood their place. They did not conquer the land. The land was not their slave, and they were not slaves to the land. The people and the land lived in harmony. The whites thought her people were lazy, because they did not farm the land. The whites thought Annie's people were slothful, because they did not build houses like the whites did. But her people knew what the land meant. It was a friend, and sometimes it was even an enemy. As a friend, it fed, clothed, and cradled them. As an adversary, it starved them so that they honed their hunting skills and sharpened their intelligence.

They could have told the newcomers this. But they didn't. Most of the white people could not understand the dialects, and her people had difficulty wrapping their tongue around white words. But that was not the major difference. Europeans were born of conquered peoples and set out to conquer others. They needed to feel the mastery of their race. Annie's people were born of the Master Dreamer's gentleness. They lived the Master Dreamer's dream.

The horse and cart pulled up to the Pearts' house. For their home, they had chosen an oasis beside a now-dry riverbed. As there were river gums growing, Annie knew that the dry bed would fill whenever the Master Dreamer sent his sporadic rains. Annie supposed this place reminded the Pearts of the soft green fields Mr. Daniel had told her about. There was a camel tethered to a date palm growing close to the river. Camels were new to her country, and Annie vowed to stay her distance. The beast merely gazed at her with a smug grin pulling at its lips. Joshua, with a child's curiosity, assumed that the camel was his friend. He would have made its acquaintance, but he glanced at Annie and knew that he was to stay. They had not come to play. Compared to the village proper, this was a cool haven. Annie thought it might be like the Dreamtime. Mr. Peart helped his wife down from the cart and left her to explain the chores.

"As this is your first day, just look around a bit," Mrs. Peart said. "I don't know where you'll sleep yet. I hadn't thought we would come back with hired help, you see."

Their home was made of the same wood as many in the area. It had a wash of white, which was new enough to glow. Few of the white man's buildings could endure the blazing sun and keep their vibrancy. The same could be said for the white man. As Mrs. Peart entered the house, Mr. Peart unbuckled the horse from the cart and led him to a lean-to shed. It was close to the riverbed and sheltered from the hot sun by three huge trees. He rubbed down the horse while Joshua watched, taking in all the owner's moves. Annie knew Joshua would be doing this particular job very soon. He was no slacker. Joshua had an innate desire to work hard and work well.

She drifted away from Joshua and Mr. Peart to explore. The grounds surrounding the house were once well tended but were now overgrown with weeds. The garden plants were rambling and untidy. Either Mrs. Peart had lost her heart for the gardens, or they had bought the house with the gardens in this shape. She and Joshua could help with these too. She turned toward the house. Knocking on the door, she pushed it open without waiting for a response. If she was to work here, she wasn't about to knock at a door every time she entered. Mrs. Peart must have thought the same thing, for she smiled warmly as Annie entered.

Her new employer had changed from her dusty dress and was now wearing a beige muslin at-home gown, which Annie thought suited her fair coloring. Her long, blond hair was pulled back into a tight bun and held with a net. On her feet were soft house shoes. Just as she was about to speak, Mr. Peart entered the house with Joshua. "I'm afraid we've gone about this rather backwards. I don't even know your name."

"Annie, Mr. Peart. Call me Annie." Despite Mrs. Peart's rather austere appearance and aloof reticence, Annie was sure that she and the woman would get along. "I cook." By the position of the sun, she knew the day was ending. She looked about her. The furnishings had obviously been shipped from England. Overstuffed chairs in a deep red color dominated the room. Dark tables sported coats of red dust. Annie imagined the chairs were covered with the same red dust, but at least it didn't show. "I clean too." She grinned at the Englishwoman. In that moment, they became lifetime friends.

Annie looked around the inviting house. There was a large bedroom, which was dominated by a dark wood bed. Over the bed was a covering of the same deep red cloth that covered the chairs. Heavy, red draperies framed the windows in all the rooms. The smaller bedroom held a small bed covered with a yellow quilt, but there were no young children about. A large closet stored what wasn't in use.

In the kitchen, Annie gasped in dismay. There was a strange-looking contraption, which Mrs. Peart called a cooking stove. Seeing Annie's consternation, Mrs. Peart said, "I'll show you how to use all these." A white sink with a hand pump was close to the stove. She had seen this before at Mr. Pedersen's house, so it was not frightening. Over the sink was a rack where dishes could dry, and over that there was a cupboard where plain white, heavy dishes made their home. She had seen dishes like these before in one of the white man's trading stores in Coober Pedy. In the middle of the room was a large, wooden table where food preparation and eating occurred. The one colorful dish was a serving bowl edged in a medium green with a cluster of purple violets on the bottom. She knew they were violets from her work with Mr. Daniel. He had owned a book with English plants in colored pictures.

Every spare moment, Annie looked at that book, trying to understand the people who came into her land. At the time, she secretly hoped that Mr. Daniel would take her and Joshua when he returned to England, and Annie wanted to be prepared when she arrived. She knew such a thing was foolish, but in her moments of daydreaming, she held onto a small hope that she would one day see the home of Joshua's father. "I think you've had a hard life," Mrs. Peart said, catching a fleeting emotion cross Annie's face. "I hope you won't find it too hard here. And I've a feeling we'll be friends."

Annie knew then that Mrs. Peart was deeply lonely in a way she was not. Annie was not thousands of miles from her home of soft, green hills and woodland violets. She could always return to her tribe. Or could she? When she had been there, she felt like an outsider, just as she felt now in this white home. No. This way of thinking was not good. For Joshua's sake, she must make a place for Joshua and her in this Englishwoman's environment. She was determined that he succeed in his new world.

CHAPTER 18

Annie and Joshua spent three years with the Pearts in Mpartwe, living in a lean-to shed that Mr. Peart had added to the back of the house. It was much better than many white people had. Over the years, she crushed eucalyptus leaves and strewed them on the dirt floor, removing the old and adding fresh. The pungent aroma kept the flies to a minimum. When Mrs. Peart saw how well they worked, she gathered leaves for herself and soaked them in a pail of water. Then she and Annie used the water to wash the floors and walls in the main house. Both Annie and Joshua were content, and he learned English rapidly. Annie was slower to grasp the syntax of the language.

In the time since they arrived, the town had expanded faster than a buzzard landing on a dead roo. A white newcomer had opened a shop to sell fabrics, pots, pans, and pickaxes to the miners. At the end of three months, however, the shop went up for sale. When Mr. Peart had come to Annie's land, it was either to mine or homestead. After arriving, he found he had made a huge mistake. Not one to give in easily, he continued to search for work in the town.

The day Annie had gathered her courage and asked for work, he had been scouting for an opportunity. His God had smiled on him. Mr. Peart had bought the shop from the previous owner with enough cash to see the fellow settled in another town. He would then send a percentage of sales to the man for the next five years. Both men were satisfied with the transaction.

Mr. Peart did not start out as a businessman. He tried talking the previous owner into staying and teaching him the basics. But, once the man decided to sell and found a buyer, he wanted to depart immediately to a more equitable climate. Mrs. Peart had little more business knowledge than her husband, but she gamely offered her help. But it wasn't until they asked Annie's help that the shop became a success. Mr. Peart contracted to be the merchant for cattle and sheep feed. This brought him into contact with the ranchers. Then he began selling wool goods made by the sheep farmer's wives. Now and again, they asked Annie's opinion on some matter. Did she think the tribesmen would trade with them? What did she think was the most desired commodity in this place? She talked them into importing more lightweight cloth for furnishings and clothing. Until then, furnishings were heavy and dark and unsuited to the hot climate. Although this took time, the changes began within a month of Annie arriving at the Peart home and offering her suggestions. This resulted in the Pearts doing even more business. The Pearts, however, were not the only people willing to change and adapt.

Annie's people didn't always agree with the whites, and many of the newcomers' schemes ruined her ancestral home, but she did admit they had one transforming idea. Those not mining for gems or farming on the hostile soil lent their muscle to placing parallel rails of steel across the land. Mpartwe became the northern end of a new railway. To cater to the travelers, a depot opened, and a white man sat at a machine sending and receiving messages. When he wasn't needed by the Pearts, Joshua had a new job as a message runner.

It was obvious to the Pearts that Annie understood the trade and had a knack for dealing with people. Her years with Mr. Pedersen and Mr. Daniel paid dividends. Her English continued to improve. Joshua made himself useful in the store by delivering orders to customers, sweeping the floor, and running errands. Around the Peart homestead, he helped Annie and Mrs. Peart tend the gardens and helped Mr. Peart with upkeep of the house. Annie was proud of his dedication to learning. One day, she asked him if he still wanted to be a doctor. He replied with a shrug of regret. "I won't, will I? My people can't become doctors for the white people."

"Who say you need to doctor the white people? Black people need medicines too, Joshua. We need doctors."

"Yes, but where will I train? There are no white doctors here. I heard a man say there are white doctors on the coast. Do you think I could train there?"

Her heart went out to him. He was born of two opposite worlds—north and south, white and black. "You go to Pitjantjatjara, Josh. I don't know if the same kalbin is there, but I sure our people welcome you, and you learn the clan medicine."

"No, Mama. I must learn the new medicine—the white medicine. It is much stronger than our clan's." He looked at her, daring her to disagree.

She knew arguing was useless. Josh believed the white man's medicine was better, and therefore it was. She couldn't contradict him. Her people were contracting the white man's diseases at an alarming rate, and her clan's medicines were ineffective against them.

"Why haven't we been back to visit our clan, Mama?"

"You know how much work we do here. Where we find time?"

"The Pearts will let us go. They'll even lend us a horse, so we can go faster."

He was breathless with his idea. Although it seemed to come suddenly, she knew he had been considering the prospect for many days. Why now? She was less inclined to revisit her home. Having lived with the white people for so many years, her Pitjantjatjara family was foreign to her. Even when she had taken Josh as a baby, they were strangers. No, she would not visit. "You go. But, Josh, the whites not think you good if you dash off across the desert. And I not think Mr. Peart will give you horse."

"I won't need a horse if I go by myself. I was thinking of you."

She grinned at him, knowing that he viewed her as old. "Mama keep up with you okay. If visiting our clan what you have in mind, you ask Mr. Peart."

Many days later, Annie and Mrs. Peart polished the fine pieces of walnut furniture, which were the few remnants of the genteel life they had left behind. Besides the dining table and six chairs, there was a sideboard with a mirror. Because the walnut furniture was prone to dry and crack in the arid outback heat, they applied beeswax to conserve the moisture. Annie took the opportunity to ask Mrs. Peart about Josh's latest whim. "Did Josh ask Mr. Peart if he go to our clan, Mrs. Peart?" She continued to rub the table, looking up briefly to intercept a quizzical look on Mrs. Peart's face.

"No. Was he supposed to? I've never given much thought to your family. I don't think it crossed my mind in all the time you've been with us. Isn't that odd?" She looked at Annie, as though she were assessing an article in the store. "Do you want to see your people? I fear I've been remiss in my duty toward you."

"No, Mrs. Peart. Only, Josh talked one day, and I said he ask Mr. Peart."

"Well, I'm sure he didn't, or Mr. Peart would have mentioned it." After her half apology for negligence, Mrs. Peart went about the house doing other chores, leaving Annie to finish the table and chairs. Annie knew that she would not mention the subject again. However capable, Mrs. Peart still needed someone for the rougher and harder chores of scrubbing and cleaning. But mostly, they needed Annie for their shop. Annie understood the country and its people in a way they would never comprehend.

Josh did not mention his proposed trip again. Annie wondered if she should broach the subject, but in a moment of illumination, she realized that Josh was testing her. If she gave him an enthusiastic *yes* to his proposal, they would be on their way to the clan. As she hadn't, Josh confirmed they were in the white world to stay, and that world was changing.

With European ingenuity, the people who developed Mpartwe were conquering the unforgiving land. Along the wide, dusty streets, the townsmen planted gum trees to shade their storefronts from the blazing sun. The trees grew, and they shaded the street and the new boardwalks along the fronts of the stores. It soon became a pleasant place to gather and exchange news or gossip with the neighbors or anyone who happened into town.

Josh, as he preferred to be called, loved to be part of the eclectic crowd. He felt important running his messages from the telegraph station to the different townsfolk. From a miner or homesteader, he sometimes delivered messages intended for the coast or farther south. His expressive face showed his delight. Annie could almost see his visions of faraway dream towns. At this time, Mr. Peart offered a tentative suggestion. He should take Joshua traveling to the coast. Josh was ecstatic. "There are bigger houses in the coast towns, Mama, and lots more people too. I can't wait to go there."

Torn between wanting him to travel to these faraway places and remaining her little boy, she turned away for a moment so he wouldn't see her dilemma. Hadn't she worked toward the day he would set out on his own? Every month when Mr. Peart gave her a salary, they tucked a little away for this quickly approaching day. At first, Josh spent his wages on items such as the white man's candy. After his initial taste, however, he gave it up as too sweet and went back to sucking pieces of sugarcane the Pearts bought from a coastal plantation. Now, Josh could hardly wait to see the source of the highly prized cane.

After much thought, Mr. Peart took the long, arduous trek to the east coast without Josh. He went with a homesteader giving up on Australia and heading back to England. They parted in Sydney, and Mr. Peart traveled alone up the eastern coast. The trip took five months, and although Josh was disappointed that he hadn't gone, Annie was glad Josh hadn't accompanied him.

When Mr. Peart returned to Mpartwe, Mrs. Peart was hungry for details about the lush, tropical coast. She begged for more particulars, and Annie worried the family would pack up and make a new start where the climate was temperate, the red dust was tamed by frequent rains, and the hot sun was lessened by a thick canopy of leaves. Worrying was a habit she had picked up from Mrs. Peart. After three years, she had become quite adept at it. She was surprised that she hadn't produced the very things she worried about, knowing the power of thought and the strength of speech. That was why her people's language was terse. There was less chance of a wayward thought or a misspoken word. The whites didn't recognize this, and she frequently closed her eyes and stopped up her ears whenever she heard curses or harsh words. In the end, she needn't have worried. She was not in jeopardy of moving or having to find another job.

After the novelty of Mr. Peart's adventure diminished, both he and his wife settled back into their routine. Yes, the east coast had much to offer. But as Mr. Peart said, their shop was doing well and Mpartwe had much to offer. They were indeed blessed. When the spring to the north was discovered, their town not only gained precious water, but it also filled with new people, bringing more business to the Peart store.

As the red dust seeped into their pores, the land crept in and lodged itself in their souls. They would stay in Mpartwe.

CHAPTER 19

Over the years, Annie and Mrs. Peart had become almost like sisters, but only almost. Between the Aborigines and the whites there existed a barrier, which only centuries of intermingling could break. The Englishwoman was expecting her first child. With Annie's people, women gave birth to all their children well before they were Mrs. Peart's age. Even among the white women, Mrs. Peart was considered a laughing embarrassment. Oblivious to the snickering of her white sisters, she was ecstatic.

The Pearts' house had been improved throughout the years. Now they had three bedrooms, an English parlor, and a kitchen. Two bedrooms remained empty. A few years before, Mrs. Peart had stitched three coverlets for a nursery cot, which she had ordered from England. Matching curtains soon joined the coverlet, but still the room remained vacant. Until now. It turned out that Annie needed this baby as much as Mrs. Peart did. Josh was fifteen and eager to leave. She needed a new soul to fill the emptiness she knew was coming.

The child, coming late in Mrs. Peart's childbearing years, presented a difficult time for her. But she carried the baby well. As her time for delivery drew near, however, it became obvious that the child was going to enter the world feet first. Annie had delivered Joshua herself, but his had been an easy birth. When she had returned to her camp with her baby son, she had helped at several births, but nothing had prepared her for the agony of Mrs. Peart in labor. Mr. Peart was beside himself with grief and guilt. There was no doctor in the vicinity, and none could be found by the telegraph man at the station.

Assuming a confident manner, Annie gave Mrs. Peart plant leaves used in her tribe for early stages of labor. Between pains, she tried to turn the baby in the womb. She knew nothing about sterilization, but for centuries her people had washed their hands in water infused with crushed eucalyptus leaves before delivery. They also used tea tree oil over their hands and the birth area. She did this now, keeping herself and Mrs. Peart cleansed with the warm, pungent liquid.

As soon as she turned the baby, the girl emerged with a piercing howl, startling everyone in the room. She was healthy, pink, and squalling. Annie cut the cord, wiped the newborn off with a cloth dipped in the eucalyptus water, and handed her to her parents. The afterbirth pulsed out a few minutes later. Then she swabbed Mrs. Peart with another pail of eucalyptus water, gathered all the soiled linens, and left to make the new mother a cup of tea. Victoria Anna, with a mop of red hair, entered the household. Victoria was followed in quick succession by James and then Timothy, who arrived just as the nineteen-year-old Joshua left Mpartwe to find his future. Annie knew she had given him most of what he needed to succeed. She had instilled in him a willingness to work at his dreams, taught him to succeed in both worlds, but she could not prevent the disappointment she knew he would meet. In Mpartwe and with the Pearts, he had known mostly kindness. She knew the larger world would not be as kind. As the three youngsters of the white woman grew, they filled the void in Annie's heart left by Joshua going alone into the white man's world.

The children matured to adulthood and accepted Annie as family. If they heard the derogatory term *boong*, they never used it around her. In their years growing up, Josh returned twice for short visits, having found an east coast life to his liking. One by one, the Peart children left to be educated. The two boys moved to Melbourne, and Victoria traveled to England, where she received genteel schooling.

This struck Annie as odd. After all, the Pearts were as Australian as any European could be. But still Mrs. Peart fretted. "England won't hurt her, you know. And I'm sure she'll return here, don't you think?" Mrs. Peart's voice sought Annie's reassurance.

Yes, it would be unnatural for Victoria not to return. The stark Australian outback had bred a boisterous tomboy. She would not fit for long in the English landscape the Pearts had described to Annie. With great conviction, she said as much to Mrs. Peart.

As the younger Pearts grew and left, Annie had more time for the store, which she loved. The Pearts had succeeded where many Europeans failed. And true to Annie's prediction, their daughter returned to Mpartwe after a five-year sojourn in England. As soon as Victoria's boat sailed into Sydney Harbor, she set out to find Joshua, whom she worshipped, and bring him along with her. The day Victoria and Joshua returned home was a great celebration for the Pearts. Annie had mixed feelings.

"Annie! Annie!" Victoria's melodious voice rose above the clank of miners' tools on their camels' backs. She had acquired more of an English veneer, but she was still the same girl Annie had delivered into the world and helped raise. Victoria had a tall Aborigine in tow. Annie could recognize him anywhere, although he was beginning to gray at the temples.

"Joshua! Joshua!" She ran as fast as her aging legs allowed and threw herself at him. She had not seen or heard anything from him in ten years. But she often dreamt of Joshua's rise in the white world.

"Hello, Annie." Joshua's voice was remote in a way she had not heard before. And he called her *Annie*. She had not expected to be called *Mama* like when he was little, or even *Mam*, which he used before he left. But *Annie*? The rudeness shocked her. Victoria and Mrs. Peart turned away from the hurt and embarrassment in Annie's eyes. The chastisement in Mrs. Peart's face went unnoticed by Josh. He went to hug Mrs. Peart, but she didn't respond with her normal enthusiasm. After giving Annie a quick hug and kiss, Victoria went off linked arm in arm with her mother, discreetly leaving Joshua and Annie to renew their bonds. Annie, unwilling to notice the coldness in her son, clung to him, grinning while joyous tears coursed down her cheeks.

Ten minutes passed before Victoria and her mother returned. Victoria left shortly after to visit her father in the store. Annie smiled happily, thinking that the strangeness of his return to Mpartwe caused her son's rude behavior. "Come, I make tea. I'm sure Victoria bring Mr. Peart for tea." She prated on, trying to cover her disappointment.

Mrs. Peart said, "I'll help, Annie. You're not as steady on your feet as you were when we first met."

"Humph! I still run circles round you, Mrs. Peart. Watch." Annie intercepted Joshua's expression. The two women were *not* equals, however much they pretended they were.

Annie very much wanted a long, private talk with Joshua, but she knew that would have to wait. She was so happy to see her grown son again that she was ready to make excuses for his boorishness. Nonetheless, she knew their relationship would never be the same. Once children break their filial bonds, they will not return to them. She didn't even want that relationship again. She wanted her son as a close friend. She wanted someone to share memories. She wanted to speak to him in Pitjantjatjara, laugh over their trek through the desert to find work, and wonder with him about his acceptance into the Sea-turtle clan. She led the way into the cool dining room just as Victoria returned with Mr. Peart.

Afternoon tea was chaotic. Mr. And Mrs. Peart both wanted to question Victoria at once. "Has England changed much?" Mrs. Peart repeatedly asked, forgetting that Victoria was born and bred Australian.

"I *liked* England, Mother. And I visited the relatives as you asked. I'm sure I learned much from the school, though I don't know how much of what I learned can be applied here." She stopped in thought, her finger tapping the side of her face. "And yes, it is a gentle, green land as you've always said. But the poverty! In some areas around London it is worse than any poverty here. In my short time in Sydney, I didn't see any of the destitution I saw in London. I can honestly say I'm glad you and father moved to Australia."

It was clear where Victoria's loyalties lay. She went to Annie and hugged her tightly, looking over her shoulder at her mother. "And where would we all be without the Annies of the world?"

"Well said!" Mr. Peart raised his cup. Annie sent a tentative glance toward Joshua. His smile was forced. She doubted anyone else noticed. Moments later, Annie retired to her little house.

Years before, Mr. Peart and his sons had built a three-room house at the back of their property so Annie could have privacy. She knew even then that privacy worked both ways. At times, the couple wanted to be away from the all-seeing eyes of Annie, the Aborigine whose presence reminded them that they needed her kind to succeed in their new world. She was not angry or hurt. That was the way of the white world and her people. The pain from Joshua's disdain was a deeper hurt by far.

Later, he left the Peart house and went to his mother's. Although Joshua had grown to manhood in the house, his lengthy absence made the rudimentary hut more Annie's than his. She knew nothing of his life in Sydney. She didn't know how or even where he lived. She could barely wait to be regaled with tales of his new life. Before he left, he had a talent for storytelling, embellishing the details of everyday events so they took on a unique mythology. Even though her English was acceptable—thanks to the efforts of the Pearts—she did not have Josh's imaginative way with words. If he had inherited the ability, it was from his English father, a blurry figure in Annie's memory. Her people's terse speech did not lend itself to Josh's picturesque talent for language. The Pitjantjatjara tribe had no need to embellish their tales. They had a deep pride, knowing they were the masters of this land. They were the ones charged with the honored task of hallowing the Master Dreamer by keeping watch over Uluru and Kata Tjuta.

All these thoughts ran through her mind as she waited for Josh. It was many years since she had last thought of her tribe. Yet deep in her soul, despite the many efforts of Mr. and Mrs. Peart to convert her to their church, she knew where she belonged and to whom she owed her life. Her beliefs were older than the whites' Christianity. Many of her people outwardly accepted the Europeans' beliefs, but she had yet to see one of her people who did not continue practicing his beliefs once the whites were absent. Besides, was there such a chasm between her beliefs and the newcomers' beliefs? She thought not. They were merely different ways of expressing the same faith. Even in the small town of Mpartwe, the variance in white beliefs was noticeable. *If they can't agree on a faith,* Annie thought, *how can they instill faith in my people?* She sat on her porch in the evening, the strewn eucalyptus leaves keeping the flies away, and she wondered about Josh's beliefs. Joshua sauntered over, looking downcast. They were mother and son; they were strangers.

"You're upset with me, Annie. Don't think I didn't notice," Joshua said.

Did she detect shame in his words? She couldn't be sure. Instead of answering, she patted the chair beside her. "How you been doin' these last years? You learn the white man's medicine?"

He sat beside her, but he didn't take her hand as she thought he would. "There is so much to tell. And much you wouldn't comprehend. The white people understand life better than your people."

She gasped. "*My* people? *My* people are *your* people too. You forget that, boy?"

"Of course not. But I choose to be white. I've met great people and have had good times."

"So, you return to Sydney? To these wonderful white people?"

She could not keep the scorn from her voice. Who were these people corrupting her son's thinking so that he refused to recognize his black heritage? How did Josh think he could forget it? As far as she knew, he had not returned to the clan since they came to Mpartwe. But then, neither had she. She sometimes thought of her clan, but time passed. As each year slipped by, her heritage faded. Nonetheless, she did not forget her people. She tried to understand Josh's perspective. He was not fully black. And yes, he should acknowledge his European heritage. To deny either would make him something he was not. Yet, she couldn't forget that his white father had left for home without a backward glance for his son.

If anyone had asked two days before whether she wanted Joshua to stay close, she would have shouted *yes!* As it was, she would now be happy to have this arrogant stranger leave. "You have doctor's office, Josh? You help our people?"

He looked ashamed and didn't answer for a long time. Then he spoke haltingly. "The European doctors don't want to teach me. I've picked up a few white cures, but there are many Aboriginal cures just as effective. Of course, no white man is letting me near him. And the blacks fear the European medicine. The only thing they want is the white man's whiskey. All I see are the boongs sitting along the road nursing jugs of joy juice. It's disgusting!" He spat the last words with loathing. Her arm swung of its own volition, her hand connecting to his sneering face. "I glad you didn't call me Mam. I ashamed of you." If she thought her words humiliated him, they hadn't. To Josh, she was the same as the boongs along the road. Her years of integrating him into white society only succeeded in making him despise his own people.

"I going to bed. You welcome to stay here. But if you don't want sleep near any boongs or gins, Mr. and Mrs. Peart will allow their porch." She entered her small shelter, too wrapped in her misery to sense his.

After a restless night, she awoke early, washed at the washstand behind her house, and put on a clean frock. When she returned through her door, she noticed that Josh had spent the night on her small veranda. She couldn't think about it then. The Pearts were early risers and liked a big breakfast, so she hurried to the house. Embers remained in the large kitchen range firebox. She stirred them and added two pieces of mulga wood to produce a hot flame.

While the oatmeal cooked, she slid fried eggs onto a large platter. With three Pearts, it was a noisy, merry meal. If not for her disappointment in Josh, Annie would have loved the din and feeling of family. But the one person she longed for was still asleep on her porch.

The meal was over too soon, and Mr. Peart hastened to the store. "I'll help out," Victoria yelled. "Are you coming, Mother?"

Mrs. Peart hesitated, unable to decide between going to the store and talking to Annie about Josh. She didn't have to say a word. Annie understood. "Mrs. Peart, you go along now. I clean up. My goodness, you underfoot all day. I never get house clean."

Victoria grabbed her mother's arm and smiled her good-bye. When they were out of sight down the road, Josh appeared in the kitchen. Annie fixed him a bowl of porridge. He sat with his face downcast, saying nothing. While he ate, she washed the dishes and let them drain on the wood drying rack that Mr. Peart made thirty years before. Finally, she could stand the silence no longer.

"Joshua, what's wrong? You come home after long time, and you treat me like a stranger—no, not even a stranger. You treat me bad. That's not the real you. That's not the boy who did jobs he not like so he learn language and ways of white people. That's not young man who want to learn medicine so he help people. It's not even little boy favored by our people's kalbin. You talk to me, Josh."

CHAPTER 20

Annie turned away, pretending to wash the dishes she had just finished. After many moments, she gathered her courage and turned back to Josh, astonished to see tears running down his cheeks and dripping into his now-empty porridge bowl. "Josh?"

"I'm sorry for treating you badly, Mama. I wanted you to be so proud of me. Nothing's worked out." He rubbed his hand across his eyes. "When I saw you, it brought back all that's terrible in my life. I hate that I'm black. I hate it when white people spit on me, but I hate it even more when the black people reject me. I thought a white doctor would be happy to teach me his medicine. But it's not like that at all. The white doctors don't want me to learn. They think all I know is Aboriginal cures. They think we are too stupid to learn white medicine. If we had their medicine, they wouldn't think they are better."

"Not all of them think that way. The Pearts don't. The people in town don't." She thought about what he had said. Yes, there was hostility in Mpartwe. And it wasn't just between white settlers and blacks. It was between the blacks themselves. Josh and she were in another's territory. They had learned the Arrernte dialect, but were they accepted by the Arrernte people? Overall, though, there was less hostility among the different Aboriginal tribes than between the blacks and the whites.

"They don't want to give us any control," Josh continued. "They want to keep us like animals, doing what they want us to do."

Annie's bitterness fled as soon as Josh spoke. Why hadn't she realized it would be harder for him than her? Two different worlds had given him life. He wandered between both but fit into neither She dreamed such beautiful dreams for him. She wondered if her dreams for Josh were against the Master

Dreamer's dream for him. Or even against Josh's own dream. Was Josh trying to live her dream or his?

"You listen careful. I don't know whose dream you trying to live. But I'm telling you now. You got to live your dream and nobody else's. That's the only way you're goin' to be happy. It's not easy. When you start your path, the Master Dreamer, he work with you to help. But just when you're goin' to win, he throws Mr. Python in your path. That's when you need to say, 'Master Dreamer, I not goin' to stop. I got to do this.' Then you step over Mr. Python, or you go around him, and you be right where you're supposed to be."

"I'm so ashamed of the way I treated you yesterday. I've blamed you; I've blamed all black people."

"You can't blame other folk for what happens to you. Your journey between you and Master Dreamer. If you know that, you happy."

"I still want to try, Mama. When I go back to the city, I'll travel up the coast a little. If I go where there is no white doctor, I may do better. I know a little white medicine, and I know what you taught me too."

As he was speaking, a thought occurred to Annie. "You remember when we go Sea-turtle clan? You had good time there. You more at home there than with the Pitjantjatjara." She stopped, remembering her discomfort with the Sea-turtle clan and Josh's happiness.

"I like both clans. I do remember, though, you were uncomfortable with the Sea-turtle people. I don't know why."

She couldn't tell him, because she didn't know. "Josh, why don't you go to Sea-turtle clan. They welcome you."

"I may, Mama, but first I will return to the coast. I do like it there, and I know you would too."

"I don't think so, honey," she said, using a term of endearment she picked up from the Pearts. "I too old now. Besides I like here."

"I know you do, Mama. I like it here too, but I guess I like it most places. Mama?" Josh hesitated, uncertain how to continue.

"What you want, boy? When you ask like that, I know it sometin' I not gonna like."

Josh laughed deeply. She was thrilled. It had been years since she heard her son's laughter. "Mama? I was going to ask why you never got another man."

His question took her aback. She had barely thought of wanting a man in years. When Josh was little, there were times she wished for a man beside her, but as the years passed, her wanting lessened. "I guess I got used to bein' alone. And when the young Pearts were growin', I never had time to think of it."

She understood why he asked. He would be happier if she had someone. Then he could travel anywhere and not worry. "I'm happy here Josh, and I don't need a man now. You think about Sea-turtle clan. I know you do good there. And," she continued, giving him a long gaze, "wear your sacred stone. It gives you the Master Dreamer's power." He had worn it throughout his boyhood, but she noticed that he hadn't worn it when he returned to the Pearts.

She had given him the skills to succeed in this dream and her eternal love, and that was all he needed from her. He left the next day for the coast with the amulet replaced around his neck.

"Did you and Josh have a talk? There was something bothering him, I know." Mrs. Peart was solicitous as she prepared Victoria's clothing for leaving and Annie scrubbed the kitchen floor. Victoria would stay for a while with her brothers, but she would eventually head for the east coast. Annie knew Mrs. Peart felt as she did. They may have different skin and different beliefs, but they were both mothers.

"Yes, he feels better now, Mrs. Peart." What more could she say to this white woman? Mrs. Peart would never understand what blacks felt or the difficulty of reaching their dreams.

"I think Josh finds it hard to fit in with the white people, Mama." Victoria came into the kitchen while her mother ironed and Annie mopped the floor. She discerned Josh's problem better than anyone, but there was nothing she could do. The time was not right for the blacks. The whites had enough difficulty;

they had no compassion left for those they considered inferior. Annie felt guilty thinking that way. She experienced only kindness and consideration from the Pearts. She had seen others, though, hunted down, kicked, or beaten. And the whites were no better with their own. The Pearts were all that newcomers should be, treating black and white more or less equally.

If Josh discerned a master–slave relationship between Mrs. Peart and his mother, it was a benign relationship. Annie could leave at any time. And if she had, where would she go? To her own people? She realized once she left the clan, she couldn't go back. She was used to the white man's comforts. Why would she want to return to the land? Was she happy? She was happy that Josh had a chance. She was happy that she fulfilled the Master Dreamer's dream to look after him.

Now she wanted a few more years to see what the new century brought. Interest and curiosity filled her heart. She had no fears for Josh. (Well, there were a few when she thought of him on the east coast.) But she knew that if he went to the Sea-turtle clan, he would do well—if the Sea-turtle clan still existed. Her world was changing. Many of her people were in confined land areas, and their food from the Master Dreamer's land was disappearing.

Annie lived with the Pearts in an interdependent relationship. Mr. Peart turned the store over to a new manager, who hired new help and gave the store his personality. Mr. Peart did not sell it, because he still hoped one of his sons would take it over. The Pearts aged and did not think of returning to England. Victoria presented them with three grandsons and one granddaughter in quick succession. Victoria's brothers both settled their homes in Sydney, and each also gave the Pearts four grandsons. Another generation of Australians was born. Annie was happy that their life here turned out so well. And the land gained more people who called it home.

Many years later, Annie had an unexpected visit from Josh. They sat on the weathered porch of the small house as they did in the long-ago past. Annie was still alone.

Josh took her hand in his. He came alone this time, but there were two visits before with his wife and their son and daughter. Annie's life would continue in Josh and his children. His father's life was diluted, for Josh had chosen a girl from the Sea-turtle clan, and his children were more black than white. It didn't matter to Annie anymore. After asking about his father once or twice, Josh was resigned to never knowing the man who sired him.

"Remember how I went to the coast after I left you that time? I met a man there, Mr. Paterson, who said he was a white man's lawyer. But he loved this land too much to sit in an office all the time. One day, we met on a beach, and he asked me to tell him stories of my life. So I told him as many as I could. It wasn't just that one day. He came to me many times over a long period. So I kept telling him stories of the Pitjantjatjara, the Arrernte, the Sea-turtle people, and how the white man treated us. How we had hopes and dreams too, but the white man didn't recognize this. The other day, I was outside a white man's home, and I heard Mr. Paterson singing a song he wrote about one of the stories I told him. He called it *Waltzing Matilda*, Mama, and everybody loved it."

"That's real nice, but jumpin' joey, you come all this way to tell me that?"

"No," he smiled. "I came to tell you that I've been treating people on the north coast—my people and a few whites. I keep busy, Mama, using medicines of the white man when I can and medicines of our people when I think they're better."

Tears ran down Annie's cheeks, attracting flies. They were happy tears for her son who had found his dream. "So, you like living with the Sea-turtle people, then?"

"I do. I wish I could persuade you to come. The Pearts don't need you now. You looked after me, helping me believe I would fit in with white and black folk. Can I make you believe I'll help you fit in with the Sea-turtle people?"

"Maybe long time ago, but not now. This my home for so long." They both looked around at her tiny house and the bigger homes going up around it. The gum trees were full, and the flower beds that she and Josh tended many years earlier were blooming vigorously. Protected by the porch roof, she and Josh were out of the hottest rays of the burning sun. This was as close to the Pitjantjatjara clan as possible without going back to them. The Sea-turtle clan was a dim, uneasy memory. Regardless of what Josh thought, the Pearts were her family. No, she couldn't leave now.

Before Joshua returned to the north coast the next morning, she stroked his face lovingly, etching each laugh line and each worry line into her memory. "Take my love. You're doin' good, my son." She knew she would not see him again in this dream life they shared.

He gave her a quizzical look but said nothing. Gathering his few belongings into a bundle, he shouldered the pack and set off. She sat on the porch in the cool morning. There was no hurry now. The Pearts had slowed their former routine, and Mr. Peart had taken to bringing his wife a morning cup of tea. Breakfast came later, and it was much lighter than when the children were growing and the parents were young.

Shortly after Joshua left, a tall, aging Aborigine man walked into the yard and to her house. His hair was gray with the years, but he strode proudly to where she sat. She recognized him immediately. "Kalbin!" When she rose to greet him, he motioned her to remain seated and took a seat beside her.

"Hello, Annie" He spoke in the Pitjantjatjara dialect. "I knew I would not see you back at our camp again, so I came to your camp instead. How are you and Joshua?"

Holding her hand, he listened as she told him about Josh and of how the kalbin had just missed her son. She knew he still loved her and she felt a fondness for him. If their lives had been different, perhaps they would have become mated. But all that was in the past. He brought her hand to his lips. "We'll meet again, you and I. In some other time and some other place. I must be going now."

After he left, she closed her eyes. The buzzing flies lulled her into a hypnotic state, and she smiled as good memories washed over her.

CHAPTER 21

"Annie's awake. Annie's awake." The love-filled sound reverberated around the hills and bounced back to her as she opened her eyes. Wallaby grinned and butted her. Python glided over, his diamond back glittering in sunlight. Mack, whom she had known eons ago, strummed his guitar, making unfamiliar music. It was different and … yes, quite pleasant.

"What is that, Mack?" she called. "That's new."

"It's called pop, Annie. You've got to catch up. You've been asleep too long." He yodeled a crescendo, and Benny appeared with Margo. Was she still giving seminars? Debbie appeared with a young child in tow and smiled happily. "It's good that you're awake, Annie. The MD will likely let you stay longer this time."

"Where is he?"

"Off sitting in the hills. You wouldn't recognize him. He's feeling much better. I think he wants to talk to you. You and he have a bond."

"Yes, I will go and find him. I'll be back. Keep the music going, Mack, and we'll have a dance." She needn't worry about Mack playing his tunes. Already, a crowd had appeared to dance to his music. Dolly showed up wearing a new blue gown. Spotting Annie, she waved gaily. Liz two-stepped over. "Nice to have you back, Annie. We'll get together later for lunch."

Annie floated across lush, green pastures, eyeing the munching sheep and the chewing cows. A horse whinnied in greeting, causing the bearded old gent to lift his head.

"You do better and better, Annie. Your soul mate learns quickly under your care."

"Are you sure I'm the only one you can send, MD? Surely, I've earned enough credits to stay here for eons."

"Eons? What on earth is that?" He laughed at his own joke. Yes, he was looking marvelously well. His robe was pristine, his beard neatly trimmed, and his flowing hair reflected beams of sunlight. "The world is getting better, Annie, old girl. Thanks to the likes of you."

"Thanks, MD. What's that I hear?" Soft, fluting tones drifted toward them.

"That's Howard. He's been learning to play the clarinet since you went to sleep. Let's dance, Annie. Let's dance, old girl." He whirled her around in his arms over the soft green hills, into the purple and white mountains, and into the red valleys. They danced and danced, never tiring. They picked up the tempo as they neared the group. "I'll leave you now. Have fun, old girl."

Off the Master Dreamer went to keep watch over his dream. "He's picked up, hasn't he?" The sibilant tones of Python reached her from waist high.

"Indeed he has. Soon we will see the end of all this nonsense and continue as we were before. When do you think he will stop dreaming, Python?"

"Soon. He wants all the little parts perfect. He wants you to be perfect too. Then we'll be as one again."

She had a feeling that soon wasn't going to be soon enough. She sank down into a patch of Irish moss, closing her eyes as she listened to Margo give her seminar on maximizing savings. A chuckle bubbled up into her throat. *Will Margo ever realize that she isn't still in the banking world? She was giving that seminar the last time I woke up.*

Annie was surrounded by friends, and a feast materialized in her honor. Afterwards, she sank into the comfortable moss, pulled out her lined book, and started to write.

"Dinner was delicious. Delicious dinner. Down Under delicious dinner."

The Irish moss was cozy. She tuned Margo out, put down her pencil, and snuggled into a fetal position in the deep, cushiony bed. Python curled against her stomach, and Wallaby lay at her back. She felt loved and so much a part of this group. In none of her earth trips had she ever felt like this. The dancing exhausted her, and the dinner made her drowsy. A nice nap. That would help.

CHAPTER 22

She felt herself straighten out. Her body was crushed by wave after wave of pulsating muscle, until she was propelled into cold dampness. A warm towel was wrapped around her, rough against her skin. Not again! She wasn't ready. *"Help me! Help me! I've earned my freedom. MD, where are you? You can't do this to me. Not to me. Not to Annie. Not to your old girl."* She looked at her pink hand clutched into a fist and let out a frustrated wail. Pink? Kicking kangaroo! She wasn't sure she liked being pink. Why did he choose now to change her color? She had been back and forth so many times, she ought to have some say in how she looked. Why did he choose to exercise his authority all of a sudden? Well, there wasn't much she could do about it at the moment, so she yawned, took in a great gulp of the putrid air, and let out another scream.

Being a child under the control of adults, who were younger souls than she, took some getting used to. But here she was helping him once again—her brother, Jeremiah. He was three years old when she was born, and he was a terror.

Jeremiah should be my protector, Annie figured, *because he's my older brother.* But it seemed she was always pulling him out of scrapes. Her daddy owned several opal mines close to Coober Pedy. He did all right, Annie guessed. They always had food and a place to sleep.

Many of the miners lived underground in old mines turned into living quarters. In the hot, dry season, Annie figured the cool temperature must be like heaven. But Annie's mama would never go into the pits. "We'll all go in the ground soon enough, Annie. I'm not going there any quicker than God wants."

Although Daddy kept a little room in that mine, he built a small aboveground house for his family. They were happy together, especially when they were aboveground. In the unrelenting sun, her mama's fair Scottish skin browned more deeply than daddy's, even though Daddy was a born Ozzie and had black ancestors.

Daddy had a deep singing voice, and they heard him singing down in the hole where he fossicked for opals.

Gotta get me a big one for my woman.
Gotta get me a big one for my kids.
Gotta hammer and poke, hammer and poke to find the big bloke
FOR MY WOMAN!

These last words were always shouted at the top of his lungs. If Mama was nearby, she tried to keep a straight face. But after a moment, she broke into peals of girlish laughter as she prepared supper or dusted their well-used furniture.

They didn't have much, and what they did have were the castoffs of disgruntled fortune seekers who gave up and went home or to the more temperate southern climate. But it didn't matter. A chair was a chair. Unless, of course, it was a sailing ship, or with two chairs, Annie and Jerry's opal mine. Most of the time, Jeremiah and Annie were outside with no need for furniture.

She was seven the day Jeremiah fell twelve feet into an abandoned opal pit. They knew they weren't allowed near the open mines. But as Jeremiah said, Daddy went down all the time and nothing ever happened to *him*. That day, Annie gasped as she looked at the limp form at the bottom of the hole. There was no one else around. Mama was several hundred yards away in the house. Daddy was down in his opal pit. She shivered in fear for Jeremiah as well as the licking they would get if they ever got back home.

Death had no meaning for her then. As her daddy said, how could you die if you were just dreaming your life? She remembered Mama's shriek when he said that. But Jeremiah sure looked dead at the bottom of that hole. She knew she had to find some way of getting down to him. There was an old shed at the back of their house where Daddy stored a rough, wooden ladder. She found it lying on its side against the wall, and making as little noise as possible, she dragged it across the sands and up the incline to the top of the mine. She struggled getting it down the hole at first. If she pushed too far, it dug into the opposite wall and knocked more sand to the bottom. If she didn't push far enough, she could not get the ladder farther into the hole. After much struggling, it was finally in place. She felt proud of herself for handling the ladder, but she was scared too. She still had to go down the ladder and wake Jeremiah.

With trembling hands, she grasped the two sides of the ladder and swung her body around to clamber down. The rungs were made for men like her dad. It was a long stretch for her short legs, and she let out a trembling sigh when her feet touched the cool ground. "Jerry! Jerry! Wake up!" To her ears, her voice sounded like the roar of the men's voices in the town tavern.

His right arm twisted under him, and she pulled it to make it straight again, not hearing the grating of bone. She kept shaking him and yelling in a loud whisper, "Please, Jeremiah. Please, wake up!" She didn't realize she was crying until teardrops fell on his still form. His face was as white as one of her daddy's opals. Again she pulled at him, gazing with adoration at his golden hair, which was so like their mother's. He was a golden boy, while her hair hung down in curls as black as an Australian starless night. Not that she saw many starless nights in the desert. Most of the time, the sky was filled with the Master Dreamer's lights. That's what her dad said, and she believed him.

She was like her daddy. His skin showed the racial mix in his blood, and he carried those ancestral beliefs in his heart. It never occurred to her to ask why she was so dark when her brother was golden light. She just knew she loved Jeremiah with a soul-knowledge deeper than she could explain. He couldn't leave her. Not yet.

Her hand stroked his yellow hair from his white forehead, which was lighter than even their mother's. She could feel her heart fill her small chest. As she crouched beside him, a tingling feeling ran from her heart, through her arm, and out her hand. A white and green shimmering light thrust into Jeremiah's pale head and ran the length of his arm. His quiet body jerked, and he opened his eyes. "Annie! I was in the most beautiful place. Why did you wake me up?" He sat up, brushing the coarse red sandstone off his bare legs. The color flooded back into his face. She looked at him. His lips were a no-nonsense line like Mama's. His eyes were the brightest and deepest blue. He shook his head to toss back his mop of yellow hair, and he straightened his long, lean body.

They were as different as coal and opals. No one would guess they were from the same family. He had none of Daddy's softer traits or playful ways. With Jeremiah and their mama, all movement was purposeful and deliberate. And often, as happened this time, the consequences came upon him suddenly. Caught unawares, Jeremiah's temper flared. He and Mama couldn't believe the world would thwart their best intentions and purposes.

"Jeremiah!" She placed her seven-year-old chubby fists on her hips and stood with her legs apart like Daddy when he scolded them. "Jeremiah! You are so 'sasperating! We gotta get out of here, or we're gonna get a lickin'. You know we're not s'posed to be near these mines. You're lucky nobody saw me get the ladder. Come on, you're gonna have to help me get up the ladder and get it back."

"Why do I hafta help? You got it here okay by yourself."

She knew he was sulking because she had come to his rescue once again. In Jeremiah's world, girls weren't supposed to rescue boys. But then, in Jeremiah's world, boys were always getting into trouble and needing to be saved. She grabbed the sides of the ladder and struggled to pull herself up. Jerry had to boost her each step, or she never would have made it out of that hole. His legs were longer than Annie's. Annie's head came just to his shoulder. It would be comforting to feel his arm around her as she leaned against him, but she knew that wouldn't happen. "I was scared for you. Really scared."

Jeremiah was intent on pulling up the ladder and had no thought of comforting his younger sister. Between them, they managed to return the ladder to the shed before anyone noticed it was gone. Jerry was still silent. If she didn't get a response before they went into the house, she knew she wouldn't get one at all. Jerry wouldn't say anything in front of Mama.

Mama's melodic Scottish voice reached them in the dark shed. "Come, children. It's time for lunch." Annie felt Jerry's hand grab her sleeve.

"Annie, please don't say anything to Mum or Dad, will you?"

"Course not. We're not allowed near the open pits." Jeremiah's face relaxed as he darted toward the house, and she followed more slowly, still wondering at his odd comments and the strange light that flowed from her hands to his body.

"What have you two been up to this morning?" Mama ladled soup into their bowls and called Daddy from his pit at the same time. "I looked out twice and couldn't see you. You weren't near any of those open holes?"

"No, Mama," Jerry and Annie said together. It was a toss-up. They could end up with a licking on two counts—one for going into the hole and the other for lying. Mama looked at them with her piercing, blue eyes, but she said nothing. She looked distracted, and it was clear she had other things on her mind. After setting the soup before them and seeing that they had fresh bread and butter with a chunk of cheese, she turned to their dad.

"Will, I'm going with the Royal Flying Doctor Service tomorrow for a checkup. Can you manage these two while I'm away? You'll have to make sure they're up and on the radio for their lessons."

"No problem, dear. You go and make sure you're healthy and strong. I'd go with you, you know that, but I think the RFDS is taking Ron Cook in too. There won't be room for me."

"Aye. I can manage by myself, and I'm sure I'm fretting over nothing."

Daddy got up from his place at the table and put his arms about Mama. He winked at the two children. "Me and the kids will be fine for a couple of days, woman. You deserve a holiday in the city."

"I," Jerry and Annie shouted at once. "You should have said *I*, Daddy. Not *me*."

"See what I mean? We'll look after each other real good. If you have to stay longer, send word, but I expect to see you back here in no time." He kissed her cheek, but she was already pulling away, her mind on private thoughts.

CHAPTER 23

Mama was away longer than a couple of days the first time. For Jeremiah and Annie, her absence was a holiday. "We do love Mama, Daddy. But you're more fun." Annie knew that she and Jerry wouldn't do anything more mischievous with Mama gone than they did when she was there. But when Mama was there, an air of sternness hung over their play. If her sternness didn't keep them totally in check, at least it kept them feeling guilty. Truthfully, Annie figured she was the only one who felt guilty. Jeremiah had no problems that way. He was like Mama. He felt whatever he did was right, so he had no reason for guilt.

Like when he fell down the opal pit. If Mama had pressed them, Annie was sure Jerry could have found a perfectly good reason for going down that pit. And he would have believed every word. He wouldn't have told Mama he was hurt, of course. Already the incident was fading when Mama went away. Annie knew she felt the most relief whenever Mama had reason to leave, although this didn't happen often. The nearby town supplied them with household goods, which wasn't much. Annie did miss Mama, though, when she went on these trips. Daddy wasn't nearly as good helping with schoolwork, though they saw he was as eager as Mama that they get on in the world.

They usually knew beforehand if Mama was going away. But this latest trip was done quietly. They hadn't known ahead of time, and Mama hadn't asked if they wanted to go with her. When she returned, she changed. She was often occupied with her own thoughts, but she was also softer. Daddy was too. Jeremiah and Annie had much more freedom — even more than before. But Mama insisted they do their schoolwork, especially

Anne Ravenoak   169

Jeremiah. She expected Jeremiah to do well, and Annie felt no resentment. She loved Jeremiah too and knew he would do well, if she could keep him alive long enough. She somehow knew it was up to her to look after him, keep him healthy, and teach him things. She figured Daddy's Master Dreamer would help.

One day, Annie talked Jeremiah into looking for honey ants. Both he and Mama were disgusted, but out of boredom, Annie guessed, he said he would go with her to protect her. Annie would have laughed if it hadn't been for Mama's next comment. "Annie, you take after your father's people. You get more like them every day. I don't know how you people expect to get on in the world when you slip back into your old ways." Her words hurt. Annie didn't understand them, but she knew there was rebuke in her mother's voice. Whatever her views, Mama didn't stop them from hunting the ants. When they returned home, Daddy was waiting for them. He took Annie's arm and sent Jerry into the house to wash for supper.

"You mustn't do things like this, Annie. You know how it upsets your Mama when you do Aboriginal things." His voice was gentle and sad.

"Daddy, what does Ab … Ab … mean?" She stumbled over the unfamiliar word.

"You and me, Annie, we carry the blood of a very old people in our veins. Mama and Jeremiah don't. They don't understand."

"You mean like Archie at the Taylor's ranch?" She loved Archie. Next to Daddy, he was her great hero. She loved the way his black and silver hair curled and the way his broad face creased into a smile whenever they met. And he always placed his hand on her shoulder and told Daddy that she was special.

"Yes, I mean like Archie. Although he has more of the old blood than we have. Still, we do have old Aborigine blood, and I'm proud of it. You should be too."

"I guess I am. But how come Mama and Jerry don't have the same blood as us?"

"Because your Mama had a man before me. That other man was Jeremiah's father. Do you understand, Annie?"

"I guess so. You mean Mama and Jerry don't carry the same old blood. How old is their blood, Daddy?"

"Their blood is ancient too, but it is not the same as ours. Mama's goes back to Scottish chieftains, and before that, to Vikings."

Annie had studied this in school, but she had not thought about it in relation to herself. Mama had never said anything about coming from chieftains, and Annie was sure Jerry didn't know. Now she had something special to tell the school when they were on the air. She stood a little straighter, anticipating the next day's lesson.

Daddy stood quietly looking at her. There was still worry hanging in the air between them. She felt it crawl up her arm and into her stomach. Daddy wanted to tell her more, but he didn't know how. "Daddy, you want to say something. I can feel it."

He looked at the desert, where the heat shimmered off the sand and a buzzard circled overhead. "Mama is sick. Real sick."

"Is that why she went away? To see a doctor?"

"Yes."

"Why can't we make her better, Daddy? I can help. You know how, and I bet Archie does too."

"Mama doesn't believe in our ways. If she doesn't believe, we can't make her well. She believes in the white man's doctor."

"But if she's sick and he's not helping, why doesn't she try our way?"

He had no answer. He caressed her dark hair and smiled a sad smile. "She may have to leave us, Annie. I think she wants to send Jeremiah to her people in Scotland."

Annie knew the day was going to be bad when she saw one of the Master Dreamer's lights wink out. To lose two of the people she loved was devastating. "When?"

"I don't know. Your mama feels fine now. But soon she won't. I don't want you and Jeremiah causing her any trouble. Do you hear what I'm saying?"

She heard more than he knew. She was sure the Master Dreamer could help Mama, and Daddy knew it. Why didn't Daddy go ahead and help her? Why did he have to wait for Mama to believe? Annie knew what she had to do. She would help Mama get well, but she didn't know when or how. "Does Jerry know?"

"No. Unless your mama told him. Jerry can't absorb these matters like you."

"If Mama hasn't told him, may I?" She was proud for using *may* instead of *can*. That was one of the latest lessons she had learned from School of the Air. She was sure she had used the word right. But then again, she should think about that. *May* indicated permission, and in a way she had asked permission. *Can* related to ability, and she wasn't sure she had the ability, either.

"We should wait a bit. It will be harder on Jeremiah, for he will have to leave all he knows and go to another world."

"Why does Mama want him to go to Scotland?" She wasn't sure she even knew what Scotland was. At the moment, all she knew was that it was not half as good as her world. She tried to fathom all these things as she thought what life would be like without Mama. She couldn't. Mama was a big part of her world, although Annie knew she would miss Jeremiah more. Why did Jeremiah have to go away? Daddy hadn't answered her question. Maybe he didn't know the answer.

Mama didn't believe in the Master Dreamer. She was aghast when Annie mentioned getting the Master Dreamer to help. "God will punish you, Annie, for being blasphemous."

"What's blasph'mus?"

"Oh, Annie, you are so ungodly. How could I give birth to an ungodly child?"

Annie noticed that Mama never said any of these things around Daddy. She had heard them talking once when she was outside the door. Daddy had told Mama not to speak ill of what she didn't understand. Mama had harrumphed and told Daddy that he must not teach Jeremiah any of that stuff. If he wanted to teach Annie, that was fine. She was his daughter. But he was not to say anything to Jeremiah.

Annie's mama tried to be jolly around Jerry and Annie, but Annie knew it was a show. She wanted to ask Mama about her sickness, but she didn't have the words. She wanted to tell Mama that the Master Dreamer didn't want her sick or hurt. But the Master Dreamer was working in his own way.

One hot day, Archie came into town for supplies, driving a wagon with a team of horses. When he went past Annie's house, she yelled to him, and he waved and grinned. Mama must have heard, because she came to the door and shouted for Archie to stop in when he had time. Annie knew Mama didn't like Archie. She was welcoming him for Daddy's sake, and Archie knew this. But he nodded as he went past.

After he completed his errands, Archie pulled the wagon to a halt at their door. Daddy greeted him with an arm around the old man's shoulder and a cold drink. They went to a canvas shelter, sat on the sand, and talked. Annie didn't go near them. She knew this was man talk. Her turn would come. Archie always saw to that. At long last, when she tired of swatting flies and watching a roo in the distance, Daddy waved her over.

"Your daddy says you think the Master Dreamer can heal your mama. Is that right?" Archie's black eyes pierced hers, and she squirmed.

"Mama doesn't believe in the Master Dreamer, Mr. Archie. Daddy says she can't heal if she doesn't believe."

"And what do you think?"

The words stuck in her mouth. She wanted to agree with Daddy, but couldn't. "I think she can."

"So do I, little one. Shall you and I do something about it? We don't have to tell your Mama a thing. But I need your help. You carry a lot of the Master Dreamer's power. I've seen it."

Daddy frowned at Archie. Annie didn't know what Archie meant. She never told him about the time in the opal pit or about the time Jerry cut himself, and she stopped the bleeding by touching his finger. There were other times, but she never gave them a second thought, for her power had always been with her, and she accepted it as naturally as she accepted eating or walking.

"What do I have to do, Archie?"

"You have to think of your mama the way the Master Dreamer does — that she is well already. And soon, you and I will get together in your head with the Master Dreamer and think these thoughts together. Can you do that?"

"Yes, Mr. Archie." She clapped her hands.

"Your daddy's job is to keep Jeremiah from distracting you while you think about your mama. Jeremiah has some of our blood too," Archie added, making Annie and her daddy start with surprise. "But I don't think his mama knows, so it's best not to say anything."

Annie looked at her dad and knew that neither he nor she would divulge Jeremiah's Aboriginal blood.

Healing Mama was not as easy as Annie thought. For several days, Mama kept to herself in her room. Annie missed Daddy's laughter and song coming from his opal pit. But he stayed aboveground, going outside under the canvas shelter for a few minutes, and then returning to see Mama. Many times, Annie was surprised to see dried tears on his cheeks, but he put up a brave front in front of them. Jerry took over making soup for their lunches, and they ate it with hard biscuits from the tin Mama kept on the back shelf.

Once, when her daddy went outside, Annie followed him to ask about Mama.

"She has a bad sickness in her chest." He circled his hand over the front of his shirt. Annie wasn't sure what he meant, but Daddy wouldn't say more.

"You have to believe Mama is well, Daddy. Mr. Archie said he would help, and he will." She couldn't understand why Mama didn't want to get well. "Why can't we ask Mama to get well?"

"No!" He shouted the word but was contrite in the next moment. "I'm sorry, Annie. I didn't mean to yell. Your mama believes in the white man's medicine. I've tried to make her use our ways before, but she says they're the work of the devil."

Annie had heard of Mama's devil. He was the opposite of Mama's God. Annie figured she was a lot like him; she always seemed to do what Mama didn't want her to. "I can ask Mama. She will listen to me." She wanted to believe it. But deep down, she knew if Mama didn't trust Daddy, she wouldn't trust Annie. Even though Annie came from Mama's belly, she was Daddy's daughter. Mama told her this repeatedly. To Mama, Annie was nothing like her. But Annie knew she had Mama's Scottish grit. It was in a different way, but she had it. Her daddy's strength was different. He liked people and understood them. "I don't think so, Annie. Not this time. Mama has made up her mind she is dying, and I don't think even you and Archie together can change that."

"I don't want Mama to die. Then Jeremiah will go away." The words tumbled out. When she realized that she uttered more feeling for Jeremiah than her mama, her face reddened. She expected a sharp rebuke and looked at her daddy apprehensively.

"It's all right, little one. You are close to Jeremiah." He didn't add that Annie would never be as close to Mama. This was better left unsaid. Once spoken, thoughts became powerful. As long as they stayed unformed in people's minds, there was a good chance they would not cause harm. Unless, of course, people dwelled on them. Annie had learned these things from Daddy and Archie. Mama would never say such things to her. After all, she was still a small child. But Archie and Daddy saw her differently.

Nothing was said to Mama. One night, about a week after her talk with Archie, Annie lay on her cot in the room she shared with Jerry. A sheet, hemmed and strung with rope, divided the room. Both had a window. Annie's faced west, while Jerry's faced south. She loved to sit on her bed in the waning light and watch the sunset. It turned the already red soil into a Van Gogh of colors. She had seen a picture of Van Gogh's sunflowers and related everything after to their brilliant hues. Annie didn't think Van Gogh had ever seen Australia, though. If he had, the red soil would have shown up in all his paintings.

Jerry's window held reflected light, but he didn't seem to mind. Jerry's world revolved around his schoolwork. Any time she looked at him, he was deep into some mathematical formula or some theory about the universe. One day, she approached him about his preoccupation. "If you believed we are living the Master Dreamer's dream, you wouldn't have to study so hard. You would know that he helps you."

"Grow up, Annie. You and your dad live in a fantasy world. When I've finished my School of the Air, I want to go to university. You make that Master Dreamer guy sound like Superman." Superman had just come into their world. One day, Daddy and Mama had gone to town and come back with the priceless comic book. Jerry and Annie were enthralled with the present and took turns reading it.

Jerry's world was the white world. Annie's was three-quarters white, but she felt more black than white, much to Mama's distaste. If Annie resembled Mama's family, she would have pushed Annie harder in her schooling. As it was, she saw Annie kept up with her work then left her daughter pretty much on her own. Mama always asked Jerry questions, and when Jerry didn't know the answer, she said, "Look it up in the encyclopedia, Jeremiah. Don't be lazy." If she asked Annie a question and she didn't know the answer, Mama just gave her an odd look.

Now, Jerry lay on his cot reading the Superman comic book by lantern light. Annie lay on her cot watching disorienting shadows dance on the sheet that separated them.

CHAPTER 24

Annie was becoming drowsy and unfocused when she heard the call in her head, much like the wail of a bagpipe, which Jerry had imitated one day for her benefit. All day she had thought of Mama, picturing her in good health. It was almost impossible, because Mama's illness paled her skin and drew it taut across her cheekbones. Annie thought she looked like a walking skeleton after the buzzards picked at the flesh. Annie knew the doctor had given Mama pain medicine, because she had seen her mixing a white powder with water. She drank it when she thought Annie and Jeremiah weren't looking. Even though mother and daughter weren't close, Annie didn't like to see Mama that way. Annie missed the tough, no-nonsense mama who drew her Scottish lips tight at her daughter's escapades.

Jerry and Annie talked about healing her once. "We can't do anything, Annie. We're kids. But when I get older, I can help people like Mama. I know I have a talent for it." His mind was set like his mother's.

She was scared! All day she had been anxious, not knowing what would happen, but aware something momentous was coming. She lay on her cot watching with a numb mind the flickering shadows cast by Jerry's lamp

The call came clearly, and she knew Archie was reaching into her mind. She didn't know what to do. She daren't cry out. How could she explain to Jeremiah what was wrong? She didn't know what was wrong. Her whole world was wrong. Mama was dying; Jerry would have to go away. Daddy and she would be left by themselves. That didn't bother her too much, but she tried to imagine life with just the two of them and couldn't. A black curtain came over her attempt.

The buzzing sound reminded her of an Aborigine ritual Daddy had taken her to when she just started walking on her own two feet. When the singsong chant began, she had lost her balance and fell close to the fire. Daddy had picked her up, and the kalbin looked at her oddly. She hadn't known he was the kalbin. Daddy had told her afterwards. For the rest of the ritual, Daddy had held her within the circle of his arms, his chin on her head. She felt comfortable there with the Aborigine people. She was certainly more comfortable than when she went with the family into Mama's church in Alice Springs. That's why she could bear the thought of losing Mama. With Mama gone, there was a good chance Daddy would return to his people. But then, Daddy wasn't full Aborigine, and she had even less black blood than Daddy.

The high chant continued. She tried to bring her full attention to the sound without letting her thoughts wander. Archie had told her she must do this to succeed. The noise grew louder, until it filled her head. It was impossible to think of anything except that throbbing, insistent sound. Gradually, she was able to discern words. "Your mama is well, Annie. Your mama is well." Over and over, the words echoed in her head, until all she knew and believed were those words. "Yes." Her lips moved, but no sound came out. If Jerry heard, he would scoff. "Yes, Mama is well." She rolled her head side to side as the mantra throbbed. "Mama is well." She pictured Mama as she was before those ill, high-colored cheekbones. She pictured her with stern but bright eyes and the no-nonsense smile that seemed to escape her lips on its own whim. "Mama is well. Mama is well." Over and over Annie thought the words quietly, until she felt her mother's health in her bones. "She is well. She is well."

She continued the silent chant in her mind for several hours. The crimson glow of the sun-swept desert sand turned to purple. The Master Dreamer's lamps hung in the sky like Mama's glass ornaments on their bottlebrush at Christmas.

Jerry's lantern was extinguished. If he had said goodnight, as he often did, she hadn't heard him. She lay in bed thinking how well Mama would look tomorrow, and as she lay there, she fell into a deep sleep.

The next morning, Daddy had porridge ready on the stove for breakfast. Mama always argued them into eating the oatmeal. It took Annie time to get used to it, but now she looked forward to the filling gruel. Daddy learned to put sugar on his. Mama insisted on salt. The two were in a constant battle over the correct porridge topping. Jerry and Annie didn't mind. Three mornings a week, they showered the porridge with salt, and they dusted it with sugar the four remaining mornings.

Daddy looked more cheerful than he had in weeks. "Mama is resting in bed today, so you need to be extra quiet. You must do your schoolwork." He looked at Jeremiah as he said this. "Annie, do you think you could walk by yourself to the Taylor's ranch? It will take most of the morning, unless you are lucky enough to get a ride. Don't count on it. The only vehicles coming through are military, unless a millionaire prince stops for my princess." He gave her a teasing smile. "I want to get a message to Archie."

"Yes, Daddy." She knew what his message said. Mama was going to be well. "I think Archie knows what you want to say, though."

Daddy looked at her for long moments. "Eat your porridge, girl." He turned to enter his bedroom.

"What was that about, Annie Nanny?" Jeremiah's voice broke into her thoughts. He started tacking on the second name after they had seen the goats on Mr. Taylor's ranch months ago. Mr. Taylor had given Daddy a can of goats' milk to help Mama when she was ill.

On their way home, Jerry had turned to Annie, "You're just like one of Mr. Taylor's goats, Annie Nanny. Always bleating about something." Annie didn't mind most days. Besides, she had a name for him — Jerky Jerry. Usually she used it when she had to get him out of another mess.

Jerry and she did their schoolwork, and then he went to his room to read. Daddy was still with Mama. Annie eased open the door and peeped in. He lay on the bed holding Mama's hand. She looked peaceful and beautiful. The stern look around her lips was gone, and her mouth pulled into a small smile. With a shock, Annie realized this was the woman Daddy fell in love with—this soft, gentle girl. Daddy opened his eyes. "Are you off, little one?" His voice was little more than a whisper.

She nodded, not wanting to disturb the serene scene. "Take bread and cheese with you and water from the well. When you come back, I'm sure Mama will be awake. And, Annie ..." She turned to him. "Thank you. Tell Archie thanks, too."

She wanted to tell him that it wasn't Archie or she who had made Mama well. It was the Master Dreamer. She didn't expect Jeremiah or Mama to acknowledge that, but she expected her daddy to know.

The sun beat down over the desert as she started out, her new sunbonnet tied under her chin.

Hot winds blew across the open sand, depositing fine, red dust all over her. She tied a rag over her nose and mouth to keep the dust out. Daddy had showed her that when she was little. She couldn't do anything about her eyes, though, so she squeezed them shut against the harsh wind and grating sand. If she had been six, she wouldn't make it. But at eight and a half, the years added strength to her legs and discipline to her mind.

She heard a strange noise behind her and turned to see a rare car coming along the road. Daddy and Mama had talked about them. "They aren't much good out here on the desert," Daddy said. The camel and horse were still the best way to travel other than the train, of course. The first time Mama went to the doctor, she flew in the biplane belonging to the Flying Doctor Service. After that, she took the train. Neither was convenient, but both were more comfortable than riding a camel or horse.

The car passed, leaving clouds of dust in its wake. She may be her daddy's princess, but the man driving hadn't stopped. The driver wore dark glasses and had a white scarf around his neck. The top of the car was open, and she saw him laughing with the young, white woman beside him. Then they were gone.

Coober Pedy was tiny and isolated. Unless you wanted opals, there was nothing to hold anyone. There had been even less before the war, but the war brought changes. Daddy said war had two sides — the side killing people and the side bringing progress. She hadn't seen any of the killing, so she thought war must be a good thing. After all, it brought automobiles like that shiny black one with its happy couple with the smiling faces.

As she glanced around, she saw a buzzard circle overhead. Dead kangaroos were common in the desert, their bones picked clean of flesh. But the couple in the car wouldn't have to worry; they were leaving the desert. Annie doubted their bones would lie in this red soil.

Melons twined themselves along the road. She knew she must not touch them, because they were poison. They looked so much like Mama's garden melons, but Mama said they were not the same. In these matters, Annie knew better than to question the grown-ups. Sometimes she thought she knew more than them, especially concerning the Master Dreamer, but for matters of this world, she trusted their wisdom.

In the distance, she spied the bright pink of a timeless rose, dazzling against the red dust. The desert willows were dusty green, and the bottlebrushes appeared hazy. But the timeless rose glowed brilliantly like the Master Dreamer's lamps hung for his people at night. Sometimes when she looked at those lamps, they changed from gold to pink to blue. But they were out of reach. The desert rose was not, and she considered picking the flowers for Mama on her return.

The first of the white clapboard buildings came into view. It was two stories high with a small store on the ground floor and an assayer's office on the second. A sign said Coca Cola would refresh her, but as she had no money, she took a drink from her water jar and sat in the veranda's cool shade. Mama and Daddy knew most of the townspeople, so all the shopkeepers knew she was Kate and William's kid. Mrs. McFarlane, the owner of the store, came out. She wore the same look as Mama. Annie didn't know what to call it, but it was a look that said she could control life and she didn't need other people. Jeremiah was the same way. Annie was more like Daddy. She needed people around.

"How do you come by here then, Annie?" The way Mrs. McFarlane asked questions always confused Annie. It had taken Jeremiah to point out when Mrs. McFarlane said *how*, she meant *why*. Annie ran the back of her hand over her mouth and put the top on the precious water jar.

"Looking to find Archie, Mrs. McFarlane. I gotta get a message to him from my daddy."

"Saw Archie in town a little while ago. See if he's over at the pub having a beer. Don't suppose you have to hurry too much. I think he's going on a walkabout, and he's seeing to his thirst first."

"Thanks, Mrs. McFarlane. I better be going before Archie leaves."

Mrs. McFarlane gave Annie one of her rare smiles, as if she counted out how many smiles she would give in a year. Annie guessed she should be pleased, but she couldn't help thinking people like that took themselves and the world too seriously.

"How's your Mama doing, Annie?"

It had taken her a while to ask, but Annie knew she was genuinely interested in Mama's welfare. "She's goin' to be okay, Mrs. McFarlane. The Master Dreamer said so."

"I'm glad you think your mama will be better, but if she heard you, she would want to curl up and die. You're so much like your daddy."

Annie knew what she meant, but it didn't matter. She left to find Archie. If he was at the pub like Mrs. McFarlane thought, he was drunk by now. It hurt Annie to see the whites sell her people whiskey and laugh when they got drunk and did crazy things. She wanted to cry every time it happened. How could her people let themselves be put down like that? She guessed she knew the answer. They lived the Master Dreamer's dream, and he had a reason.

She found Archie at the Desert Inn on a small, unpaved street. The red dust settled over him, and she stirred up more as she walked to him. "Ho, Archie! I thought I'd have to go to the Taylor ranch to find you."

CHAPTER 25

Archie was propped against the pub under the shade of a gum tree. The whites of his eyes were all red, and the blacks were unfocused. Spittle drooled from his open mouth, and dozens of flies lit on him, drawing moisture from his drool. A leafed branch lay in his limp hand, and Annie wormed it out of his grip to brush at the buzzing flies. "Archie, Archie! Wake up you no-good fool of a bugger." Her daddy's words echoed from her lips.

Two white women tsked their way down the boardwalk as she tried to wake Archie. She didn't know if they were more upset about her or Archie. Daddy had told her often not to copy the way he talked when he was with Archie or his other black friends. Mama had forbidden her to go with Daddy on his infrequent trips to friends, but Daddy persevered and took Annie with him. "You have Jeremiah, Kate. All I have is Annie, and I want her to learn about our people. I know ..." Daddy held up his hand against Mama's argument that Annie was hers too. "But she is also mine. I don't disagree when you teach her the ways of your people, and I would ask the same courtesy from you." Daddy could be quite eloquent with the white people, just as he could talk pidgin English when he was with his less verbal friends.

What made Mama angry, Annie thought, was that Daddy looked more white than black. Maybe she hadn't known about the black part when she married him. But his black ancestry was noticeable in his wide face and broad nose. Then again, Mama probably didn't care that he looked a little black. It was stressing his blackness that made Mama's lips tighten into two thin, pink strips. Annie wondered if he did it on purpose. When she gave it thought, she decided Daddy loved his family too much to be juvenile like that. Daddy's heart was as large as the desert, and Archie's was too. She poked him harder.

"Archie, you drunken fool of a bugger. Open your eyes. You want to go on a walkabout, that's okay. But don't let yourself sit here to be laughed at." She shook his arm and watched as his head lolled to one side. Suddenly, she noticed that there were no moans like Archie usually emitted in one of his "bouts," as he called them.

She was confused. Mr. Jacks, the pub owner, opened the door and looked out at the commotion. "What's up, Annie?" Used to seeing Archie out cold on the sidewalk, Mr. Jacks ignored him.

"Look at Archie, Mr. Jacks. There's something wrong with him."

Mr. Jacks glanced over. "He's sleeping it off, Annie. Leave him be for a while. He'll be okay."

"No, Mr. Jacks." Her breath caught on a sob. "No, Archie isn't okay. Look at him."

Mr. Jacks went over and shook Archie as she had. There was no response other than the clusters of flies dispersing. He put his finger on Archie's neck. "I'm afraid he's gone on walk-about, Annie. For good. I'll have to get Harry to take him back to Taylor's ranch. They'll have to deal with his body." Harry was Mr. Jacks's helper, and it often fell on him to cart Archie back to the ranch. This would be the last time.

"The drunken, bloody fool," Annie screamed. Tears washed down her face, and the flies sucked at the new moisture. She kicked Archie in the leg. "Drunken, bloody fool."

"Watch your tongue, Annie. If your Ma heard you cussing, she'd give you a good tanning, she would. You'd best run along back home. There's a girl. You can't help Archie now."

She knew he was right. She couldn't help Archie. They had worked together the first and only time last night. She could still hear the incessant, high-pitched humming in her head. Archie did more than channel the healing power to Mama. He had taught Annie her first real lesson in healing. There would be no teachers after Archie. Daddy's people were losing their skills faster than a steer lost its life in the desert. She turned away from Archie's discarded carcass and tried not to think of buzzards gorging themselves on his flesh.

Her bare feet scuffed the dust of the road, sending up clouds of red grit as she hurried back to Mrs. McFarlane's store. The veranda was empty except for a wooden bench and a sorry-looking pink geranium drooping in a black pot. She was thirsty and hungry but doubted anyone would give her anything to eat. Archie would have. Even if he spent his money on beer, he would have found her a biscuit or a piece of cheese. She cried out for Mrs. McFarlane, who came running to the door. "What's the ruckus, Annie? Did you find Archie?"

"He's dead, Mrs. McFarlane. He's dead. The no-good bloody bugger is dead."

"Hush that mouth of yours, Annie. Wherever did you hear such language?"

She was more shocked at Annie's words than the death of one of the kindest men Annie had ever met. She didn't understand. Yes, Archie drank. But so did lots of white men, and their drunken ways were far more disgusting than Archie's.

It never occurred to her that *no-good bloody bugger* held as much censure as anything the white woman could say. They were just words. It was like Mama calling one of the miners a *kraut* or Mr. Fujimoto a *Jap*. If Mama said that's what they were, then that's what they were. Annie liked Mr. Fujimoto very much. He was a shoemaker in Coober Pedy, and Daddy often took shoes and leather goods to him to repair. He was a quiet, soft man, and like Archie, he always gave her a smile and a nod. Not too many grown-up people gave little kids that much respect.

Daddy had said she shouldn't talk about people that way, and they weren't responsible for the war. As she stood on Mrs. McFarlane's porch, Annie thought of Mama getting well and how young and pretty she looked with Daddy at her bedside. Mrs. McFarlane was still looking at her, waiting for her reply.

"Archie's dead, Mrs. McFarlane. He's there outside the Desert Inn."

"Well, it was bound to happen sooner or later. The way he drank, it's a wonder he's lived this long."

"Daddy sent me with a message for him."

"Well, you must go back to your daddy and tell him about Archie. He was Archie's friend, you know. Your daddy would rather hear it from you than one of the miners in the pub." She turned to go back inside the cool shop but stopped. "What was it you had to tell Archie?"

Annie didn't want to say. It would be all over town and make Daddy the butt of jokes. She knew how people reacted to the primitive ways. Mrs. McFarlane wouldn't have believed it anyway. "He wanted Archie to know Mama seemed better. Mrs. McFarlane, could I have a drink of water before I go back home?"

"Yes. Fill your bottle from the well at the back of the store. Then you'd best be running along."

"Thank you, Mrs. McFarlane." Daddy and Mama had taught both Jeremiah and Annie to be polite. People were more willing to help if you gave a *please* and *thank-you*. Annie knew Jeremiah had fewer problems getting along with white people. After all, he was one of them. Although Annie was too, she had that strain of black, which caused whites to draw back. If they understood they were all part of the Master Dreamer, they wouldn't treat blacks that way. But they didn't. They thought their white God, sitting on his heavenly throne with his white, flowing robes, was superior to Annie's Master Dreamer. She retraced her steps out of town and onto the newly surfaced road, which allowed army vehicles access to and from Darwin. They weren't so isolated that they didn't know what was happening in the world. Annie didn't understand any of it, but she had heard Mama and Daddy talking after Jeremiah and she had gone to bed. At one point, Mama discussed taking Jeremiah back to Scotland, but Daddy pointed out their town was less likely to become part of the war than Scotland. It had hurt terribly that Mama did not mention taking Annie too.

On the way home, nobody passed Annie in either direction. A lone buzzard circled overhead, looking for its next meal. She knew she wouldn't be it. The Master Dreamer looks out for those on his mission. Daddy had told her the Master Dreamer was especially looking after Archie, for he always seemed to get Archie out of his scrapes. In a way, Annie guessed, Archie was a lot like Jeremiah. They got into one problem after another. But Archie seemed to float into problems. Jeremiah sought them out. And most of Archie's problems were caused by drinking. When he wasn't drinking, he was smart and worked hard. When he was drunk, the only thing he was good for was sitting on the roadside while the whites laughed at him.

Her legs began to cramp from the long distance she had traveled, but she had to keep moving. Daddy had told her that. If she stopped for a rest, her legs would refuse to budge another inch. Gazing at the shimmering heat making the desert dance, she detoured from the road to pick a pink blossom from the timeless rose. She loved the desert in all its dresses. Mama had told her about the green grass, vibrant flowers, and cooling trees of the coast. Annie remembered them from a trip she had taken with Mama and Jeremiah. Jeremiah could hardly sit still when he saw the ocean. The water made Annie cringe. She felt safer in the desert.

On the coast, the Master Dreamer's lamps didn't hang as close to earth. In the desert, she felt she could almost touch them. Daddy told her that the Master Dreamer hung them out just for her. Mama had told her once not to pay attention to Daddy's stories. They were stories handed down by a heathen people. Daddy had overheard her and became angry.

"My stories are no less important than yours, Katie." His tone was gentle but chiding. When Daddy was in that mood, he and Archie were similar. "Your people tell stories to explain what they don't understand. My people do the same. But I think our people understand this world better than your people do."

Mama's voice was sharp. "I don't like the way you put so much emphasis on this Master Dreamer of yours. You don't hear me telling the children that God put the stars in the sky or the kangaroo in the desert. But that is what I believe. I know Darwin talked about the species evolving, including humans, but I still say God is the master planner." Mama's voice wound down as she realized what she said.

"See, we just call them by different names." Daddy was jubilant. He went over to Mama and hugged her waist, dancing her around the floor until she was breathless and laughing. Annie loved it when she saw them like that. It made her feel loved knowing they loved each other. She knew Mama loved her just as much as she loved Jeremiah. But Jeremiah took after her, and she couldn't help but feel closer to him. Annie had the same feeling with Daddy. She knew all this, but she couldn't have vocalized it. She just knew. The same way she knew, clutching the blossom from the timeless rose and plodding along the dusty road, that Mama was well.

Reaching home, Annie found Mama in a chair at the table. Her face was pale but happy. Daddy made her a cup of tea and held her hand across the table, smiling into her eyes. He looked up as Annie entered the doorway and handed the blossom to her mama.

"You're back." Daddy's voice was soft. "Did you give Archie my message?"

"The no-good bugger is dead." She could scarcely contain the tears as they clogged her throat. On her walk home, she had asked herself if she would have been so upset at Mama's death. She guessed she would have, but Mama's dying didn't seem real now.

Mama looked at her with shock. "Hush up those words, Annie. Wherever did you hear the likes of that?"

"Uh, I think she heard them from me. I've said words like those before when I found Archie drinking. But you mustn't say those words," he said, turning to Annie. "They don't sound good coming from a young lady."

"Daddy, don't you care Archie is dead?" She squeezed her eyes shut against more tears threatening to fall.

"Yes. I care, little one. Believe me, I care. But Archie is ... was old. Nobody knows how old. And he drank too much."

"Are you sure he is the one who helped me get well, Will? I can scarcely believe it."

"Yes. Positive. With Annie's help, of course."

Mama looked at her. Annie didn't expect her to say thank you, because she didn't even understand what role she had played.

"Where is Archie? I suppose I should go into town and look after him — take his body back to his people." Daddy uttered the words she wanted to hear.

"I found him sitting outside the Desert Inn. He had flies all over him. Mr. Jacks said he would get Harry to take him to the Taylor ranch."

"I like the Taylors, but they won't think to return him to his people. They'll want to bury him in the cemetery outside town with the white people. That won't do at all." Tears glistened in his eyes. "Archie was once a kalbin." Annie watched as her dad brushed tears off his face.

"What's a kalbin, Daddy? I didn't know Mr. Archie was anything. Is a kalbin important?"

"A kalbin is a high priest, little one. And it hurts me to see Archie brought to this."

"He brought it on himself, Will. You can't deny it. And he wasn't a Christian priest, so it doesn't matter." Mama was back to her normal self.

Daddy didn't get to town in time to rescue Archie's body. Harry delivered Archie's remains to the Taylor ranch, and Mr. Taylor buried Archie in the cemetery outside town as Daddy predicted. Daddy was quiet for several days after Archie's death. Annie didn't feel like talking either. Jeremiah kept pestering her to look for bugs in the desert with him, but she didn't want to. She knew why Daddy was quiet. He felt bad because Archie was buried in the white man's cemetery.

There was a church in town that was dug out of the sand hills for all the white people and some of the Aborigines too. A cross made from mulga wood stood at the front of the church, and somebody had scratched outlines of two fish into the pebbly surface of the walls. There were chairs set up in two sections with a center aisle leading to the altar. Annie went there once with Mama. Daddy refused to go. Annie was surprised that Mama went. She was as much underground there as she was in the opal pits. The same dampness permeated their clothes and skin. But Mr. Taylor did not take Archie to the church in town, but to the adjacent cemetery. When he had approached Mr. Taylor, the rancher told Daddy that Archie received a "proper Christian funeral."

Daddy knew there was no sense pushing for an Aboriginal funeral for Archie. Mr. Taylor had no quick way of letting Archie's kinfolk know he was dead. All he could do was tell another ranch hand and hope the word spread to Archie's people. At first, the Taylors and their hired hands went around with glum faces, but then life at the ranch carried on as before. The same thing had happened when one of Mr. Taylor's work horses died.

When Daddy returned home, he walked away into the desert and sat there a long time. She wondered if he was talking to Archie or the Master Dreamer. Afterward, he came back to the house, and he looked happier than he had been in a long time. Mama continued to get well, and soon they were all back to their old ways. Annie didn't worry about Mama anymore. If the Master Dreamer had made Mama well, then she would stay well. There wasn't much point in making people well just to let them die.

CHAPTER 26

Jeremiah was obnoxious now. He had become chums with two other boys in town, and the three of them delighted in teasing Annie for hours. She was eleven the day he and his pals went looking for bugs in the desert. Annie trailed behind, but they made it clear they didn't want her tagging along.

"It's the way boys are," Mama consoled the crying Annie. "They go through a stage where they like to be with other boys. Soon, you'll want only girl friends to tell your secrets to, and you won't want Jeremiah around."

Mama was looking healthier and happier than Annie ever remembered. After her illness, Mama changed toward her. She wasn't hard, but Annie often caught her looking at her with eyes full of questions and fear.

The day Annie followed Jerry, Nick, and Josef into the desert, the hot sun blazed as they made their way to the shade of a desert oak. Annie kept a short distance behind. Jerry sat close to a desert rose and put his hand under the pink blossoms. Both Josef and Nick yelled in unison. Jerry pulled his arm back sharply, but not before a snake sunk its fangs into his hand. "Oh crikey, Annie, I'm bit." Jeremiah's frightened yells sent the other boys running back to the row of houses for help. Jeremiah's hand swelled and red stripes zigzagged their way up his arm as he thrashed.

"Hold still, Jerky Jerry." Annie was more annoyed than frightened. It didn't escape her notice that he cried out for her rather than his beloved chums. He didn't want her around, but when he was in trouble, she was the one he turned to first. "Hold still. You can't talk to me. I have to concentrate." He kept surprisingly quiet.

The high-pitched buzzing began in her head and took over her whole body. Her hand clutched Jerry's wrist, but she thought only of the buzzing. Red and blue flashes whipped across the desert in quick succession, followed by a blinding white light. She watched until the buzzing ebbed and the light disappeared. She knew there would be no mark on Jerry's arm when she looked.

"Thanks, Annie." For once, Jeremiah's voice was small and frail instead of loud and taunting, as it was on most occasions around her. Shouts assailed them from across the desert, and they both looked up.

His two friends came back with Daddy right behind them. They were all breathless in the heat, and she watched sweat pour down her dad's face. He wiped it away with his sleeve. "What have you gone and done now, Jeremiah? You're going to be the death of your mother yet, you are."

"I got pricked by the desert rose, but I thought it was a snake bite, Dad." Jerry's voice brooked no argument.

Daddy looked from him to Annie and back again. Jerry's friends both shouted at once. "We saw the snake bite his hand, and he was sure yelling enough."

"Well, whatever it was, it seems cleared up now. You all better come back to the house for lemonade. Besides," he said to Jeremiah and Annie, "your mother and I need to talk to you. After you have your lemonade, you two boys run along home."

The long walk back to their little house with the corrugated tin roof and square, brick walls was hot, dusty, and quiet. Annie couldn't tell what everyone was thinking, but they all seemed absorbed in their thoughts. They went past one of the dugout houses where the temperature remained cool. She thought they were rather nice, but with Mama's fear of the underground, she knew they would never live in one. The people who lived in them built lovely porches to sit and watch the play of light and shadow across the red desert sands.

Annie knew their small house was well built for the town. Most of the people who mined for opals cared little about where they lived. Annie guessed Mama made theirs better. She was sure Daddy wouldn't have minded living out his days in his opal pit. But Mama had come from Scotland, a very civilized country, and that made the difference.

She never knew how or why Mama ended up with Daddy out here in the desert. Mama didn't fit in with the rest of the mining families. She was not a snob, but she lived differently than most of the people here. Annie saw the many differences between Mama and Daddy, but the Master Dreamer knew what he was doing when he brought them together, because they were sure happy.

But now, both Mama and Daddy looked worried. Mama poured lemonade from a pitcher she brought from Scotland. It was her prized possession. She enjoyed it as much as Jeremiah enjoyed collecting and looking at his bugs. Josef and Nick gulped their lemonade, muttered their thanks, and left for their homes. Daddy, Mama, Jerry, and Annie remained around the table.

"You two know there's a war on, don't you?" Daddy began. They both nodded. It was hard not to know when all the talk was about those *damn Japs*, and Mama explained how food was rationed. Jerry and Annie were never allowed to say they disliked Mama's cooking. They ate it, because they knew there would be nothing else.

Mama and Daddy had a shortwave radio besides the one they used for schooling and the Flying Doctor Service. Through static and censored newscasts, they kept up with world news that had seemed so distant to the people of Coober Pedy. Jerry and Annie had war games down to a science. He was always on the side of the Allies, and Annie was either German or Japanese. Jerry would cast her in the role of enemy, because her skin was darker, her stature was shorter, and she had an Aborigine nose. *Besides,* Annie thought, *being on the side of the Allies makes him feel good.*

Josef, whose family was from Poland, understood war more than they did. His father joined the fight to save his homeland and left his wife and two children behind in Coober Pedy.

Nick's father also left Australia early in the war to protect Greece. Daddy was fully Australian, and until the Japanese bombed Darwin to the north, he did not acknowledge the threat of battle. Mama had, and she worried constantly about her Scottish family. As Annie had never met any of them, they were faceless people that Mama always sent parcels to. Mama stored little items in a cupboard until she had enough for a parcel. Once, Annie found chewing gum there. She sneaked the gum and, sitting on the red sand out of sight, chewed it all.

Mama didn't say she was disappointed. She explained that her people in Scotland were on strict rations and couldn't get little treats like that. Annie and Jeremiah didn't get treats like chewing gum and candy, either. They were on rations too, but Annie figured they weren't as rationed as the Scottish people were. And because she had swiped the gum, she didn't enjoy it all that much.

Even though Australia had joined the British early in the war, many in their small community felt they were distanced from the fighting. But the war stretched into the nooks, crannies, opal pits, and sapphire mines, calling the people to its cause. Miners made more money from their work in war factories than they ever did in their pits and mines. Daddy had more skills than opal mining, but he said he wasn't about to lend his help in any factory. He chose to fight the enemy himself. Mama was both proud and upset. Daddy was his usual jovial self. "I'm going off to join the army, Annie. That's where I can help the most. I want you to be a big girl and help out your Mama and Jeremiah." He winked at her. She was eleven years old but not a little girl. She knew she had abilities neither Mama nor Jeremiah had, and it would be her job to help if they needed her.

"I'll be the man of the house while you're away." Jeremiah puffed up with pride. Annie choked on her lemonade. She loved Jerry with a passion, but she was not blind to his shortcomings.

"Good-O, mate. That's the kind of stuff I like to hear. You look after your mother and sister, and I'll be back in no time at all. We'll reclaim Australia lickety-split. Then we can get back to our lives."

Annie felt that her heart would burst with love for her dad. He was not one to put anybody down. Even though Jeremiah was not his, Daddy loved him as he loved Annie. Mama came to him with a son, and Daddy saw that son as part of the woman he adored. Annie wasn't sure that Mama even realized Daddy's vast capacity to love. If Mama had not been ill, Daddy would have wanted a dozen kids. But Mama *had* become ill, and Daddy nearly lost her. That changed his focus entirely. He needed Mama more than he wanted more kids.

Daddy's leaving didn't seem quite real. After a tearful farewell to Mama, Annie expected to see him back after supper. To take their minds off Daddy's absence, Mama turned the meal into a festive occasion. In this hostile desert, Mama worked her own miracle. She created a small garden to one side of the door, where she grew the Scottish vegetables she missed from home. All their wash water and dishwater went to appease the thirsty soil. Nothing was wasted. The vegetable peelings were returned to the garden, until the stony soil gave way to adequate gardening ground. They ate new potatoes, carrots, and fresh tomatoes. They didn't have any meat, but they did have fresh goat's milk and cheese.

Once a week, they went into Coober Pedy for mail. An air of excitement always pervaded their walk, because Mama made mail day an adventure for everyone. Before Daddy went away, Mama had looked forward to letters from Scotland. Although Jeremiah and Annie didn't know the writers of these letters, the mail always set Mama on one of her memory trips. She would tell them all about the highlands and the glens, the purple heather and the yellow gorse bushes, and the wandering sheep on the laneways. She talked dreamily of the ocean roaring against the cliffs, licking away a little bit of rock with each flick of its salty tongue. This was always explained with her tongue flicking away at a chunk of ice, their treat for the long walk into town.

Months after her dad left, the three had walked to town for mail. They each received a letter from her dad. Annie didn't know what he said in Mama's letter, but in the ones to Jeremiah and her, there were black lines crossing out many words and *Censored* written in black across the envelope. Daddy said they were holding their own against the Japanese. He never called them Japs like Mama. Thinking of him, Annie asked Mama about Mr. Fujimoto. No one had seen him in the area for many weeks. Some said he had joined the Japanese navy. Others said he went underground until the war ended. Annie pictured the pleasant man living in one of the opal pits and wondered if she could find him. Mama's face tightened. Annie knew she shouldn't have asked.

"I don't know, nor do I care. The Japs took the Malay Archipelago, New Guinea, and the Solomon Islands. They've bombed Darwin. How can you ask about a man like that?"

"But, Mama, it's not Mr. Fujimoto's fault. Mr. Fujimoto isn't even in the war."

"I don't want to hear another word about that man. Your father says he is doing well …" Her words trailed off as they heard a noise above. A plane droned overhead. Mama grabbed them, and they flattened themselves against the outside wall of Mrs. McFarlane's store. The war had come to them.

CHAPTER 27

Three years passed. Annie turned fourteen, and Jeremiah turned seventeen and took on new responsibilities helping with the Royal Flying Doctor Service and delivering telegrams. Their dad's letters became scarcer, and their mother became quieter. They both took to calling her *Mum,* and the three of them waited out the war. Jerry and Annie grew into adulthood, and Mum grew away from her desert life, becoming more discontented with her life in Australia.

The Japanese succeeded in raiding many Australian cities and towns. Alice Springs to the north, more inhabited than Coober Pedy, became a communication center for the war. Nevertheless, Coober Pedy was close to the road connecting Adelaide in the south to Darwin in the north. Often, they saw Army jeeps raising dust as they sped past.

One day, Annie found her mother crying in her room. Thinking she could help, Annie went in and put her arm about her mother. Mum sobbed even louder. "Annie, there is nothing you can do. I'm lonely for your dad, and I'm lonely for my people. I hate Australia, and I hate Coober Pedy more. This godforsaken hole isn't fit for anybody to inhabit. Why did I ever come here?"

"Why *did* you come here, Mum?" Annie questioned her mother's choice herself. *She* was born here. This was her home, but Mum had come from a gentler land, which, Annie figured from her mother's descriptions, even with its crags and outcrops and wild ocean wind couldn't beat Coober Pedy for desolateness. Even at fourteen, Annie saw how the rough town ate at a person who didn't know it as she did. On the rare trips Annie took to the coast, she felt stifled by the humidity and greenery.

Mum loved it. To Annie, the ocean was mysterious, and deep, and unsettling. The soft air crept into her lungs and suffocated her. Not Mum. Mum became a girl again in the gentle climate. She romped with Jeremiah and Annie in the waters, splashing and giggling. It was fun in its way, Annie decided, but it could not measure up to the desert.

Jeremiah, like Mum, loved the water. Annie saw his spirit grow as it never did in the desert. Mum's face glowed when she said, "We'll go home to Scotland one day, Jeremiah. Just wait. Then you will feel the sharp gales from the North Sea and splash in much colder water. This is like taking a bath." Their bond excluded Annie. But that was okay, because there was a bond between her and Dad. Some people didn't understand things like that. They wanted everybody to love them all the time. But Annie understood, and so did Jerry. When Jeremiah wasn't nattering in his big brother voice, he could be quite perceptive.

Mum stopped crying and set about gathering their laundry to wash. Annie and Jerry helped her haul water from a cistern to wash sheets and blankets. As they worked, Annie noticed Mum become quiet and cast glances toward Jeremiah. Annie could see that she wanted to talk with Jerry without Annie's presence.

"Mum, we're finished here. Is it okay if I go to town for mail?" Annie could see her mum's relief as she gave her nod of approval.

Going into town for mail, oceans and tall palms were the farthest thing from her mind. She understood more about the war and knew Darwin, although distant from Coober Pedy, was closer than it seemed before. War was different when it was far away. When it called on your doorstep, your ideas changed. The war caused Jeremiah and her to grow up fast. Jerry took more accountability for chores along with the Flying Doctor Service. Annie wanted to do more.

She clutched their ration books and left to visit the few buildings in town. A wind came across the desert, raising red dust devils and pinging tiny grains of sand into her eyes. She walked with her head down against the hot sun and drying wind. Her dark curly hair protected her head unlike Jerry's gold hair, which needed the protection of a hat. With her head bent and the wind rushing past her ears, she didn't hear the army vehicle pull up beside her.

"Want a lift, girlie?" The voice was an American drawl. She had heard that same voice over the radio when it talked about the war in the Pacific. Sharply, she turned her head. Two men in camouflage outfits looked at her.

"I'm going into Coober Pedy, Mr. MacArthur, sir. You're going down to Adelaide, I expect."

There was a short silence. General MacArthur spoke again to the other man. "Tom, it looks as though your people did a great job of disseminating information."

"Most of our people come from other countries. They'd naturally want to keep up with events. Hop in, girl. We'll swing by the town and drop you off." His voice was Australian, and it was then she realized that he was Thomas Albert Blamey. Her dad had been quite proud when one of their own was made Commander-in-Chief of the Allied Ground Forces in the southwest Pacific.

She pulled herself into the back seat, and the vehicle picked up speed. Mum warned her about talking to strangers, especially soldiers. "They are a long way from home, Annie. Sometimes they crave a woman, and it doesn't matter how old she is or who she is." Still, Annie felt safe with these two men. Their talk picked up where she imagined they left off. General MacArthur, the Supreme Commander of the Allied Forces in the southwest Pacific, was detailing his plan to wage an offensive against the Japanese in the Coral Sea. As he deftly handled the steering wheel, Lieutenant General Blamey nodded his head. Once in a while he would add a few ideas. They were interesting to Annie, but she was more absorbed in watching the landscape change with their speed. It was different than viewing it up close while walking. The ride was short. When the vehicle stopped, General MacArthur looked Annie in the eye. "You mustn't say a word about anything you heard. Is that understood?"

She swallowed. "Yes, sir." She nodded at both and ran away to Mrs. McFarlane's store. She wouldn't say anything. Besides, she didn't understand what they had talked about anyway.

"Hello, Annie. How come you here today?"

It was on the tip of her tongue to say she rode in a Jeep with two army generals. "Mum sent me in for a few things."

"You look hot, Annie. Would you like a drink from the well?"

Annie wasn't hot, not like she usually was after walking into town. But as she didn't want to say anything about the ride, she accepted the store owner's offer and handed her the grocery list before she went out back and pulled up cool water in a pail, plunged in the dipper, and took a long drink. By the time she returned to the store, Mrs. McFarlane had put the few groceries in Mum's woven basket. Annie pulled a knotted handkerchief from around her neck and took out the coins to pay.

"Your Mama always seems to have money on hand. Not like the people who run up a bill and pay every four months or so. What with no opals being sold and all."

She wasn't sure what Mrs. McFarlane expected her to say, so she said nothing. This wasn't the first time the store owner hinted at the source of Mum and Dad's money. Annie mentioned it to Mum once, and Mum snorted, "Old busybody." Annie shoved her arm under the basket handle. "Thanks for the water, Mrs. McFarlane." About to turn and leave, she felt the older woman's hand on her arm.

"How old are you now, Annie?" Her eyes squinted behind her gold-rimmed glasses.

"Fourteen, ma'am. Fifteen in five months." A sudden thought occurred to her. "Mrs. McFarlane, do you need help in the store? I'm quite good with customers, and I'm good at organizing. I understand merchandising costs and mark up ..."

"Oh, no. I wasn't asking for that reason. What with the war, I can't afford to hire anyone else. People don't have money to buy like before. No, I was just curious. Young people grow up so fast these days, especially those with nigger blood in them. Why, your Daddy won't recognize you when he comes home. It's quite a lady you've become."

Annie knew what Mrs. McFarlane was suggesting. Embarrassment flooded through her. Mrs. McFarlane was hinting at the same thing Mum had warned her about. She was glad she hadn't said anything about the ride into town with the two officers, even though nothing happened. Annie decided not to say a word to Mum either. Thanking Mrs. McFarlane for the groceries, she left and walked back to the main road. The walk home would be much longer than the trip in, and Annie made sure it was longer still. If she was home too soon, Mum would want to know how she made the trip so quickly.

Time passed, and her mum grew quieter and more distant. They listened to the radio and knew fighting had escalated. General MacArthur moved his headquarters to Melbourne to be near the war zones. This was what the two military men had discussed the day they drove Annie into town. Afraid she might let a word slip, she put their conversation at the back of her mind. It wasn't just the war plan she was afraid of leaking. She also wanted to hide what Mrs. McFarlane said to her that day in the store. She couldn't tell how Mum would react, but she suspected she would take Mrs. McFarlane's view. To be certain, Annie kept the incident to herself.

Dad's letters home became scarce, and then there were none. The sole topic of discussion became the war. Jeremiah grew quieter along with Mum. He was yearning to enter the thick of battle. This surprised her, as Jeremiah did not seem a likely candidate for fighting. Annie knew it wasn't the fighting that appealed to Jerry. He still wanted to be a doctor, and he constantly badgered Mum to let him join some service group or other. Mum said she needed him at home, and that he did his share by taking messages for the Flying Doctor Service. Annie knew Mum feared being left with no husband and no son.

Annie was sixteen when the Allies invaded the Philippines. The danger of a Japanese invasion of Australia was over. They had received no word from Dad in months, but there was no official notification of injury or death, either. Annie was sure he was not dead. Knowing Dad, he would have let her know, even if it meant finding Archie in the Dreamtime and hooking up a telegraph system to her brain. Nineteen-year-old Jeremiah was ready to take undergraduate studies at the university. He and Mum grew closer, and both grew ever farther from Annie.

When the war was declared over, Coober Pedy resumed its reason for existence. Men who had dug in the opal pits before the war returned to their lonely occupations. Several relished the mining even more. Deep in their holes, chipping away at soil, they didn't have to carry on inane, polite conversation. They could chisel away and live with their memories of fighting or gather at the Desert Inn for a beer with their comrades. Dad wasn't part of the group.

They still hadn't heard from him, and there was no official letter from the military or Red Cross. Then a battered and torn envelope reached them. It was notification that Will had been wounded. Through the Red Cross, Annie and her Mum found him in a Melbourne hospital. He had lost both legs. Tears of joy ran down Annie's cheeks as she took his hand. He was missing his legs, but his heart and mind were the same. Mama held back, and Annie saw the look of disappointment in her dad's face. She wanted to scream and push Mum toward him. Dad's words came quietly. "Let me speak with your mum for a bit, okay? There's a lovely park outside where you can sit or walk around."

Holding back tears, she kissed his cheek and gave a weak smile. It wasn't fair that Dad had no legs. Mining for opals had been his life for as long as Annie remembered. Sitting on a bench in the hospital grounds, she thought about everyone who fought to keep their land safe. They were lucky he came back, except she knew Dad wasn't feeling so lucky. He still had months ahead in the hospital. But at least he could see and speak. There were many in his ward that could do neither.

She sat and watched the jacaranda trees in bloom and wondered what would become of the family. Jeremiah would go to university. She couldn't say that she longed for more education, not like Jeremiah. He wanted it so badly he could barely contain himself. His grades were high enough that he could apply for a scholarship. Mum was quite proud of that. Dad would have a hard time providing for them in the days ahead, so Annie gave some heavy thought to her future. If she could get a shop job, she knew she would do well. From some deep recess, she pulled up knowledge of retail trades. She knew what customers liked, what they wanted, and how to get it for them.

The sun went down behind the tall buildings before her mother came through the hospital's double glass doors looking for her. Annie waved and smiled. Mum had been crying, but Annie could see her back stiffened in resolve. "Annie, we have to talk. Your dad and I decided I should take Jeremiah back to Scotland. You know he would have a better chance there, what with my relatives and all. We have no one here. I'm asking if you want to come with us, or stay with your father."

Annie had to make a decision. If Mum left Dad, he would have no one. His birth family had dispersed to different parts of Australia and beyond. He could contact a few, but Annie was sure he would not. Dad would be determined to make it on his own. She sensed that his black heritage was a sore point for many of his European relatives, and Dad had no desire to go abroad in search of distant kin who may or may not accept him. Annie was caught up in a dilemma. Dad needed her. Jeremiah needed her. She knew others would find that odd, because Jerry was quite talented. But that was the problem. Although he was academically gifted, he had few skills for putting his talents into practice. She always felt an obligation to steer him in the right direction and keep him safe. Then again, maybe he needed independence—to get his feet wet without her or his mother's presence. Annie wondered whether her mum could let him go when the time came.

"Mum, are you leaving Dad for good, or are you coming back once Jerry settles in university?" She knew the answer before she asked, but she needed to hear her mother say the words.

"I don't think I will come back, Annie. This is not my home. I loved your dad." She let the past tense settle around Annie like a shroud. "I did at first. When he sang his silly songs and laughed and teased. But that's not the same man in there. A confident, jolly man went to war, and I don't know the man who came back."

Annie understood more than her mother ever said. The man who went to war was whole. The one who came back was not.

CHAPTER 28

Her dad dried his tears with the sleeve of his hospital pajamas and forced his lips into an infectious grin. "Well, Annie. It's quite a lady you've become. You'll wow all the Scottish boys — from Aberdeen to Oban, from John O'Groats to the border. 'Tis a beauty you are. Annie," he said, grabbing her arm. "I didn't say anything to your mum, but I've a good opal hidden in a metal box in the pit. If you sell it, you won't have to worry about things for a time."

"Why would I want to sell it? It's yours. And we might need it for a fresh start in a new place. I don't think you want to return to Coober Pedy, do you?"

"I wouldn't be much good there, Annie. Can you picture me climbing up and down ladders to my pit any day soon? I'll have to be fitted with new legs, and then I'll have to learn to use them. But don't you worry about that. You'll be starting a new life with your mum and Jerry in Scotland."

She had resolved her dilemma as she returned to the hospital ward. "No, Dad. I won't. I belong here, and Mum knows that. She and Jerry will get along fine without me. You need me." She beamed, feeling the last few hours had matured her.

"Annie, I can't ask you to do this, girl. You're what? Sixteen? You should be going to parties and meeting other young people. Besides, girls should be with their mums."

"You don't believe that. You know Mum and I are not as close as you and I. She has always preferred Jeremiah."

"Oh, Annie, don't say that. Your mum is a fine woman. It's just that she fancies Jeremiah as a doctor, and she has her sights set on big things for him. You take after me more," he said, hugging her to him. "You have soul-knowledge, Annie.

Deep down, you understand things that others take a lifetime to learn."

"All I know is that I love you, and I believe I can help you. I have to go now, Dad. Mum is waiting. We'll sort things out, and I'll be back."

He nodded, trying not to appear too happy, but she knew he was. Her decision to stay gave him something to look forward to. It would fill his days until he was released from the hospital.

Their return to Coober Pedy took longer than their trip to Melbourne. When they left the small town, they had begged a ride with the Royal Flying Doctor Service. Bus service was erratic at best, and the train station was a distance from their home. For their return, they set out on foot, carrying one small bag of clothing and two jugs of water. Annie was used to making camp in the desert. Mum was not, but as she knew her time in Australia was ending, she was quite willing to make do with whatever accommodation they could find.

The long journey afforded them time to talk, and it was the closest to her mum she had ever felt. Her mum was beginning to view Annie as a woman rather than a little girl. Annie hadn't told her about the ride in the jeep with the two generals, and she didn't tell her now. *There are some experiences in life,* Annie thought, *you should keep to yourself.* She didn't want to listen to a lecture on propriety from her mother. Plus, she was sure if a car or jeep or even a camel came along, Mum would be the first to beg a ride.

No one came along the road the first day out. At dusk, they found a bare stretch of red sand and put up a small lean-to overhead. As the land was almost deserted, they didn't have to worry about modesty. Besides, across the flat landscape, they could see vehicles coming miles before the driver could see them.

There were places in the desert with water, if you knew where to look. Dad had showed her how to find them, and she had passed the information along to Jeremiah. Mum didn't know about them. Her mum's excursions alone in the desert were rarer than her tight smiles. When Annie returned with a kangaroo pouch full of cold water, she passed it to her mum, who gave her a tired look. "You're at home here, Annie. More than Jeremiah or I will ever be." She gave Annie a long look, and Annie could read the sadness in her eyes. For all their differences, Annie was still her daughter. They loved each other with a casualness born of strength and knowledge. Annie understood her mother as her mum understood her — without words. "You're staying, aren't you?"

"Yes. And you're going to Scotland." She wanted to add that Jeremiah had needed her once, but now he could survive alone.

"Annie ..." Her mum struggled for words. "When I was so sick, I know you and Archie helped me get well."

"Mum ..." About to deny it, she felt held back by an invisible hand on her throat.

"No, don't dismiss your soul-knowledge, Annie. You think I don't see these things in you. You think I love Jeremiah more and understand him more. Well, I do understand him more. But I love you as much as I love Jerry. In many ways, I love you more. But I'm afraid of you. I know you have a power to heal, and that scares me. I don't know whether you are with God or the Devil."

"Mum, I don't believe in your Devil. And your God is the same as my Master Dreamer. I don't understand the power either. But you were not the first one I healed."

"I know." She looked at her scuffed shoes, covered in red dust.

"You know?"

"Yes. Remember the time Jerry hurt his arm?"

Annie remembered back. Jerry and she had been playing in the shed, and Jerry ran headlong into the rough metal wall. He was bruised, but Annie knew there was nothing more wrong with his arm. He had to be taught a lesson, so she let him suffer the bruises and scrapes. Seeing that Annie recalled the incident, her mum continued. "The next time I went into the doctor's for my illness, I asked him to look at Jerry's arm. He took an Xray and remarked on how well the old fracture healed. I didn't even know there was a fracture, but I'm sure you remember."

Annie did remember. It had been the year before Jerry bruised his arm. That time, she knew he was hurt and had healed him. When she didn't answer, her mother went on. "Then there was the snakebite, when your dad told us he was going to join the army. Jerry told me that he was certain he was bitten, but after you held his hand, he could find no sign of it. You scare me, Annie. But I know if I leave you in Australia, you'll survive. Neither Jerry nor I will survive for long out here."

She wanted to tell her mum that there were other parts of Australia, not just the desert. Mum and Jerry could go to the more temperate climates along the east or south coast. Nothing held them to the desert. Farther south, people grew the grapevines her mother loved. She wanted to say that Sydney, Brisbane, Melbourne, Adelaide, or Canberra were good cities, but Annie knew her words would be wasted.

It wasn't just the desert her mum was leaving. It was Dad. Whatever brought her here and held her for seventeen years was gone. Annie felt she had a good understanding of her mum. Living in an isolated desert town with close relationships and few distractions resulted in enhanced perceptions. Her mum would feel a bit guilty about leaving Annie, but she would not feel guilty about leaving Dad. Her mother had decided throughout the war years that she was returning to Scotland. And she found a perfectly good reason for going. She wanted Jerry to attend the university in Scotland. There was no thought about letting Jerry go by himself. If her life were different, she might have allowed him to test his wings alone. But as things stood, she needed him more than he needed her.

They ended up walking three-quarters of the way to Coober Pedy, and then a man in a Model T Ford picked them up. It was Mr. Walker, the new grocery store owner. A returning army veteran, he set up shop in the isolated town rather than one of the more populated cities. He seemed to like her mum a lot, but when he heard she was returning to Scotland, his enthusiasm cooled.

Annie's mother sat in the front seat, a kerchief tied round her head against the wind and sand. The car was not new. It had been around since long before the war, but Mr. Walker polished the black body and cleaned the leather seats until the whole thing sparkled. He prattled on about his prized possession until Annie thought her mother would jump out and walk. But she continued to smile and nod at every little detail. Annie watched her, fascinated. Her mum had never showed any interest in automobiles before. She had a way of making men feel important. Resentment stabbed Annie. Her mum had already drifted away from her dad, and there was no turning back.

She tried to catch her mother's eye, but the woman refused to look at her. If Annie were older or if she weren't mum's daughter, they would have laughed at the situation. But her mum wasn't about to change her behavior to suit her daughter. And she wasn't going to discuss her love life with the daughter of the man she was leaving behind. As it was, Mr. Walker let them out at the edge of town, and Annie and her mum walked to the north end. They arrived home and were greeted by Jeremiah. Glad to see them, he punched Annie on the arm as his hello, and he grabbed Mum, dancing her about and pecking her on the cheek. She glowed, and Annie knew they belonged together in Scotland.

It didn't take long to sell their few belongings and book passage for Mum and Jeremiah. Annie packed a small bag of her prized possessions. Her mum made her two new dresses and a pair of coveralls like the women wore in the factories during the war. Annie had never worn coveralls, but she could see the advantages. When they bought the material at Mrs. McFarlane's store, they had purchased a pair of sandals for Annie at the same time. It was the second pair of shoes she had owned. In the desert, she rarely needed any, but if she was to stay with her dad in the south, she would need shoes on her feet. As her mum said, they made her look more ladylike and presentable and would afford more comfort in the cooler climate.

"Are you sure you will be all right? Alone here with your dad?"

Annie nodded, unshed tears clogging her throat. She would have felt happier and safer in the desert. But with Mum and Jeremiah in Scotland and Dad legless in the hospital, that would not be the case. Dad could not come back to this place. She had to go to his.

Now that all the preparations were performed, time passed slowly. There wasn't anything holding them to their small house and the opal pit, yet they stayed. *Change always does that,* Annie thought. *What people know is comforting. What they don't know is terrifying.* She believed she felt more terrified than either Jerry or Mum, though.

The day for leaving arrived. Jerry took her hand, many words unsaid. "You'll come and visit, Annie. And when I'm finished with university, I'll come back here to visit you. And I'll write. I promise."

"We'll all keep in touch, Annie," her mum added. They were on their way to Alice Springs to take the train to Sydney. From there, they would embark on a ship and sail back to the craggy hills her mum called home. New people waited to move into Annie's home. She had found the opals her dad secreted in a small box in a hole in the wall, but she didn't tell her mum or Jeremiah. It surprised her that Mum didn't know about them, but with the war raging around them, she thought it was better that they hadn't known. That way any occupying power could not force them to reveal the opals' hiding place. Mum did not seem short of money, so Annie assumed she had funds from her Scottish family. Annie added a leather thong to the pouch and put it around her neck under her dress. Her dad needed the opals more than Mum or Jeremiah did.

They said their good-byes on the road leading out of town. Mum and Jeremiah were getting a ride with Mr. Walker in his black car, while Annie headed south on foot, a water canteen slung across her shoulder. When she was a short distance from Coober Pedy, she left the road and walked through the desert where she felt safer than on the white man's road. The time she had spent observing Mum with Dad and with Mr. Walker made Annie more aware of her body, an awareness Mrs. McFarlane set in motion.

As she scuffed through the red sand, she examined her feelings about Jeremiah and Mum. It surprised her to realize that she bore no ill will toward them. They were right. She would fit into the Scottish society as well as they would fit into the Aborigine society. Mrs. McFarlane had said once that love made everything all right. She referred to Annie's mum and dad when she said it. Annie knew that Mrs. McFarlane was wrong. There were things that even love couldn't make right. One of them was trying to grow a mulga tree and an English rose in the same soil. It was like Mum trying to grow primroses in the desert where only the desert rose flourished. She guessed the secret was adaptation, but people were stubborn and forced their wills onto any situation. Either they succeeded, or they didn't. Mum hadn't.

Under different circumstances, Jeremiah could have loved his desert home, or at least the Australian continent. Annie spent a few hours contemplating how their lives would have changed if Mum had died. Her dad would have put Jeremiah into one of their own universities so he would have been able to practice medicine here. This contemplation did not last long. Dad had told her once never to live life on what-ifs. One never knew when the Master Dreamer would cut short his dream, and you would be left with nothing but a universe of what-ifs. She concentrated instead on surviving the desert and getting to Melbourne.

CHAPTER 29

She was two days into the desert when she felt her throat tighten. She sipped her water sparingly, wondering what was happening with her body. She could not recall ever being ill. She raised her head and looked around. "Now is not a good time for this," she said to the blue sky and the red sand. Ignoring the dull ache, she plodded on with her few possessions on her back.

She used the boomerang that her dad had made many years before and caught a small rabbit. Jeremiah had tried both the boomerang and the throwing stick, but he had more luck with his BB gun. They didn't have many store-bought toys, but the gun, which Mum saw as a food source, was Jerry's Christmas gift one year. It went with him to Scotland, a memory of his desert past. She toted a pot for water and cooking, her meager clothing supply, the boomerang, the opals, and nothing else. Finding herself putting her hand to the pouch around her neck, she forced herself not to betray the opals' hiding place. She had no idea of the opals' worth and brought them along only at her dad's request.

She was not lonely on the trip. There were kangaroos bounding across the red sands, buzzards circling overhead, and the occasional dingo howling. A dingo followed her for a few miles, but sensing she wasn't about to become its meal, it slunk off in search of other prey. She hadn't seen any wallabies about and took the only rabbit that crossed her path. But she walked continually slower, her limbs refusing to obey and her throat burning. On the fifth day, she was forced to find a desert oak and curl up under it, shivering and scared.

Images danced before her. First was a black male of prehistoric Australia. She knew she loved him and had helped him somehow. *Thank you, An-ee, for showing me how to live and heal.* A kalbin appeared. *Forgive me, An-ee. You were right.*

A blond Englishman appeared. *Annie, I am so sorry for the way I treated you. But you are strong, Annie. Much stronger than I ever was.* A young boy floated across her line of vision. *Thank you, Mam, for showing me the way and for showing me how to heal.*

Jeremiah leaned over her, smiling. *Thank you, Annie, for showing me how to heal and live.*

If she had shown them how to live, why couldn't she will herself to become well? She thrashed on the sand, her hand hitting the bundle she carried. "Mum! Mum!" Her voice was a whisper lost in the leaves of the desert oak. A buzzard swooped down and sat watching her as she cried out. It spoke. "Annie! Annie! Pull in the power, Annie. Pull in the power. Breathe deeply. Pull in the white light. Pull in the healing light. Call on Archie, Annie. Call on Archie."

She started to cry. Mum and Jerry had left her. Dad was lying in the hospital wounded. She was alone. She was sick. Hot tears drenched her fevered face. Her throat was too swollen even to sip water. She could not will her limbs to move. She sobbed, but her cries choked her even more. Suddenly, Archie appeared in kalbin dress. He smiled at her. *"Is this any way for a healer to be, little one? Pull in the power, Annie. Pull in the power."*

She clutched Archie's hand and breathed as deeply as possible through her aching, swollen throat. In her fevered mind, she knew what she must do. She visualized the white light and pulled it in through her crown chakra and into her throat chakra. The healing light turned blue. Down into her heart, the light became a healing green. Into her solar plexus, and it was yellow, and into her sacral chakra as orange. Finally, she pulled it into her root chakra as red. It spread throughout her body as a white, healing light. Archie gave her a huge smile. *"You did it, Annie. I knew you would."* She lay on the red sand for hours in a deep sleep, and when she awoke, she had only a slight sore throat.

The climate was cooler as she neared the southern cities, but it was still mild enough to go barefoot. As she approached the hospital in Melbourne, she found a town pump and let cold water wash over her sandy feet. Taking advantage of the cover from a dense bush, she pulled off the coveralls that she had worn against the flies, put on one of her new dresses, and slipped on her new sandals. Walking into the hospital, Annie glanced at herself in the glass window and liked what she saw. Her face had resumed its tan after her illness, and one would never know she had recently been ill. She would keep that information to herself. Her dad had enough worries.

Once inside the hospital, she had another setback. When she explained her mission to the desk clerk, she was informed that her dad was moved from the hospital in Melbourne to a rehabilitation hospital in Adelaide. Annie's face registered her consternation.

"Oh dear! You had no idea, had you, love?" The clerk put her hand on Annie's arm in concern.

Annie shook her head and felt her shoulders slump. The prospect of seeing her dad had kept her going on the long journey through the desert. Now she was further from her goal. If she had known he was moved, she could have headed in the direction of Adelaide at the outset and been there sooner. As it was, she had shifted east each day until she came to this metropolis. She had only the few pounds and shillings her mum gave her, and she had no idea how far the money would go in the city.

"Well, I suppose it's the hospital's fault nobody informed you. Wait here a moment, love, and I'll get the almoner for you." The clerk shuffled down the brown, linoleum-covered corridor, her rump swaying side to side. In another situation, Annie would have found it comical. She had no idea what or who an almoner was and less idea of why she needed one.

The clerk returned a few moments later with a hunched man in tow. He had a kind face and piercing blue eyes behind gold-rimmed spectacles. Annie liked him immediately. Despite no physical resemblance, he reminded her of Archie. Archie was a full-blooded Arrernte; this man spoke with the rounded British voice she had heard on BBC radio. "You're in a bit of a pickle, I hear?"

Annie had no idea what he had heard, but obviously the clerk gave him bits of information gleaned from her assessment of the situation. "I came to pick up my dad, but the clerk tells me he was moved to Adelaide." She had no intention of telling him she would be walking the distance, or that she had walked into the hospital after weeks crossing the hot desert. To them it was unthinkable that a British subject was in such needy straits.

"You'll have to take the train to Adelaide. It leaves tomorrow morning at six sharp. Our hospital has vouchers for people who need them ..." His voice trailed off. He waited to see if she would accept his offer. Annie had no qualms about doing so. She was not about to divulge the opals she carried. Not knowing what the future would bring, she clung to the few pounds and gems like Scrooge in Mum's battered copy of Dickens' *A Christmas Carol.*

With the train voucher as well as one for food and another for a hostel, she left the hospital feeling easier than at any time since she had left the desert. Not being accustomed to big towns, she felt at a loss, and Melbourne's size staggered her. Stopping to check out the hostel, she asked Betty, the woman in charge, to tell her something about the place.

The town was already a hundred years old. Sitting as it did along the harbor of Port Phillip Bay, Melbourne was a beautiful example of a planned city. It began as a gold rush town and continued as a manufacturing center. A half hour later, Annie wandered the wide streets looking at the universities and schools, watching the day students in their school uniforms playing or sitting on the lush, green grass.

It was nothing for her to spend hours walking in the desert, but she was unused to walking on such hard pavement. Her hand clutched at the money in her pocket, and without giving it further thought, she boarded a tram for the first time. At that time of day, there were few riders. It was mostly shopping housewives chattering away to their neighbors. For a while, it was a novelty to sit and sway gently side to side as the streetcar swayed down Collins Street. She was reminded of the hospital clerk's rump.

When a traveler pulled the cord to exit, she got off too. She didn't know where she was, but with her sense of direction, she knew how to get back to the hostel. On the north side of the Yarra River, she paused to gaze at the parliament buildings and businesses grown out of the gold rush days. To the east, she spotted a green park and decided to stroll along to it so she could run her bare feet through the cool grass.

The south side of the river was not as beautiful as the north with its planned city. The other side was filled with factories, spewing out smoke from their chimneys. You weren't supposed to notice the south side, Betty said. People looked in disgust at the dirtiness and barrenness of the south side, yet Annie could see it was the essential part of the city. She was amused how people always tried to hide the plain facts of their lives. In Coober Pedy, nobody ever thought of doing that. If you were an opal miner, that's what you were. There was no sense trying to pretend you were anything else. It seemed Melbourne wanted to be something it was not. It wanted to be the north side while ignoring the south side. Annie knew she would never fit in there and was glad that her dad had been moved.

Cultured voices floated about her as she sat on the grass, and she wondered how the voices from the other side of the river sounded. She was sure she wouldn't hear them that afternoon in the park. The south side voices were hushed as their owners worked hard in the warehouses and factories. Those voices would be heard only on holidays when families boarded the streetcars and rode to the park for an outing. After an hour, tired of the greenness and the flowing voices, she slipped on her sandals and walked back to the hostel. The aroma of soup wafted through the open door, reminding her that she hadn't eaten in hours.

She didn't have to worry about waking up in time for the train the next morning. At five, the rattling of carts along the hallway penetrated her dreams. Breakfast was being prepared, but she had to leave. She looked longingly at the breakfast cart as she signed out at the desk. Before she could even ask, a portly woman, who looked remarkably like the hospital clerk, came over and gave her a bag with a roll and butter for her journey. Annie thanked her and was out the door and running for the streetcar by 5:30 AM.

Arriving at the train station with five minutes to spare, she had no time to look around. The conductor was already picking up his step stool for departure. He slowed as he saw her running. "Just made it, you did, Miss." He looked at her voucher and saw that she was heading for Adelaide. "Two cars down on your left. Hurry it up now. Do you have luggage?" She shook her head and did as he said. Considering the hour of the morning, a surprising number of people held seats on the Overlander. After taking a seat next to a kindly looking, gray-haired woman, Annie found there was only one daily train to Adelaide, and thankfully she was on it. She settled down to experience the twelve-hour ride.

The woman reminded her of Mrs. McFarlane, though Annie was sure she didn't delight in pert innuendo. The woman, who announced herself as Mrs. Moore, was departing the train at a halfway stop and chattered on about seeing her daughter and grandchildren. The woman asked about Annie's parents, and when she learned Annie's mum had returned to Scotland and her dad was in the hospital, her lips tightened. It intrigued Annie the way people's lips tightened when she mentioned Mum going home to Scotland. "Couldn't have picked a worse time, she couldn't. What was she thinking?"

"I'm used to looking after myself, Mrs. Moore. My brother and I were raised to be independent."

"Humph! Looks to me like *you're* the independent one. Your brother is with your mum. Not much independence there, love. And what with your dad wounded and all, it's a sorry mess, it is."

"You don't think Mum should have gone back home then, Mrs. Moore?" Annie contemplated the woman's words. Mrs. Moore hadn't seen how miserable Mum had become, and she certainly hadn't seen her face when she saw Dad legless in his hospital bed. "Mum is quite a strong person in many ways, Mrs. Moore. But I know she wouldn't have been comfortable around Dad for long. My mother doesn't like illness or disabilities. Yet I saw her struggle with a vegetable garden, struggle with her own illness. I guess we all have strengths and weaknesses."

"You're wise for one so young. We sent our daughter to university, and she still isn't as wise as you. Well, love. I wish you all the best. I do."

They were an hour away from Mrs. Moore's stop, but she had nothing more to say. Annie spent the time observing the passing scenery. As Mrs. Moore rose to retrieve her luggage, she pressed a folded piece of paper into Annie's hand. "This is for any emergencies. You don't have to pay it back, and this is my daughter's address if you should need it. Hope you find your dad all right, Abbie." Annie was about to correct the woman, but then decided against it. They had only met for a few hours, and what difference did it make if she called her Annie or Abbie? They would not meet again. Mrs. Moore would tell the story of the strange girl she had met on the train and how her mother had gone off to Scotland and left her alone. Then the whole incident would slip into oblivion.

As the woman alighted from the train, Annie waved good-bye and settled back in her seat, still clutching the folded piece of paper. After some time, curiosity overcame her, and she opened her hand. Along with the address of the woman's daughter were two one-pound notes. Tears pricked Annie's eyes. The woman did not dress like she was well-to-do. She thought back to their conversation. Yes, Mrs. Moore definitely said she and her husband owned a hardware store. Annie vowed to repay her, but at the moment she bought food from the rail dining car to fill her empty stomach. The Master Dreamer was looking after her. The money in her pocket would last another few days.

The dry cheese sandwich was nowhere near as tasty as the roll and butter she had that morning, but she was famished enough to eat the whole thing in three gulps and followed it with two cups of tea. As she would get no more of her mum's homemade bread, Annie decided to get used to what she could get.

The clacking train wheels sang *Waltzing Matilda* with every mile passed, and her eyes became heavy with sleep. She didn't want to close her eyes, for she didn't know what the Master Dreamer had in store next. He hadn't warned her that she would become ill. He hadn't let her know that she wouldn't find her dad at Melbourne. He had let her walk those long miles for nothing. But if she hadn't, she never would have seen the beautiful city or William Butterfield's magnificent St. Paul's Cathedral with its statue of Matthew Flinders, the first seaman to circumnavigate the coastline—well, the first seaman the white people knew. Coober Pedy had nothing to compare.

In front of the older St. Patrick's Cathedral was a statue of Daniel O'Connell, an Irish patriot. Taking eighty-two years to complete, the cathedral was finished in the early years of the war. Annie smiled as she thought how her schoolteachers would react to her knowledge of Australian history. It was the one and only subject in which she had surpassed Jeremiah in marks. She may not have been their best student, not like Jeremiah, but she could hold her own in Australian history. She had even told them some things about Aboriginal lore that she was sure they didn't know. Congratulating herself on her memory reminded her of Jerry, and she was homesick for the first time. She wondered where Mum and Jerry were and what they were doing.

It had taken her weeks to walk the distance from Coober Pedy to Melbourne. In that time, Mum and Jerry would have arrived at Sydney and booked passage on a ship to the northern hemisphere. Their journey was taking them thousands of miles away in distance and unbounded miles in remembrance. She once heard Mum say that absence makes the heart grow fonder.

CHAPTER 30

It was supper hour and city movement had thinned by the time the train arrived in Adelaide. Annie wasn't hungry. Now that she was here, she was anxious to find her dad. Alighting from the train, she asked the Station Master the hospital's location and set out on foot with his directions in hand. It wasn't a difficult task. If she thought Melbourne was a well-planned city, Adelaide was even more so. William Light drew the plans for the city in 1836, Mrs. Moore had said between admonishing Annie's absent mother and chatting about her grandchildren. He chose a flat area of land with Mount Lofty on one side and the sea on the other.

In Adelaide, she was closer to the desert, which had been her home. Whether it was made by her mum's God or her dad's Master Dreamer, the land was impressive. Annie heard little about Mum's God making the cities and towns of the world, though. According to her dad, the Master Dreamer made everything. His helper, Boodjammula the rainbow serpent, formed the streams in the Dreamtime to keep his skin wet. That accounted for the mighty Murray River in the south and the Yarra river, which split Melbourne into two cultures. Annie figured Mum's God wasn't interested in helping his people in this way.

She found her dad in the physiotherapy ward, trying out his new legs. When he saw her, his grin spread so wide she nearly cried out. How could her mum leave him? Dad was a softhearted man, not given to cursing and swearing like a lot of men she knew. If he displayed wrath at times, it was to rail against the drunken ways of his black kin. He wanted so much to see his people advance that when he saw them mishandling liquor, Annie saw a little of him shrivel.

"You're back then, lass. Tell me all about it." He hobbled to her, steadying and balancing himself with his hands on the rails.

"Come on, girl. No tears. There's a girl." He brushed the tears from her face and steered her towards a wheelchair where he promptly sat down, relief on his face. "You push your old dad, girl. There's a lovely bench outside." She grabbed the handles and did as he asked.

"How's your mum?" His first thought would always be for her mum, whether she was here or miles away. Annie wanted to yell at him. She was the one who stayed for him, not Mum. Mum left him behind to fend for himself. She couldn't say that, though, because she loved her dad and knew he would be hurt. And she understood her mum's reasons for leaving.

"She was fine, the last I saw her. I left them when they turned north to Alice Springs, and I turned south to come here." He hadn't asked how she knew he was moved to a new hospital. "I went to Melbourne. Nobody told us you'd moved."

"What! The hospital told me they notified your mum a week before they moved me here. Well, it's no matter now. You've found me. It's gorgeous here, Annie. I have to stay a bit longer to get used to my new legs, but then you and I can go and explore. Would you like that?"

"Yes." He didn't ask how she got from Coober Pedy to Melbourne and Adelaide or how long it took her. She wanted to tell him about becoming ill on the desert, but she knew he was wrapped up in his own problems and did not have time for hers.

"Don't you want to know how I got here from Melbourne, Dad? The hospital gave me a voucher to stay the night in Melbourne and a voucher for the train. They said that if they made the mistake, they should compensate. On the train, I met a wonderful lady, Mrs. Moore, whose daughter lives about halfway between here and Melbourne. When Mrs. Moore got off the train, she gave me two pounds." Annie was prattling on, unable to stop herself.

"Do you have no money then, girl?" He gave her a quizzical look, a frown creasing his brow.

"I have the opals you told me to get, and Mum gave me three pounds. But I was keeping it until I needed it. I walked from Coober Pedy to Melbourne. You know I don't mind walking. Must be our ancestors coming out in me." She tried to joke with him, but he was clearly upset.

"I asked your mum to make sure you had at least twenty pounds to get you started." He spoke quietly, almost unwilling to let the words exit his mouth. "I sent my pay each month."

"She was caught up in leaving for Scotland. And I didn't want to part with any of the opals. I know you're counting on them." Pulling the pouch from around her neck, she emptied the seven opals into his palm. He stared at them. "There should be one more, Annie. A big one. These aren't good opals; they won't fetch much." He swallowed hard.

"This is all I found. Mum must have taken it."

"Your Mum has many opals. Each time I found an exceptionally nice one, I gave it to her. And she had money from her family. There was more than enough for their passage to England, their transportation to Scotland, and Jeremiah's education."

"But nobody was taking opals during the war. Mum may have spent her money during the war and used the opals for passage." Annie was searching for answers. It seemed odd Mum did not bring up the subject. She saw her dad make a determined effort to be cheerful.

"So, Annie, how much have you got then, girl? Enough to hang in with your dad for a while?" He put his arm about her shoulders.

"Six pounds. I guess I'll have to find a job, in a shop if possible. I understand the retail business, though I don't know how. I thought I would look after you, but I can see the best thing is to get work."

"I have a war pension. That will take care of most of our needs. We don't need much, girl. At least I don't. But I imagine you will want a few shillings for yourself. Maybe you can get a part-time job." His voice became almost a whisper, and there was a distance in his eyes. "I love you around me, but I can take care of myself, good legs or bad."

"Have you ever thought of going back to our Aborigine people?" It was a question that was on her mind for several years, ever since Archie enlisted her to help heal Mum.

"I don't belong there, girl, any more than I belong to my white kin. Much less, I'd say. I had two black grandparents, and you had two black great-grandparents. Funny, isn't it? You and I seem to carry our black ancestry more than our white."

Annie thought they related to their black parentage because they lived physically closer to the people, while she never saw nor learned to love Mum's Scottish relatives. The one letter Mum received after she decided to return was quite sharp in its rebuke. Annie's Scottish grandmother could no more understand Mum's decision to leave Annie behind than could Mrs. Moore on the train. She had to admit, deep down she expected Mum to realize she had made a mistake and send for her. She wasn't going to wait around for it, though. Besides, at the moment, Dad needed her more than Mum or Jeremiah did.

If Jeremiah were on his own, Annie would say he needed her close by. But with Mum to look after him, she doubted Jerry would miss his sister too much. He would be in university and finding new chums. But she did look forward to hearing about his new life and would always worry about him.

Her dad left the hospital about a week after she found him. He healed well, considering his substantial loss. Once he learned to maneuver on his new legs, they set out. Her dad walked on crutches, and she carried his bag and handled his wheelchair. The bus station was nearby and they found a seat. Waiting, her dad pulled a stone amulet from under his shirt. "This is yours now, Annie. It protected me in the war, but it was always meant for you. Archie gave it into your keeping, but your mum wouldn't let me give it to you. She said it was pagan and against her God." He placed the stone around Annie's neck, and it slipped beneath the collar of her dress.

"Did you know Archie asked me about this once? He thought I already had it." Annie fingered the small stone, warm against her skin, and she knew it was powerful.

"He asked me about it too and why you didn't have it. It's hard to explain beliefs to someone who is not open to them. Archie didn't understand your mum's beliefs, and she didn't understand Archie's, so I didn't give it to you before."

Adelaide was on the edge of the desert area they had left, and although the green grass, cooling trees, and flocks of birds were refreshing, she knew Dad wouldn't be happy until they were back close to Coober Pedy or Alice Springs. They talked the matter over at length, but in the end, they decided to let the Master Dreamer guide them. After all, this was his dream they were living, her dad said with a grin.

She wondered why they had to suffer to fulfill some fantasy. But when she mentioned this to Dad, he gave her a black look telling her she shouldn't question the Master Dreamer's motives. She didn't place the Master Dreamer on a pedestal the way her dad did or the way Mum placed her God on one. She knew he wasn't sitting in judgment up in the sky somewhere. When she had said as much to her mum one day, she slapped Annie across the face in horror that she would blaspheme her deity. After that, Annie kept such thoughts to herself.

They endured the long, hot bus ride to Alice Springs. Annie wondered how her dad's Master Dreamer could dream up such purgatory. *Why do I always think of him as Dad's Master Dreamer?* she thought. When they alighted from the bus, Dad had difficulty getting down the steps, and the bus driver helped him.

Annie felt she had come home. She loved Coober Pedy, but there was an aura about Alice Springs that grabbed her heart. She knew the place. Seating her dad in his wheelchair and guiding him as fast as possible, she told him she had dreamt for three straight nights about finding a store where she would work. Two blocks away from the bus depot, she found the dry goods store that she dreamed would be there. She felt for the amulet. In the window was a sign: HELP WANTED. She went in, leaving her dad outside with his jaw hanging open.

"Good afternoon. Are you the proprietor?" She turned on her best voice.

"Yes. Mr. Peart. What can I do for you, young lady?"

"No. It's what my father and I can do for you, Mr. Peart. We're here to help out in the store."

He stood bewildered by her forthright attitude just as Dad was outside. Finally he managed, "I need only one person."

"Then, you've got her." She tried to remember all the things she had learned over the years from Mrs. McFarlane in Coober Pedy. She knew she would be good at the job. "I see many of your groceries are still rationed. I'm sure more will come in as the factories and businesses get going again." She glanced about the store. "Do you import your wool, or are you buying from the sheep ranchers here?" From somewhere came a familiarity with Mr. Peart's business, and she carried on a knowledgeable conversation. She guessed the Master Dreamer had heard her questions and decided to prove he knew what he was doing.

"What do you say, Mr. Peart? I have my father outside. He's a wounded war veteran. I can look after his needs and look after your store too. If you don't need Dad, I imagine he can find a job elsewhere."

"Well, you do sound as if you know what you're talking about. So, yes, the job is yours. As for your father, I believe the shoemaker down the street is looking for help."

"Thank you, sir. Now, when do you wish me to start? We have to find living quarters first, and I can be here soon after that. And we'll check out that shoemaker." Annie found she could be quite businesslike when prompted. She hadn't taken on that role too often and would have to perfect it. The irony of her father working for a shoemaker did not escape her, and she wondered how her dad would react.

Mr. Peart's eyes twinkled. "Young lady, you've told me how good you are, and that I need you, but I don't recall you giving me your name."

"Annie, Mr. Peart. Call me Annie. Now, do you know where Dad and I can find living quarters? It doesn't have to be much, at least for now. Even a boarding house to start."

"Well, Mrs. MacDonald has a boarding house over on the next street. I'm sure she would love to have two paying boarders. Shall I ring her for you?"

"Please, Mr. Peart. We can pay her the first week's rent. Tell her Will and his daughter Annie are in town." She was walking on air and felt like singing but managed to control her exuberance. Dad would be surprised. He hadn't expected such good luck.

Mr. Peart ended his conversation with Mrs. MacDonald and hung up the phone. "When you and your father are settled, come back and I'll show you around the store. I don't suppose I have to show you too much. You sound as though you've had a good deal of experience."

She didn't want to do anything to make Mr. Peart reconsider his assertion, so she thanked him and walked back into the shaded street. Dad was sitting under a striped awning when she left, but now he sat on a bench at the edge of a wide street. He was looking worn, and Annie knew the ordeal of the bus ride and the newness of their situation were wearing on him. However, she approached with a grin.

"Done. I start as soon as we find a place to stay, and we already have that. We'll go there now. Then you will go and meet your new employer, the shoemaker. I know you haven't got the job yet, but you will get it. Our Master Dreamer is looking out for us. Unless you would rather rest for a bit first." She added the last thought hesitantly.

"A shoemaker?" They both broke into loud laughter at the irony. Dad did not like being viewed as less than capable, so she knew he would do well at the job. He looked at her in amazement and chagrin. "And where did I get such a go-getter daughter? And a bossy one at that?"

She laughed. "Come on, Dad. We're going to Mrs. MacDonald's place, which is just one street over. I hope it's as lovely as this street. I feel like I've come home. Do you have that feeling?"

"Can't say as I have exactly that feeling, but I do feel good about our coming here. Especially as you have a job the minute you arrive."

CHAPTER 31

Three years at Alice Springs passed in a blur of activity for Annie and her dad. She made friends and became an invaluable asset to Mr. Peart's store. Wherever he went, her dad was feted as a war hero. He never talked about his war experiences. There were a lot of men like him, Annie noticed. They went off to fight the enemy, but found the real enemy was within. Often you had more enemies at home than on the battlefield. And the young men paid, Mrs. MacDonald said before supper one evening. The generals, like the ones who gave Annie a ride, did the planning at a safe distance from the front.

Dad was happy. But he had the disposition to accept whatever the Master Dreamer dreamed for him. Annie wouldn't hear him singing to Mum down in his opal pit anymore, but he sang as he helped Mr. Hebert, the shoemaker. Together they turned out beautiful shoes and tuneful melodies for their customers. Her dad never talked about Mum. He knew she wouldn't come back. He did ask once if Annie had heard from Jeremiah, but no news came from them in three years. She wrote a letter to Mum in care of the address of her Scottish grandmother, but she hadn't received a reply.

If she wasn't cherished by her Scottish kinfolk, Annie was appreciated by Mr. Peart. When business was slow, he regaled her with stories of how his great grandparents came to Australia to begin a new life. He told her how they hired an Aboriginal girl named Annie, like her. Mr. Peart liked to jest that he was carrying on a family tradition when he hired her.

For Annie's part, she felt she belonged to his family more than to her own, barring Dad and Jeremiah. Mr. Peart and Dad got along well, and often the three men, Mr. Hebert, her dad, and Mr. Peart, harmonized in song at the local pub. Of course, they needed to limber up their voices with a drink or two first. This worried her. She kept thinking of Archie and finding him dead from drink.

"That will never happen to me, Annie, so stop worrying." Dad looked her straight in the eye, and she knew he told the truth. None of the three drank to excess, and she worried little about the other two, anyway. If they wanted to get drunk, it was okay with her. It was their family they would contend with. Still, she never saw any of them drunk.

One day, there was a letter in their post office box from Mum. It was addressed to Annie, and Annie saw the disappointment in her dad's eyes. He didn't say much, but he turned away, feigning interest in the kangaroo leather he was working into a handbag for Annie's birthday. Dad was hard-pressed to keep secrets, and that purse was on his mind from the start of his job. Once her dad learned the rudiments of leatherworking, Mr. Hebert gave him a piece of kangaroo hide, and he set to work making the handbag. Now he bent over the work, pretending to be absorbed as she tore open the letter.

My dear Annie,

I hope this finds you and your father in good health. Jeremiah and I are both keeping well. Jerry will be going into his third year at the university and has won several honors. Even I am surprised how well he is doing. Your grandmother dotes on him, so of course he is spoiled. He says he isn't, but you know Jerry. He is still clumsy, and now he doesn't have you to bail him out of his scrapes. He told me one day they were in the laboratory doing experiments when a test tube shattered in his hand. No one was badly hurt, thank goodness. Jerry had a few minor cuts, and he remarked that he wished you were here to heal his hand.

Would you believe sometimes I miss the hot air of the desert? I had forgotten how humid and damp Scottish weather can be. When we visit your uncle along the coast, the sharp winds are so biting they go right through a heavy coat. I try to picture what you would think of Scotland. I'm sure you would be homesick the whole time. I feel guilty for leaving you behind, but your grandmother says to let sleeping dogs lie. That time in Coober Pedy is in my past, and you belong to that time.

I do miss your dad's laughing voice and singing from the opal pit. I did enjoy Will at first. But I went to your dad when I was newly widowed. I was alone with a son and without money. I was scared what would become of us. That is when your dad offered me a home. At the time, it seemed the best thing to do. I knew he loved me more than I ever loved him, but he was willing to accept that. I don't know why he never married before. He never talked about his life before we met. When you came along, his life was more than complete. You are his life. I know you feel the bond between you, just as you always had a special bond with Jerry. Please try to forgive me for leaving you. You are much better there than here. I will try to get Jeremiah to write. I know you must miss him. We both recognize that you were always there to help him. Well, I hear your granny shouting that supper's on, so I will end this. I don't know why I am writing to you, except I had the urge to do so. If you are still with your father, please convey my deepest appreciation to him.

Love, your mother, Katharine

"Mother sends her love to you. See? The words are right here." She put the letter under his nose, assured he wouldn't read it, although he loved to read anything he could get his hands on. She didn't have to worry that she changed her mother's appreciation to love. Mama did not write to him, and that said it all. She could convey her love all she wanted, but if it was secondhand, it was no love at all.

Annie sat for a long time at the window reading and re-reading that letter, trying to find a hint of love or real regret. There was none, either implicitly or directly in her words. Annie was part of a time that her mother would rather forget. What was it she said? The weather. Sometimes, she longed for the hot weather. Not, *I long for you.* Or *I long for your dad.* She longed for the weather.

Her dad sat engrossed in his leatherwork until the room darkened. Annie went to him and put her arms around his shoulders. He had lost a lot of weight since returning from the war, but otherwise he was in good physical health. She wanted to ask him why he didn't marry again. She knew his answer. He loved Mother. There would never be anyone else for him. When she gave it thought, and she often did, she felt she should live alone. It would force him to find a woman to replace her, but she couldn't do it.

Mrs. MacDonald rang the gong summoning her ten boarders to supper. Annie and her dad had the best rooms, and Annie felt sure that Mrs. MacDonald had a soft spot for Dad. Her husband had lost his life in the war defending his country. Annie wondered if she resented Will for living when her husband hadn't. But Mrs. MacDonald could see that Will had his own problems. Annie thought, though, their landlady would be happy to help him bear them.

The table was set with good china as usual. A lamb roast graced the middle of the table, and a gravy boat sat at each end. Mashed potatoes in two bowls were placed by the middle chairs, and dishes of carrots and brussels sprouts added color. Mrs. MacDonald always had fresh, nourishing food for her boarders. They were the family she never had with her lost husband.

Few people have a talent for that, Annie thought. It was a gift to make others feel at home. That's why she and her dad were still there after three years. They had earned enough to buy a small house, but Annie couldn't see that happening soon. She didn't miss having a home to fix, and Dad felt more comfortable here than he ever would in his own home. Mrs. MacDonald gave him the womanly attention he missed from his wife. Not sex. Annie didn't think that entered their relationship. Dad was too aware of his wife rejecting his legless body to offer himself to another woman. Annie doubted he could withstand that again.

For the most part, they were content. Her dad worried that she had not found a beau yet. Annie liked young men, and there were a couple she dated casually. But Dad was looking for signs that she found the man she was going to marry. He felt he held her back, but she felt no need for the company of men her age. At the back of her mind was an ephemeral feeling. She felt as though she waited on the edge of a great climactic event. If anyone asked her about it, she couldn't explain it. She just knew something was about to happen. She had told her dad about healing herself in the desert, but he looked at her doubtfully. He did allow her to use the power on him, though, when his body ached from phantom pains, or he was exhausted from work. He asked her once if Archie appeared each time. When she told him he didn't, he looked at her quizzically, not knowing how to handle the situation. Annie laughed. She didn't understand it either, but she knew the power worked.

When her dad tried to push her out of what he called the *nest*, she laughed and told him that when she was ready, neither he nor all the king's horses would hold her back. She was eighteen and a half, not in any hurry. Besides, she had never mentioned it to her dad, but she often had a feeling that she could only call a suspension of time and life. She didn't know what it was, but it caused her to view life in a more detached manner, as if she were standing outside her life and looking on.

"You're not pining for Jeremiah, are you, Annie? You can't mother your half-brother forever, you know." Dad peered at her over his new reading glasses as he put down the newspaper with a sigh. He was sitting by the window in a comfortable chair that Mrs. MacDonald had slip-covered in floral chintz, making their suite of rooms cozy. Most of the boarders had single rooms, but she and her dad had two bedrooms and a sitting room. They didn't have a kitchen, as they took most of their meals with Mrs. MacDonald. They did have a kettle, however, and it was now singing on a hot plate in one corner of the room. Annie went over to make a pot of tea.

"No, Dad. I wish Jerry would write, but I'm not missing him in the way you mean. I know Jerry will do well. After all, he had your influence for many years."

"And yours, Annie. Don't discount your influence in all our lives. Annie ..." Her dad hesitated, not knowing how to say what was on his mind. "Do you remember Archie saying that Jeremiah has some Aboriginal blood?"

"Just that one time when I was little, but I think Archie was mistaken."

"Archie said once he was certain there was Aboriginal blood in Jeremiah's background. I know it's hard to believe with his blond hair and blue eyes and your mum's aversion to all things black. I never said anything to your mum, and I ask you don't either. Your mum may not have known. Or if she did, she wouldn't want anyone else to know."

The tea was steeped, and she took it to him. He put out his arm for the cup and smiled at her. "I know you think I'm a worry wart, Annie," he said by way of changing the subject. "But you are my daughter, and I want you to be happy. I don't see how you can be happy looking after an old man like me."

She laughed. "If it were anyone else, I would think you were fishing for a compliment. You are still a fine-looking man, and at forty-eight, you're young enough to make half the women in Alice Springs swoon. Why haven't you gotten another woman?"

"Oh, Annie." He took a sip of his tea and sighed again. "No woman would want a cripple like me."

"You're wrong. Just because Mum couldn't accept your injuries, doesn't mean there aren't women who would love to have you. No! Don't deny it. You can't tell me you aren't aware of the way women fawn all over you. Mrs. MacDonald for one." She leaned down and kissed his cheek.

"You make a great cup of tea, Annie. I'm sure that's your Scottish side coming out, however much you'd like to renounce that heritage." He took another long sip of tea. "Annie, don't be too hard on your mum, all right? She tried to make a go of it here, but it was never meant to be. And don't be bitter she left you here. If you look deep in your heart, you will find that you would never be happy anywhere but Australia."

"I know that. And I do forgive Mum, I do. At least I forgive her for leaving me here. But I don't know if I can forgive her for walking out on *you* when you needed her most."

"You know what, Annie? Your mum and I both know you are beyond us in maturity. And she knew what she was doing by letting you stay here with me. You influenced Jeremiah all his young life, and it was time for you to let go. Besides, you're good for your old man, girl. Now, I guess we better get to the supper table. No sense in getting Mrs. MacDonald's dander up."

Neither of them wanted that. For all her good suppers and clean rooms, Mrs. MacDonald had a fiery temper to match her red hair. Annie put their cups in the sink by the hot plate, and she and her dad went downstairs to Mrs. MacDonald's succulent meal.

Three weeks later, Annie was surprised to find a letter from Jeremiah at the post office. Her fingers itched to open it, but she finished her work before she let herself tear open the envelope. She thought of waiting until she met with her dad, but after the episode of her mother's letter and her dad's disappointment, she decided to open it as she left the store. Instead of hurrying to fetch her dad from the shoemaker's, she sat on the bench for a few minutes and nodded to a couple of customers entering the store. With trembling hands, Annie tore open the letter.

My dearest Annie,

I know you must be disappointed that I haven't written before this. My excuse is university life is very hectic. I barely have time to say hello to Mother or Grandmother these days. I finished my pre-medical courses and will now be starting my medical degree. I don't know how often I've thought about you, but it has been quite often lately. Do you know why? The other day, one of my chums and I were talking about how great we are going to be as doctors. My friends have this conviction they will be like gods. Well, I have that feeling too. But every time I think that way, I picture the way you healed Mum and the day you healed my arm in the opal pit. And then there was that time the snake bit me. I lost track of how many other times. I guess I want to say I know there is more to medicine than handing out pills. And here is something that will smack you in the face. I just found out from Mum I have a little Aborigine blood in me – not as much as you have, but some. She wouldn't tell me any more, and I think she hopes it won't show up somewhere down the line.

I can't tell my chums, because they all look at me askance when I mention you and Aborigine healing. They love to tease me whenever I get on the topic. They call me The Witch Doctor's brother. I don't have any real healing power like you. I want you to know that you taught me a lot. And believe it or not, you made me more humble.

Mum says to tell you we are all fine, and she hopes you and your dad are fine also. I will write again when I have more time. I don't know when that will be, though.
Your loving brother, Jeremiah

When Annie met up with her dad, she said Jerry had sent a letter about his studies. She didn't want him getting his hopes up about her mother only to have them dashed again. Annie felt she had enough love in her life to last her for years. The fact that Jerry felt humble about his skills told her there was hope for him, and she had done her work well.

There was nothing for her to brag about in his remarks about healing. She knew she did nothing but act as a conduit for the Master Dreamer. She was like a water pipe bringing water from the hills. She still had problems thinking of the power as Mum's God, because she was sure her mum's God wouldn't enlist her help.

Other than the letter, she and her dad talked about their work and the customers in their two shops. It was a leisurely stroll home at the end of a busy day. "Dad, I want you to do something for me that you may not like." Annie gave him an intense look and saw him start.

"What is it, Annie?

She reached beneath her collar and drew out the stone. "I want you to send this to Jeremiah. He'll know why, and he will not throw it out, I promise."

Her dad stared at her, his mouth open. "Oh, my. I hadn't expected that."

"Jerry just told me in his letter he has some Aborigine blood in him. He just found out, and I know this is the right thing to do. I also know he will come back to Australia and stay to practice medicine. I bet it will be up north around Darwin."

"It's just as Archie said years ago. But why me, Annie? If this is what you want, you should send it to him."

Annie glanced at the sky and saw the intense blueness above. Looking over at her dad, she saw he was happy and relaxed, if a little shocked at her request. Mum's lack of a message had not upset him as Annie thought. He was resigned to putting that part of his life behind him, and he was getting stronger every day. Annie knew he would make it. He might even take her advice about Mrs. MacDonald. Yes, her dad would be okay. Jerry would be okay. She was pleased. She put her arm in her dad's, and her warm smile was reflected on his face. That strange feeling came upon her again. She felt a sharp stab of pain in her chest. Suddenly she knew what the power was, and then there was nothing.

EPILOGUE

A shimmering light danced about her, and she delighted in the warm glow. Mum, Dad, and Jeremiah all faded into a collage. Soft choral music filled the air and disappeared. It was replaced by a lilting Celtic reel. She was awake. A soft nose nuzzled her arm, and she looked up to see the smiling face of Wallaby. "Welcome back, Annie. It's good to see you awake again."

"It seems like I never slept, Wallaby. How long was I dreaming this time?"

"Time? What is time, Annie?"

Real time, kneel time, feel time, heal time.
Time is now, and it is none.
It is here, and it is done.
It is here and never was.
Time stands still; time flows.
Like a river it comes and goes.

"Where is everyone?"

"They are all here, Annie. Look around you."

She looked about her. There was Joseph flying his kite. Elizabeth danced with a man whom Annie thought she recognized but couldn't quite place. Iris was playing with Radar, her small dog with the pointy upright ears. Python appeared in their midst. "Hello, Annie, old girl. You ready to complete your recording of your history?"

"Python, I haven't seen you for ages. Why not, I wonder?"

"You've been dreaming in a different direction, Annie. You moved away from me."

"But aren't you the one who made all the rivers in Australia?"

"Not really."

"Where's the MD now? Usually he's here to greet me. Have I offended him?"

"I don't think so, Annie. But you still have a little to learn. All the time you've helped Jerosh/Josh/Jeremiah, you've been earning points for yourself too. Don't think you've been the one on the giving end all the time."

"Time? Did I hear someone mention time?" Wallaby romped over.

"Figure of speech, old fellow. Figure of speech. Don't get your tail in a knot," Python hissed.

Wallaby looked offended, and Annie tried with a great deal of difficulty not to laugh. It felt good to be awake once more. She knew she wouldn't have to dream again unless she wanted to.

Python glided away, and she saw the Master Dreamer appear in his gleaming white robe. He looked happy. She remembered the time he was upset and crying into Wallaby's pouch. Now, his long hair was silver and shining under a golden light. Wallaby pranced over and joined Python.

"Hello, Annie, old girl. Glad to see you back with us."

"H—h—hello." She found herself stammering. "Why do I feel everything is different, MD?"

"Because it is, Annie. You've done a remarkable job, woman." His voice boomed over the green hills, just as she remembered. "I'm proud of you, Annie. You've proven yourself worthy of the next step."

At first she saw Python, Wallaby, and the MD. Then she saw the MD and Python. Then there was only the MD. He had absorbed Python and Wallaby. "Are you ready, Annie?"

"Yes." As she moved closer to him, he disappeared. She kept walking and found herself enveloped in a white light. She knew! She was part of the great warm glow of light and power. Jerosh, Joshua, Jeremiah, Master Dreamer, all the people in her several lives were ONE.

ONE LIFE.

ONE DREAM.

ANNIE'S DREAM.

The raven's tale has been told,
New today, yet centuries old.
Nothing in life is as it seems.
Dare to live your very own dreams.

978-0-595-47176-8
0-595-47176-5

Printed in the United States
111633LV00005B/7/P

9 780595 471768